Indivisible Line

By
Lorenz Font

Books by Lorenz Font

The Gates Legacy Series

Hunted - Book 1

Tormented - Book 2

Ascension - Book 3

Reckoning - Book 4

Redemption - Book 5 – Coming soon

Indivisible Line

Feather Light

Pieces of Broken Time

The Prodian Journey Series

Rise of Alpha

Indivisible Line

By
Lorenz Font

Second Edition

Published by Talem Publication

Paperback ISBN- 978-0-9977823-0-1
E-book ISBN- 978-0-9977823-1-8

Cover Images - © Jose Antonio Sánchez Reyes | Dreamstime.com
Cover Artist - Claudia Trapp/Phantasy Graphic Design
www.phantasygraphicdesign.com

Interior Design - Jennifer McGuire | JEMBookDesigns.com

http://www.lorenzfont.com

A big hug and kiss to my Bunny. Thanks for stepping in and taking charge, and for giving me all the time I need to chase my dream.

This is for you.

Chapter 1

"I have no idea how you can stand it."

"What are you talking about?" Sarah Jones shot a glance at her best friend.

"Living here," Lily Markham muttered with indignation, darting a challenging look in Sarah's direction.

Sarah remained unimpressed, not putting much stock in the statement. Raising her long legs onto the desk and crossing them at the ankles, she shrugged her shoulders, refusing to be baited into expressing agreement with her friend's complaints.

"I can't wait to leave this hellhole," Lily whined. It had become a regular habit for her.

"Why are you so hell-bent on leaving this place? I've been out there before." Sarah waved her hand toward the window to indicate the vast open space encompassing their home and whatever lay beyond it. "To tell you the truth, you're not missing much."

"Because . . ." Lily showed her fingers and began ticking off her reasons. "One, this is a dead-end existence. We'll live and die here. Two, I can't be with Trimble here. Three, the laws are suffocating. The whole tribe looks at you like you're entertainment. You want more?"

Sarah shook her head in response. Lily was a friend who understood Sarah's misgivings and fears, but she was also blunt, honest, and often afflicted with foot-in-mouth disease. These attributes gave Lily the firepower to sling words and facts at Sarah, making her question both her sanity and her commitment to following the orders given by their tribe.

For years now, Lily had never failed to express her distaste for the laws of their land. She was most vocal in her criticism of the unfair denial of technology she believed they should be enjoying, as well the impending arranged marriage that would take place in the not-so-distant future and would rob her of the chance to be with the man she loved.

For the most part, Sarah didn't mind it, but there were times when she disagreed with the decisions of Ahila, their Tribal Chief and her father. She often thought their modest town could use some better equipment for the clinic, another computer for their solitary school, and other newer gadgets to help usher their tribe into the modern era. However, Ahila had refused each suggestion, citing the requested items as trivial and unnecessary.

"What we have is enough," her father often said, and each time, she'd clamp her mouth shut and leave the topic alone. All the other elders, at least those who were not yet senile, tended to agree with him. They still embraced the old ways. Lily called them "old school," which happened to be an apt description of the deciding members of their community.

"No, I get what you're saying." Bitterness now laced Sarah's tone. "So if you're so unhappy being here, why don't you leave? Just like the others." She couldn't make herself turn her back on her people and the only home she'd ever known, and she envied those who could. The truth was that she lacked the guts those who had left possessed and had put to use.

Many kids her age ran away at the first chance they could find. They left the suffocating traditions behind not just because they loathed the slow pace but more because of the fear of stagnation. In their eyes, there wasn't much the town could offer for their futures.

"I can't leave," Lily protested with a soft cry, jerking back as if she'd been slapped in the face. The reason behind her refusal to pack her bags and go was no secret—Trimble Meda. The complication still remained. He was betrothed to Sarah.

"I thought so. If I were you, I'd stop acting like you have the ability to pick up and leave anytime you want. People are starting to talk, and we don't want Father to hear about what you've been saying. You know he won't hesitate to give you the boot." It wasn't a threat but a fact. Sarah hated talking to Lily in such a manner, in particular when it came to Trimble. Still, like it or not, there were some things they couldn't change, no matter how much they may have wanted to.

For Sarah, following the rules had always come easy. She had grown up with a stern father, who knew very little about how to show affection. Ahila governed his Gwich'in tribe and their little enclave in Beaver, Alaska, with an iron fist. He had lost her mother before Sarah had reached puberty, so he had brought up his only child single-handedly in the best way he knew. Her father was strict and unbending. Their house had felt more like a military base than a home. Within its walls, rules were to be followed and no questions asked.

"You shouldn't be so accepting, Sarah. You're engaged to someone you don't love. I'm sick of all this self-sacrificing crap. Would you really rather be an obedient daughter and a slave to your people than living your life the way you want?" Lily seemed to regret her words as soon as she'd spoken them. She cupped her hands over her eyes. "I'm sorry. You don't deserve that."

Sarah shrugged. "Maybe I do. I don't know."

The two women lapsed into silence and listened to the roaring of a moped's engine as it whirred by and the chirping of the birds in the nearby forest.

Sarah fixed her gaze on the fishbowl that sat on her desk, watching the goldfish swim around in endless circles. Her reality sucked, and she knew it. Was she doomed to be just like the goldfish, swimming around in circles? There was nothing to look forward to in the future except marrying a man she didn't love. Sure, everyone considered Trimble an excellent catch—he was the good, solid, hardworking kind of man many women hankered for. However, Sarah knew that a loveless union would be just the beginning of her troubles to come. How far would she and Trimble allow their extreme tradition dictate their fate?

"I have to go." Lily stood in an abrupt movement. She brushed away her brown hair, which clung to her tear-streaked face, and ran for the door. On her way out, she grabbed the little basket that contained her knitting supplies.

Sarah felt sorry for her friend, but there was nothing she could do. Traditions were important, and she wouldn't defy her father's wishes. *Even if it means sacrificing your happiness and freedom?* a little voice in her head asked.

"Yes."

Now wasn't that creepy? It was one thing to hear voices in her head, but answering them out loud was downright disturbing.

Somewhat disconcerted, she continued to stare at the fish in its bowl. Its repetitive, stagnant life was not so different from her own. She was up at five every morning to do her chores. Between taking care of her father and herself, there wasn't' much time left for anything else. Her father was a simple man, doing little and saying even less. However, his demands were larger than life.

Life with the chief was like living by herself. The most excitement in her twenty-six years came when she had been accepted to UCLA with a free ride to obtain her undergrad. Afterward, the tribe had started forking over the tuition for her to attend med school. That gesture alone made it impossible for Sarah to even consider turning her back on her tribe. She was stuck living with their stifling traditions out of a deep sense of loyalty and obligation. So, she'd curbed her dreams of leaving town and had resigned herself to spending her life serving her people.

My life is as exciting as pounding a nail into a piece of wood. Sarah snorted at the thought.

Although she was due back in Los Angeles in a month for the start of her final year, she was now home for the summer break to help out as much as she was able. There was little excitement in their sleepy town, so a part of her daily routine was to jog around the neighborhood each day. Running kept her sane and provided her with an excuse to socialize with her neighbors.

Her four-mile circuit pretty much covered the radius of the entire inhabited town. Beaver offered the peace and serenity many people sought. If you were looking, finding yourself in surroundings like these was almost too damn easy. You could hear yourself think, and having Mother Nature in your backyard made it all the more enticing. The town offered picturesque mountains, lush rivers, and abundant wildlife, all ready for one's enjoyment.

How miniscule and dull Beaver seemed, though, when compared to the life she had experienced in Los Angeles. The city was a fascinating melting pot of every type of people imaginable, and she'd fallen in love with the place as soon as she set foot on campus her freshman year. Sarah adored her second home. Living in a big city had always been her dream as a child growing up, and Los Angeles offered large helpings of fun and excitement. It made her feel like a child in the middle of a candy store.

Adjusting herself on the tattered leather chair, Sarah stretched her tanned legs before slipping them underneath the desk. She picked up the book she had abandoned upon Lily's arrival and returned to the page she'd been reading. Most days, the suspense-fiction she preferred could take her mind off things, but today her attention continued to wander. Still bothered by Lily's words, she abandoned her book and stared outside the window.

Passing the time in Beaver could get tricky since there was nothing much to do. Over the past month since her return, she had methodically arranged, rearranged, alphabetized, and indexed all medical inventories, from supplies to medications. Bottles, bins, and containers were labeled, and all instruments had been sterilized in case of an emergency—not that she'd expect any.

Her father had allowed her to work here as an assistant, trusting she had enough knowledge to help with common illnesses within the tribe. The absence of a full-time physician was the driving force behind the tribe's decision to finance her medical degree. After she graduated, she would be expected to serve the tribe in return. Being a doctor had been a lifelong dream of Sarah's, so she accepted that her education came at a price.

Lily knew how she felt, but she never understood Sarah's acceptance and dedication. Sarah loved her father, and despite the constant urge to spread her wings, she wasn't planning on leaving. She was proud of her heritage. While she understood the town's limitations in terms of growth, she hoped that, one day, she could help usher in acceptable changes to keep its people moving forward. With that goal, she could embrace what was being asked of her and serve her tribe.

In this day and age, children left the comfort of home to be on their own. Sarah never felt the need to do that, though. Being a doctor was what mattered most to her. She knew that once she qualified, she would be instrumental in helping the town in moving forward.

The one consideration that took the luster out of her ideal existence was her dreaded marriage to Trimble. Sarah still hadn't lost all hope that her father would realize what a gargantuan mistake it would be to push forward with his plan. She hoped to persuade him to allow her the freedom to choose when the time was right, but for now, she'd go with the flow.

You don't have a backbone. You're letting him run your life, the little voice in her head nagged.

"Oh, shut it. Papa's sick, and aggravating him is the last thing I'm going to do. For now, I'll concentrate on getting my degree. When he sees that I've succeeded, I'm sure he'll ease up on me."

You sound so sure your plan will work.

It would. It had to. Using her continued medical services as a bargaining chip, she'd be able to convince him that an arranged marriage wasn't necessary.

Will it work? It was a constant, nagging question that surfaced whenever uncertainty started creeping into her thoughts.

These days, boredom was her constant companion. Trimble's brush with a black bear had been the most action she'd seen all month. He'd sustained deep gashes in his back that had required several stitches. Other than that, it was most often cases of the flu, infections, and routine checkups. Sitting and waiting for patients to come meant endless hours of unproductive time. Her job had its rewarding moments, but the downtime seemed endless. Sarah longed to get some action, an honest-to-goodness hard day's labor. But what could be expected from her small town of Beaver with its population of just one hundred thirty-six? Thanks to pregnant Leonor Kassi, the head count would be increasing soon. Funny how one birth could send the dull and sleepy town into an excited frenzy.

They had a running joke around Beaver: "Your business is everybody's business." Truth be told, there was nothing people didn't know about each other. If you slept, pissed, or attended the tribal meeting, it was common knowledge. Despite the open spaces Alaska had to offer, it seemed like the residents of their little town were all crammed together like sardines.

Hours later, the walkie-talkie on the desk crackled, signaling an announcement from Kenny, the town liaison. Everyone called him Jack, the nickname stemming from his multiple functions in the tribe. Not only was he their town spokesman, but he also could see to plumbing needs or even fix any electrical problems. A town as small as Beaver required everyone to multitask in order to survive within the limited confines of their land, and Jack did an admirable job of living up to his name. Fairbanks was a half an hour away, but it was the nearest big city they could rely on for important supplies, postal needs, and a connection to the outside world.

The clinic's radio sounded—it was their cheapest but most reliable means of communication. Certain areas, such as the town hall and the clinic, had access to phone lines, and there was one cell tower on the outskirts of town. They didn't need additional towers. No one could afford cell phones with their meager incomes anyway. The tower had been built for the tourists and hunters, who happened to be their number-one source of income.

The Gwich'in's, also known as the Caribou People, were still dependent on the caribou, which were a vital source for food, clothing, and tools. The animal still held a sacred place in their spiritual beliefs and was a source of guidance in their traditions. The caribou was used for both their livelihood and sustenance.

Fishing came third on the list of income generators. Beyond that, there was nothing much their town had to offer, in particular to outsiders.

Many were opposed to letting the tourists in, but the need to survive won. So they opened the Caribou Hunting Expedition Company to assist avid hunters and provide them with a safe hunting environment. Much of their business came from repeat customers, and word of mouth didn't hurt. The income brought much relief of their financial woes. Now that it was the peak of the summer hunting season, it was the best time to attract tourists and let them spend their savings for the thrill of a lifetime.

Trimble worked for the expedition team, acting as the guide, driver, and gofer. This not only made him more popular amongst the female population but also a precious asset to their town's booming business. As was to be expected, everyone loved the idea of Sarah and Trimble together. A marriage between the most popular guy and the soon-to-be doctor seemed ideal. Well, she may not have agreed, but there was no sense in worrying about something beyond her control. She'd cross the bridge once she got to it. Defying her father's arrangement wasn't something she had the nerve to attempt just yet.

"Sarah!" the radio blared, pulling her thoughts back to the here-and-now. She snatched the transmitter from the table and pressed the button.

"What's the matter, Jack?"

"We're showing a movie in the auditorium in fifteen minutes. I don't think you want to miss it," Jack teased from the other end of the line.

"What is it?" Sarah pulled herself up and walked to the window. Glancing outside, she noticed a storm brewing from the north. There was a chilled bite to the wind sneaking in through the little gap in the window. She slammed the window down, making the foundation shake a little.

"*Underworld: the Awakening*," Jack's excited voice announced.

He didn't have to say another word. Sarah grabbed her jacket, which had been hanging over the back of her chair, and hurried to lock the clinic. She hoped that Dr. Ancheta would be able to make his rounds to their town soon so she could have a chance to spend some time with Lily and smooth over their argument.

Sarah draped her jacket across her back and set out at a brisk pace toward the center of town, a quarter-mile stretch of shops, stores, the town hall, and a small eatery. It left a lot to be desired if you were a tourist. Aside from hunting, the town didn't have much to offer. The stale appearance of most of the structures coupled with the raggedy storefronts added to the dilapidated look their downtown sported. Hardly the attractive atmosphere guests would clamor for.

She sighed and kept walking, head bowed low to block the lashing wind and the fierce drops of stinging rain from hitting her face. Upon reaching the town proper, she spotted a few people running to get into the auditorium to avoid the now pouring rain. She broke into a run as the first flash of lightning struck.

"Hey, glad you made it." Jack greeted her at the entrance with a big smile and a brotherly hug.

She returned the embrace with fervor before shrugging off her wet jacket. "You had me at *Underworld*," she answered with a laugh.

"Trimble's waiting for you," Jack said, holding the door open for her.

Sarah gave a mental groan, and her steps slowed as soon as she walked in. She did not relish the idea of putting on a show for other people's sake. This was the time when she wanted to scream *to hell with your stupid tradition*, but of course, she never did. Her father's wrath was something she could do without.

She glanced around, taking her time to wave to neighbors and friends. Trimble beckoned her to the spot he had saved for her toward the front of the auditorium. The entire town had showed up, just like a big reunion. Most faces she recognized, but a few unfamiliar people stood out. They must have been tourists aching to find something to do after hunting hours.

She caught sight of Lily on the opposite side of the first row of seats, staring ahead and trying her best to conceal her emotions. Whenever Sarah and Trimble had to make a show of affection, even though Lily knew it was to appease the elders, still made her sour. All Sarah could do was to keep the PDA to a minimum for Lily's sake.

"Hey." Trimble gave Sarah the customary peck on the cheek. That was the extent of their effort to maintain their façade.

Several giggles sounded from the seats behind them, but Sarah didn't bother shooting glares that way. The kids didn't know any better—none of them had to put on a show like this, ever. "Hi." Her voice came out clipped. Out of the corner of her eye, she could see her father watching them. He sat on the far side of the first row, next to Trimble's father and mother as well as Mr. Vittrekwa, his closest friend.

Trimble, as if on cue, took her hand just when the lights dimmed. It was a show they had to put on for everyone's sake. They both hated doing it, but there was no way to avoid it. Once the auditorium had gone dark, lights flashed from the projector in the back of the room straight through the makeshift monitor up front. Sarah lost no time in pulling her hand from Trimble's grasp and inching away a tiny fraction, just enough to get some space without making her father suspect anything. As far as the chief was concerned, he had arranged a worthy and ideal union between two people.

"Who cares about being in love in the beginning?" her father had once said, sounding like an authority on marriage and all its intricacies. "You'll fall for him before you even know it."

Somehow, she doubted her father's declaration, but she'd chosen not to argue.

Don't you just love the scent of honesty? It makes me question your state of mind sometimes, the stupid voice inside her head shouted at her. And I'm not stupid. You are.

"Shut up." The words escaped her lips before she could stop them. She cupped her palm over her mouth and slid down in her seat at once, hoping no one noticed.

"Sarah, what's going on?" Trimble whispered.

"Nerves." That was all she needed to say.

Trimble nodded in understanding. They rode the same waves, experienced the same doubts, and grappled the same fear of the fate they'd soon be facing together.

There was nothing wrong with Trimble. In fact, he was an attractive man. He was just not the man for her. One thing for certain, there'd be a lot of women who would question Sarah's mental health if they knew she wasn't attracted to her fiancé.

So, who's the man for you?

She'd better seek Dr. Ancheta's help as soon as possible. These voices were getting troublesome. The fact that she was answering them posed a bigger problem.

Who *was* the man for her? That was the million-dollar question.

Exactly.

Not giving in to the mental taunting, she wouldn't dignify the strange voice's commentary with an answer. Instead, she focused on the screen and tried her best to concentrate. After all, movie showings, a new release in particular, didn't come to their town often. This had to be a special arrangement Jack had made for all of them. *Bless his heart*, Sarah thought.

The rude blaring of the alarm clock shook Sarah out of her sweet cocoon of sleep. Banging her hand down on the snooze button, she smiled at the remnants of the picture-perfect future her imagination had conjured.

Without opening her eyes, she basked in the sweet vision of her dream. It had been so vivid that she could almost believe it had been real. She'd seen herself as the head of the trauma department at Fairbanks General Hospital. Dressed in a starched, white lab coat over blue scrubs, she was racing to the ER to perform an emergency brain surgery on a car accident victim. Her elation in that moment did not come from another person's misfortune. Instead, it had something to do with her pride in her contributions to the medical world. Her expertise, experience, and invaluable service meant saving the lives of countless people and forging avenues toward a better future. Yeah, it sounded like a dream all right, but it was her life-long aspiration, now well within her grasp. One more year, and the moment she'd been waiting for would arrive at last.

Except the picture was all wrong. She'd be stuck here in Beaver forever, instead of blazing a trail through the ER of a big hospital. Sarah sighed, feeling conflicted and hating herself for wanting more. Why couldn't she just accept that her future included a husband she didn't love and keeping her work confined to a small clinic?

The alarm went off again. This time, she slid the button all the way to the right, shutting off the snooze feature. Sarah took one pillow and placed it between her thighs, rolled onto her side, and studied the veins of old, chipping paint on the walls. God, she had been planning to repaint her room for ages, but after one month in Beaver, she still hadn't gotten a chance thanks to her full schedule at the clinic. Despite the lack of demand for her services, her father had insisted that she make herself available for long periods every day.

Shutting her eyes, her mind wandered back to Lily's bellyaching the day before. There was no doubt her best friend would've taken off at the first opportunity if she'd been able to leave with Trimble at her side. That was the crux of her friend's dilemma. Lily and Trimble were in love with each other, and she didn't have the heart to leave him behind. Therein lay the problem, since he and Sarah had been promised to each other since they were children.

Being her father's daughter, she was subject to one of the traditions of the tribe. Ahila had to make one sacrifice as a rite of passage before he would be heralded as the tribe's leader, and so he had betrothed his first-born to a suitable family. So she and Trimble had been paired up, even before they had taken their first steps or uttered their first words.

And that was that. No ifs, ands, buts, or whys. You just accepted what was handed to you.

Regardless of her feelings, she didn't have the courage to criticize the arrangement. This unwillingness had earned her Lily's favorite words—*sad*, *unfair*, and *cruel*. Being Ahila's daughter had definitely complicated her life. Throughout their childhood, she, Trimble, and Lily had tried to think of ways to break the arrangement. If he eloped with Lily, it would enrage and shame their families. Sarah and Trimble tried talking to their parents to discuss the possibility of dissolving the arrangement but to no avail. They both had been turned down so fast they still reeled from the experience.

"You will be a suitable wife to Trimble when he becomes the next leader of our tribe," her father had repeated once again when he'd sensed her resistance to the betrothal. Suitable? He made it sound as if they were pairing clothes instead of discussing his daughter's eventual fate.

Still, the three friends continued to concoct scenarios during their summer breaks in high school, looking for an acceptable excuse to sever the deal. Most were flimsy at best, leading them back to where they'd started, the clock still ticking away like a time bomb waiting to detonate.

Their wedding had been scheduled during the winter solstice after her graduation from med school, which was in a year. Then what? She'd live a long life devoid of real love, never having known the true meaning or feeling behind the celebrated sensation. Sarah had no unrealistic notions about marriage, being well aware of the sacrifices associated with the union. It was a binding tie that was expected to achieve a greater sense of purpose and service that would help lead their people into a better tomorrow.

Fantastic! She rolled her eyes and blew a harsh breath. To her, it sounded more like a nightmare. This future with Trimble might as well be damned even before it began. Heavens! The whole situation could take forever to fathom. Choking back the wave of nausea that blanketed her while thinking of her eventual destiny, she tossed the pillow aside, got up, and marched out of her bedroom.

The creaky floor complained under her weight when she crossed the hallway to the bathroom she shared with her father. He knew her schedule, and he deferred to her more pressing needs before getting ready to set out on his tribe-related tasks.

"Good morning, Papa," she said in a cheerful voice before closing the door behind her. She heard him grunt in reply and smiled to herself. The man didn't have an affectionate bone in his body. Dry as toast, his emotions were often masked and guarded, as if displaying sentiments diminished his pride and sense of self-respect. To Ahila, caring and providing had more to do with putting food on the table, planning her life, and seeing her preordained future come to pass.

It took her less than ten minutes to wash her face, brush her teeth, and comb her hair. Donning her raggedy running outfit of shorts and tank top underneath a faded UCLA sweatshirt, Sarah hustled out of the house with a casual wave to her father. She stopped on the porch, giving the quiet street a brief assessment. Darkness was waning and was beginning to give way to the pink tint of the sun cresting on the horizon. There were two ways that would take her to her usual path—either left or right.

Instead, she decided to run toward the outer lying wilderness, a decision that would be frowned upon by her father and the rest of the male population. While the tribe wanted to believe the forest was safe, it was home to hungry bears and occasional wolves. As a general rule, these animals would not attack unprovoked unless cornered, but accidents did happen. Sarah pulled down the hood of her sweatshirt and started walking to the left toward the wooded area.

The minute she cleared the rows of houses, she quickened her pace. "Dotson'Sa, what do you have planned for me today?" Yeah, she'd been reduced to calling out for the Great Raven to answer her prayers for guidance, strength, and well . . . *something* constructive to occupy her time. "Can you give me something more exciting than reading and rearranging the supplies for the hundredth time?"

A nippy breeze shot across her face when she broke into a jog to get her heart rate up. There were a few people walking in the street—early risers, just like her. They waved at her as she passed by. She raised her hand to wave back before breaking into a faster pace.

~

Hours later and a few pages away from finishing the book she'd been reading, the walkie-talkie blasted with a resounding crackle.

"Just when I'm getting to the juicy part," she muttered. She picked up the portable radio, but her eyes never left the page. "This is Sarah," she grumbled, before releasing the button and resuming her reading.

"Sarah, it's Trimble." His voice boomed from the speaker.

She shook her head at the unnecessary introduction. Who wouldn't recognize his deep voice even with their eyes closed?

"Get ready. Place a call to Dr. Ancheta, if you can reach him."

"Get ready for what?" Sarah shot up out of her chair, dropping the book on the desk to pick up the transmitter again. "What's going on?"

"We're bringing in a gunshot victim," Trimble's voice rumbled over. "We're a few minutes away."

Heavens! She'd asked for action but not this.

"Okay, I'm calling Dr. Ancheta now." Sarah sprang to her feet and skidded across the room to get to the phone that was attached to the wall. Dialing with feverish speed, she waited for an answer, but the voice mail kicked in instead. While the message played, she made mental notes of what to do when the group arrived. "Dr. Ancheta, you have to come right away. We have a gunshot victim. I don't know the patient's condition yet."

That was the problem with not having a resident doctor. Dr. Ancheta was based in Fairbanks, but he had taken on the task of visiting the neighboring small towns to help out. He traveled nonstop, and there was no way of knowing if he would be able to get there in time.

Sarah grabbed her lab coat from the hanger behind the door and put it on just as the sound of screeching tires and shouts rang out from the street. She peered out the window while soaping her hands.

Curious Gwich'ins started filling the street, and the same question marked their faces: *What the hell is going on?* The once-quiet and sleepy afternoon had turned into a circus. People closed in on the jeep, making the process of unloading the passenger cumbersome.

"Please, step back!" Sarah heard Mark Simpson, one of the expedition employees, yell.

"Sarah?" Trimble's voice echoed in the tiny clinic when the pounding of heavy footsteps got closer.

"I'm in here." Sarah snapped the second glove on her hand and removed the plastic covering from the exam table. She flicked on the big industrial lamp, and the dim room came alive, bathed in light.

Trimble, Mark, and Mr. Compche, an elder in their community, rushed in. Between them they carried the body of a bloody, unconscious man. With trepidation, Sarah shot a look in Trimble's direction, her eyes posing the question she couldn't make herself say out loud.

"You have no choice, Sarah. If you don't do something, he won't survive." Trimble knew her well enough to know what she needed to hear. Ethical or not, she had to do something. She had sufficient training to know what to do in these types of situations.

Where the hell is Dr. Ancheta?

She gave a grim nod. "Put him down on the exam table, but be careful," she instructed, rushing to get the instruments she'd need to perform the impromptu surgery. Laying her tools on a steel rolling cart, she heard the men make grunting sounds while they hoisted the man up onto the table. Looking over her shoulder, she noticed the length of the man's body made the other, average-sized men look rather small in comparison. Fatigue marked their faces, especially that of old Cyril Compche. The weathered eyes shot a brief glance at Sarah before they flickered back to the patient.

"Did you try to call Dr. Ancheta?" Mr. Compche asked, still catching his breath.

"I did and left him a message."

"I heard he's in College today. No telling how soon he'll get here, if he can even make it before this man . . ." Mark's voice trailed off.

Running back to the exam table, Sarah picked up the stranger's wrist to check for a pulse. Faint. His breaths were shallow. "Bring the oxygen tank here," she ordered, and Trimble jumped to get the breathing apparatus. Once the oxygen tank had been rolled closer, Sarah grabbed the mask, placed it on the man's face, and adjusted the elastic over his head.

She picked up the scissors and cut through the man's expensive-looking snow parka and the layers of thermal shirts underneath. Shoving aside the garments and examining the blood-soaked skin, she found the entrance wound. It was located in the lower abdomen, and there was no exit wound, which explained the decreased external bleeding. She shook her head and took a deep breath. Time was of the essence, and there was not a moment to lose.

Sarah glanced at the man's face and silently implored, *Please don't die.*

Already in "doctor mode," she started barking out orders to Trimble since Mark was standing motionless next to the table with his face frozen into a shocked expression. "Trimble, grab the IV bag and bring it here."

Her sharp command made everyone in the room jump, but Trimble sprang into action. He came back with the bag within seconds.

"Hold the bag upside down, then hang it on the pole." She was working at a feverish pace, connecting the cannula to the IV bag and placing a tourniquet on the man's arm. When she found the vein, she inserted the needle with practiced ease.

"What can you tell me about him?" she asked while she inserted the syringe and taped it into place.

"We don't know who he is. We heard the gunshot, and by the time we got there, he was already unconscious."

Sarah pursed her lips and shook her head, feeling an indescribable cloud of despair wash over her.

"Where is Lily?" Precious seconds were ticking by, and the sooner she worked on the victim, the better his chances of survival. Her eyes returned to the man's face, noting its regal features despite the pallor of his skin. *Don't you dare die on my table!*

"She's coming. I sent someone to get her." Trimble's calm demeanor had fallen away, but it was understandable. It wasn't every day they saw a white man—or anyone for that matter—get shot on their land.

"Check his pockets to see if he has any identification," Cyril, who had been leaning against the wall watching the process, suggested. His expression was unreadable while he observed Trimble slip his hand underneath the man's body to fish for a wallet.

Trimble shook his head and moved to the other side to try again. "Nothing. He has nothing on him."

Sarah's head shot up. "No identification? How could a tourist have traveled here without any? Don't you guys have that as a prerequisite for each hunter you take with you?" It seemed odd that the company would agree to bend the rules for anyone, let alone allow him to get injured on their watch. "Who shot him?"

Trimble shrugged. "He is not a part of our touring group. We found him three miles off the clearing after Mars caught his scent. As far as who did it, your guess is as good as mine."

A gust of wind swirled around the room, followed by the sound of the clinic's front door opening and closing. Lily burst into the room, holding her sewing supplies. She worked as an assistant in the clinic in addition to being the town's seamstress.

"I hope I'm not too late." She gave a curt nod to everyone in the room before focusing her attention to the unconscious man. Her eyes widened. "What in God's name happened to him?"

"Lather up," Sarah ordered in a brisk tone.

Lily sprinted to the sink and scrubbed her hands. "What do we have here?" She put on surgical gloves while she looked over the work Sarah had already started.

"Gunshot wound to the abdomen. The bullet penetrated here." Sarah pointed to the site, just below the belly button. "But there's no exit wound, so we have to get it out now before it does any more damage. I think I might have to operate." She hated hearing the uncertainty in her voice.

Sarah had a good idea of what needed to be done, but she wasn't certain if she had the authority to make that decision. Under the circumstances, she might need the blessing of the tribal leader before she could proceed.

Cyril spoke as if he'd read her mind. "Sarah, shouldn't you ask your father first? This is not your choice to make." There was a strict law in their land: all matters involving "white folks" had to be brought before Ahila before any decisions were made.

"We're talking about a life here, Cyril! This is the one chance he's got. There's no way to get him to Fairbanks fast enough."

"One white man gone isn't going to be missed." His harsh words stunned them all, including Cyril himself, and he turned away on his heel in shame.

"Cyril!" Sarah gasped at his insensitive remark and its implications.

He stopped at the door and looked over his shoulder. "Fact is, we only have adequate supplies for the tribe, Sarah. What if an emergency happens and we don't have enough for our own people?" Cyril left on that note, but the weight of his question lingered.

Sarah chose to ignore it.

"No one is dying here, not if I can help it." She nodded to Lily, who held an injection of Demerol, the best thing they had for pain.

Oh Dotson'Sa, what am I going to do? This man is going to die.

No, he's not. You're going to do whatever you can to give him even the slimmest chance.

Conflicting thoughts raced through Sarah's mind while her hands moved faster than they'd ever done in her life. Shootings in Beaver were unheard of, and this scenario was not something they'd ever expected.

Lily handed the needle to her. Sarah knew she had to work fast. Without giving in to the dread and nervousness trying to claw its way into her system, she did a mental assessment and clamped the line. She injected the needle into the port and mixed the solution and medication by turning the bag from end to end. "Now, you two," she said to the men, "can you go find Mr. Vittrekwa so we can transport the patient to Fairbanks as soon as possible?"

Trimble and Mark scurried out of the room, leaving an air of fear and exhaustion in their wake. Sarah tried to draw some reassurance from her knowledge of how determined Trimble was to save this mysterious man.

"He's losing blood," Lily reported.

Sarah glanced at the clock. They had to hurry, but the Demerol hadn't taken effect. She couldn't bear the thought of cutting through the man's skin without painkillers. Lily continued to wipe away the steady flow of blood that came from the patient's wound while Sarah scrubbed with Betadine to prepare for surgery.

She felt her breath hitching while she counted from one to twenty as slow as she could. Less than a minute later, she gave up and started the painstaking task of cutting through the skin. Sarah gritted her teeth until the sound resonated in her head. There—a small incision, but big enough for her to work with.

The unconscious man groaned. It had to be from the pain.

"I'm sorry," she whispered.

Sarah slid her fingers into the incision, separating the skin and the muscle underneath it, and widened the gap with her fingers. She probed until she found the bullet. Thank God. It hadn't penetrated deeper than she'd expected, missing vital organs. She felt a little glimmer of hope. Still, Sarah had her work cut out for her, and she cursed under her breath. She was in way over her head with this situation, but in Dr. Ancheta's absence, she had no other choice but to proceed.

Beads of sweat trickled down her temple. With the clinic's not-so-modern instruments and limited provisions, the man would have to be airlifted to Fairbanks as soon as Mr. V, pilot of the only local bush plane, could be located.

The ticking of the clock was loud in her ears while she continued to work on her patient. It took her an hour to remove the bullet while trying to remember bits and pieces of information she'd learned from med school. Her actions would have definite repercussions, but she had no time to debate right and wrong. Infection could set in, but at that point, she'd rather take the risk so that he could live. She'd deal with the consequences later.

Lord, talk about bad timing. Of all the places to get shot, it had to be in Beaver, where antibiotics weren't always available. Due to the cost, the clinic was unable to always keep them on hand.

"Are you done?" Lily patted her back.

It was now out of their hands. Sarah had given him the best fighting chance possible with what limited resources she had.

"Almost." She looked at the patient and rubbed his arm, hoping for the best.

Her back ached. She'd been leaning over the guy for what felt like hours. Sarah bent her body forward and backward until her spine gave a snap. Then she began stitching him up, hopeful that her sloppy work would hold up until they could get him to the hospital in Fairbanks. She wrapped big wads of dressing around his belly, with drains leading out of the wound. Afterward, she placed a Foley catheter, and then hung it on the steel rod at the side of the bed.

Sarah sighed and sent a heartfelt gratitude to Dotson'Sa for his help getting both her and her patient through the surgery. "That should do it." She patted the stranger's arm again, marveling that he was still alive.

With the adrenaline receding, Sarah sank down on the chair, exhausted. Her stomach growled, alerting her that she'd skipped dinner. Her father would've heard the news by now. It was just a matter of time before he made an appearance. The weight of the decision she'd made now came bearing down on her.

She hoped she'd saved a life. Sarah had yet to take the Hippocratic Oath, but by Dotson'Sa, she'd done what she knew to be right. Snapping off her latex gloves, she threw them in the biohazard bin and then let out another big sigh. A sudden wave of nausea hit her, and she ran to the sink. She heaved, but nothing came out.

"Are you okay?" Lily rushed over and rubbed her back.

Sarah nodded. After heaving several times and coming up empty, she gave up and washed her face with cold water, welcoming the coolness on her skin.

"Go home, Lily. I'll stay with him until they can transport him to Fairbanks."

"Okay. Do you want anything to eat?"

Sarah shook her head. Even if she'd been hungry, she wouldn't dare eat anything until the churning in her stomach settled down.

The screeching sound of an alarm blared across the room. They bolted to the monitor to check the read-out.

"Sarah, his blood pressure is dropping," Lily screeched, paling at the reading on the EKG monitor. "We have no blood in stock. What are we going to do?"

Sarah checked the reading. It was dangerously low. The patient could go into shock.

Her heart kicked in high gear. "Hook me up. We can't waste time."

Chapter 3

The walkie-talkie crackled, and Lily rushed to answer it. Trimble was talking even before she had the chance to say anything. "Mr. V is on his way. Dr. Ancheta was in a surgery in College but is flying to Fairbanks right now. He'll meet the patient there."

In all of her twenty-six years of existence, Sarah couldn't recall making a life-altering decision until that day. One thing was certain—in the coming days, months, or even years down the road, she'd always look back on that day and be proud of her actions. She'd done many things she regretted, but saving a life would never be one of them. Ever.

Time wasn't on their side. The facts were that it was past midnight and they had no available bags of blood for transfusion. Sarah needed to make a hasty decision—and a difficult one—taking matters into her own hands.

At all levels, this singular act had *dangerous, daring, and dumb* written all over it. However, if they were lucky, it might give him a fighting chance. Every passing minute, his condition became graver. Either Sarah transfused him with her blood, or let him die. The choice was clear.

With the continued warning blaring, Sarah wiped away the sweat running down her face and pieced her scrambled thoughts together.

"You heard what I said. Hook me up!"

Having made up her mind, she glanced with impatience at Lily, who'd been glued to her spot, staring at Sarah like she'd sprouted horns.

What was the worst that could happen? He'd develop an allergy, run a fever, have trouble breathing, or his pressure could drop much lower? In Sarah's mind's eye, those side-effects were a small price to pay if it meant saving his life—if he was even able to live through the night.

Unethical? No doubt, but given the direness of the situation, she felt the gamble was warranted. It was a major decision that might lead her into serious trouble and could forever alter the course of her professional life. Even so, she wasn't going to stand there and watch someone die.

"You're . . . you're kidding, right?" Lily stuttered in disbelief.

One look at Lily, and Sarah knew what her friend had to be thinking. She knew she was acting crazy, stupid, and impossible, but she still wouldn't change her mind. "Do I sound like I'm joking here?"

Instead of letting her friend's negative reaction slow her down, Sarah began moving toward the drawers. She pulled one open, rattling bottles and instruments while she retrieved an IV line and needles. Taking the scissors from the table, she cut through the bag and emptied all of the liquid in the sink.

"My blood type is O-positive, so that makes me a universal donor."

Lily made no attempt to move except to follow Sarah with her eyes, a dumbstruck expression on her face. "And then what?"

"We have no other choice in this situation. C'mon, Lily, I can't do this by myself. I need your help. If we don't, he'll die!" Sarah gathered all the supplies she needed and placed them on the metal cart next to the exam table.

"Have you lost your mind? Do you know how much trouble we'll be in? I can't be an accessory to this insanity," Lily cried in frustration.

Sarah just shrugged. She had no time to waste on trying to convince her. With hurried movements, she pulled out a chair and sat down. She breathed in and out, needing to calm down before she started the process, and prayed that her lack of food and the task ahead wouldn't make her sick.

"Help me, Lily," she pleaded to her friend, who still stared at her with brown eyes filled with uncertainty.

The machine beeped again, and that made Lily spring forward like she'd been linked to a coil. "What do you want me to do?"

"We'll have to do a direct transfusion." Bold, yet utterly stupid. Sarah wasn't even sure it would work. At that point, though, she was willing to try anything.

Lily stared at her again, looking more bewildered than ever. "You'll do what?"

Sarah handed her the end of the plastic IV line. "This is going to be tricky. I have to be positioned higher than him to allow gravity to force the blood downward." She put one foot on the chair and stepped up.

Lily remained baffled. "What are you doing?"

"Lily, look at me. Focus," Sarah commanded while fitting one end of the line with the needle, then taping them together. "Do the same thing with the other tip."

Lily gave her head a quick shake before jumping to the task.

Sarah straightened her arm. "Hold the other end of the line, and insert the needle into his vein. We have to do this at the same time. Ready, Lily? Ready?" Sarah slid her needle into an exposed vein and cursed under her breath. Wincing, she waited while her blood began to trickle down the tube. "Lily, find his vein. Do it now!"

With trembling hands, Lily tapped the unconscious man's arm several times before she found one and was able to inject the needle into his skin.

Trying to balance her feet on the chair and keeping tabs on the flow of her blood, Sarah trembled but remained focused. While she watched the transfer happen, the weight of her action began to sink in, just like the blood traveling from her body and into the patient's.

"Let's hope that this beautiful white man is worth the trouble," Lily said with a sigh, her body straining to maintain her position over the man's arm, making sure the transfusion continued.

Repercussions were inevitable, but Sarah would worry about that later. Right that minute, her mind was focused on the task at hand. "For me, there's no white, black, brown, or yellow. This is how it should be. I wouldn't be able to forgive myself if I didn't give him a fighting chance." She glanced at the man again.

For the first time since he had been brought in the clinic, Sarah got a good, long look at him. She noted the perfect blond hair that fell on the side of his face—matted but still perfect. His features were rather forbidding, even in his unconscious state. The defined jawline framed well-proportioned lips that were pale and parted slightly. The suggestion of dimples on either cheek made her ache to see him smile. Then there were the long, dark eyelashes and the contoured nose, all coming together to create a striking, attractive package that kept her eyes glued to his face.

Her heart began to race. *What is wrong with me?* Shaking off another wave of nausea, Sarah closed her eyes and concentrated on breathing. Her knees weakened underneath her, but she kept on inhaling and exhaling. A few more minutes and it would be over.

In her short life, Sarah hadn't met a man who evoked the well–documented "butterflies-in-the-stomach" phenomenon. Now here she was, staring at a complete stranger with her heart banging against her chest in a frenzy. This man was just too perfect, too beautiful almost. She was even gladder she'd managed to keep him alive. He'd make a woman happy someday, if he hadn't already. Instinct made her eyes travel to the man's ring finger, and her heart skipped when she found it bare.

"Tell your father that. You know you're going to be in big trouble."

Lily's warning startled her.

"I'll cross that bridge once I get to it," Sarah replied, hoping Lily had missed her ogling their patient.

Sarah glanced down at her arm. She'd given him more than enough, and anything more could be hazardous for her. Already feeling lightheaded, she slipped the needle out of her skin, and blood started trickling out. "After it drains, remove the needle."

Lily nodded, watching while the remaining blood disappeared into the man's arm.

Her legs feeling shaky, Sarah stepped down, gripping the chair's arm to steady herself when the room began to spin around her.

"Are you okay?" Lily shot her a worried frown.

"Yeah." She closed her eyes.

After a minute, her equilibrium settled, and Sarah walked to the hazard bin to deposit the bag, tube, and needle before moving toward their supplies cabinet. She took one alcohol swab and dabbed at the blood from her arm before securing a bandage on the open site. The room swirled. It was most likely the fatigue setting in. Suppressing the urge to empty her stomach, Sarah hurried to the sink and braced her hands on the edge.

Footsteps sounded behind her when Lily approached, placing a hand on her shoulder. "You did the right thing."

Stifling the tears pooling in her eyes, Sarah blinked several times before turning to face her friend. "I hope so, but why do I get the feeling that my action is going to cost me something much more important?"

Lily searched Sarah's face, her expression softening. "You're not regretting your decision, are you?"

"Not one bit." Sarah shook her head. Her conviction remained solid, but events had caught up with her at last. She stumbled forward, and Lily caught her arm, pulling her into an embrace.

"What now?" Lily whispered.

"I don't know. I guess time will tell." Tears began to spill, and she was powerless to fight them. She held Lily in a fierce grip. Too many protocols had been broken, and she'd crossed the ethics line, which no doubt would anger her father. Her body shuddered as the reality of her situation hit her hard. Lily embraced her with tenderness, rubbing her back in soothing circles.

They stood there for a long time. The only sound audible was Sarah's sobbing and the steady beep of the EKG monitor. After another minute ticked by, Lily took one step back to scrutinize her friend's face.

"Hey, I don't mean to burst your bubble, but I believe you're promised to the man I love. So why don't you feast your eyes now?" She gestured to the stranger.

"What do you mean?" Sarah wiped her eyes with the back of her hand and turned, her gaze wandering in the direction of the examination table.

"Give that good-looking man one last look, because you'll be Mrs. Meda very, very soon."

The sadness in Lily's voice shattered Sarah to pieces. She knew how much Lily and Trimble loved each other, but the cruel fact remained. She and Trimble would be tying the knot soon. They were expected to continue the long bloodline of their ancestors and would be held accountable for ensuring the survival of that legacy. Though their hearts abhorred the idea, their sense of responsibility superseded their own desires.

Sarah asked, "Why do I need to look at him?" Her eyes traveled again to the man's face, questioning her attraction. She noted his even breathing, but his pained expression still lingered. Unable to turn away, she wondered what color his eyes were. She had met many boys at the university, good-looking ones, yet this man took the prize. He was stunning and oozing male vitality, even in his deplorable state. The bare chest peeking out from the thin white sheet made her want to run her hand over it to feel his body. Sarah shook her head and tried to dispel the overwhelming sensation coursing through her.

The two women heard voices outside of the clinic, and then Trimble, Mark, and Mr. V entered the room with a raggedy stretcher.

"Is he ready?" Trimble asked, shooting a quick glance in Lily's direction.

"He's all yours," Sarah said, getting the IV from the pole and handing it to Lily. She heard a weak moan and saw the man shiver. After retrieving a thicker blanket, she wrapped it around his body.

"I did what I could. I'm rooting for you, and I'm going to pray that you make it," she whispered, rubbing his arm in the process. It felt good to tell him how she felt, even if her words meant nothing to the unconscious man.

While Trimble and the others worked fast to transfer the patient onto the gurney, Sarah couldn't help the feeling of sadness that swept over her. She had no idea if she'd helped or made things worse for him.

In a matter of minutes, she heard the roar of the car engine speeding away. She sighed and turned to Lily. "Why don't you get out of here?" Sarah walked over to the desk and collapsed on the chair, her tired muscles screaming in protest.

"Okay." Lily grabbed her purse and produced an apple. "Eat," she ordered.

Sarah took the fruit and wiped it on her coat before taking a bite. "Get some sleep, and come back in the morning." She pointed to the door by way of dismissal.

"Do you think he'll make it?" Lily looked at her with eyes that mirrored her own uncertainties.

"He survived the operation. That's all I can tell you. We'll have to see if his condition improves." Sarah glanced at the now-empty table. Her heart started pounding against her chest again. *I will pray for him.*

"Okay, I'll see you in the morning. Do you need anything before I leave?"

"No, I'll be okay. Thanks."

"You're welcome. You know what? I was happy to help." Lily smiled and turned to the door. "I'll be back in the morning. Try to get some sleep."

When the doors had slid shut, Sarah leaned back in the stiff chair and closed her eyes, collecting herself for a moment. It had been a long evening. She made a mental note to stop asking Dotson'Sa for action. After tonight, she'd rather deal with common colds and flu any day.

She put the apple down on the desk, not feeling hungry despite her empty stomach. While the remnants of the receding adrenaline drained out, she stretched her legs under the desk and stretched her arms upward. It felt great, her tense muscles relaxing after hours of intense rush. She knew she was too tired to walk home. She'd sleep here and clean up in the morning. Sleep sounded very good now that her body had slowed down into a pleasant, dull rhythm. Massaging her scalp, she could feel lethargy begin to seep in, and she embraced the short reprieve she needed after the tense evening.

It was two in the morning when she woke. Even with the little nap, she still felt drained and exhausted. She made herself get up to turn off the lights.

Her back was screaming at her. Staggering back to the desk, she sat down with a weary sigh. Notes. She still had to write them, so sleep had to wait. She turned on the desk lamp and pulled one of the drawers open, took a paper, and began documenting the events of the evening: each procedure she'd performed, the dosages of Demerol given, and the vital sign readings that led to the spontaneous blood transfusion.

Once she'd finished, Sarah reviewed what she wrote. This record would have to be reviewed by Dr. Ancheta once she found someone to take it to him in Fairbanks in the morning. Man, that part made her cringe. It wouldn't go well if they found out she wasn't a licensed physician. But what could they do, revoke a license she didn't even have yet?

A bubble of hysteria rose up her throat, making it impossible to swallow. With the quiet surrounding her, the full weight of her actions descended on her, making Sarah second-guess her decision to save the man's life. Could this one incident destroy her chance to become a full-fledged doctor? Had her dreams ended tonight?

Sarah glanced at the empty, still-bloodied table a few feet away, and she hoped he was worth the effort.

Since everything had happened in one quick blur, going over the entire incident made her head ache. Reading and re-reading what she wrote was another thing. Her eyes fluttered closed several times and began to water when she strained harder to keep them open. At long last, she paused to take a short break, resting her head on her arm, but exhaustion won. She soon fell asleep, her notes sitting under her nose, and her long, black hair splayed all over the table.

The mind had a cunning way of alerting the rest of the body when it was in the midst of trouble, either through pain or other sensations, like throbbing, burning and soreness. Such was the case for Greg as soon as he surfaced from his blackened haze. He realized at once that he was in deep shit when he tried to move his body and everything felt somehow disconnected. A series of sharp, stabbing twinges radiated through his body before converging on the lower part of his abdomen. It felt like someone had left firecrackers inside his stomach and lit them all at the same time.

It was burning, exploding, hot and unimaginably painful.

He tried opening his eyes, but their sheer weight made it difficult. Moaning, he reached around for something to help push himself up, but the pain shot through him again and he'd have doubled over if he hadn't been lying down.

That smell . . . what was it? The scent of metal came to mind, just before another searing ache emanated from his gut, burning until he stopped every attempt to move. Greg took shallow breaths to control the intense ache inside him. The more shallow his breathing, the less throbbing he had to endure. He tried lifting his heavy lids again, but his eyeballs just strained hard against the barrier and rolled up instead.

What in the world was wrong with him? Greg opened his mouth to speak, but the dryness in his throat made it impossible to get a word out. His throat was a scorching burn, as if someone sandpapered his mouth and left it to dry in the sun. A faint, raspy moan escaped his lips.

Although he'd been trying to regulate his breathing, he could do nothing to prevent the shaking of his body, which intensified the spasms. His body was vibrating from the cold shiver he was experiencing. Again, he was helpless to do anything but moan.

A rustling sound came from his left, and soft footsteps approached. Then a soothing, warm hand touched his forehead. An unfamiliar voice filled with gentleness spoke to him.

"I did what I could. I'm rooting for you," the voice assured him before a warm hand caressed his sensitive skin, bringing him warmth. Minutes later, darkness prevailed once again.

Chapter 4

Greg managed to pry his tired eyes open after several attempts. The pain had been terribly real, and he couldn't get anything but moans out of his mouth when he tried to speak. The room was dim, but there was adequate light filtering through the gaps of the blinds. He looked around in confused haze.

Where was he? The stark white walls held no frames, no pictures—nothing to give away his location. Greg's eyes swept around the place, and he noted the modern equipment next to his bed. There was also a constant beeping from another machine that he couldn't see. After several attempts, he was able to raise his hand, but even that simple action drained him of energy. His confusion grew when he noticed a tube attached to his arm and the stale scent of blood wafting around him.

Then he remembered.

⁂

"Ready?" Cade McPherson grinned at him from the pilot seat of their rented DeHavilland bush plane.

"Sure am." Greg propped himself up next to Cade. After pulling out the set of headphones hanging on the dash, he adjusted the earpiece before donning them.

Cade had planned this hunting trip and made all the necessary arrangements. This time, Greg had agreed to rough it, backpacking in the wilderness instead of employing the services of a guide, like they'd done in the past.

Flying and hunting had always been a passion the two friends shared. They had met when Greg's father, Gregory Jr., brought Cade on to help Greg when business took him to out-of-town meetings and presentations. Cade had soon become his right-hand man.

"Let's find out what Beaver has to offer this time." Cade grinned before he powered up the plane. The engine whirred efficiently, and the lone propeller spun to life, spinning wildly while Cade turned his attention to the GPS. Keying their destination, he checked his watch and spoke to the man in a little shack that consisted of the control tower.

"Beaver, here we come." Greg saluted.

A deckhand waved at them, signaling their ready position and clearing them for takeoff. What had made them decide to go on their own? That was an easy one. They'd joined many expeditions before. Hunting in the Adirondacks for bucks, they'd traveled to Calvert Hill in Illinois for their prized trophy, the white tail deer. They flew west to Tehama, California, to hunt for wild pigs and to West Yaak, Montana, to hunt for moose. But Alaska gave them more bang for their buck. From the rugged and remote areas to the variety of wildlife, Alaska offered one of the most ideal hunting conditions out there. The backdrop didn't hurt, either. Greg couldn't wait to get started.

Once airborne, he removed his earpiece and pulled binoculars from his backpack. This trip had been planned about three months earlier, and now that the wait was over, he began to imagine the hunting prospects. Wolves were in abundance in Beaver, and Greg had been salivating at the possibility of encountering one. He'd also been looking forward to the unbeatable rush and the play of the hunt.

After their departure from Fairbanks, it took them half an hour to get to Beaver, where they circled a planned area close to the sandbar of a river. Once their plane had been safely anchored, they set off on foot, hunting rifles in hand and their gear strapped to their backs.

This trip also doubled as an escape from the ugliness of his impending divorce. Greg sighed while they made their way through an opening in the vast wilderness awaiting them. Cassandra was a socialite he'd met a few years back. At first, it had seemed like a perfect union—a beautiful woman and a powerful businessman. He'd had no qualms marrying her, despite the negative feedback about her character. "Gold-digging bitch" was one of the mildest labels he'd heard applied to her.

Greg had shrugged it off. With her beguiling beauty, he had been taken in—hook, line, and sinker. He'd offered her the prettiest diamond money could buy, and they celebrated one of the biggest weddings in New York City history and honeymooned all over the world.

In a way, his money blinded her, and that had set them up for bigger troubles. As the old saying went, it hadn't been long before "the honeymoon was over." All of the predictions came true when Cassandra demanded more than he was willing to give her—she wanted a family. Even though he desired one as well, he couldn't bear the thought of having children while in a failing marriage with a philandering wife.

Sure, he'd known all along, but he stuck it out long enough to see if things would change over time. When the last, little sliver of hope had been snuffed out, he'd filed for divorce, and the rest was history.

She'd be looking at half his net worth, which in plain lingo would make her a billionaire. With any luck, all that money would appease her and soon mark an end to their long, drawn-out court battle.

Two days into their trek and still coming up empty handed, Greg and Cade stopped at a clearing. It was a safe enough place to pitch their tent.

Looking back, Cade had been pressing more than usual for details about the divorce and Cassandra. Though Greg hadn't found the questions odd at the time, he could now guess the motive behind the shooting—the bastard had been screwing his soon-to-be ex-wife. That had to be the reason. Nothing else fit. But why?

Greg's head began to ache as pieces of information came flashing back. He'd often seen them talking, perhaps standing a bit closer together than was normal, but he'd shrugged it off. A man's best friend and wife *could* develop a natural friendship—there was no need to make mountains out of molehills.

Would things be better for them if he were out of the picture altogether? That must be the case. Otherwise there was no need for Cade to go to such great lengths to get rid of him. Still, the bastard had been sloppy at best. Since the botched murder attempt, Greg had sworn to make sure to extend the same hell to his so-called friend. Simple as that.

No one attempted to kill Gregory Andrews III and lived to talk about it. His fists clenched at the thought how he'd been taken out like an animal, shot and left for dead. He'd get to the bottom of things. The first thing to worry about was getting out of this place, wherever it was, and getting home. Then he'd start planning payback.

The sound of moaning jolted Sarah awake. She bolted from the chair and rushed to check on her patient. His eyes were closed, although his mouth moved as though he were trying to speak. He made no audible noise except a faint groan, and his body shook.

Sarah's instinct led her to place a comforting hand on his forehead. It was not a surprise that the skin was hot to the touch. The stranger jerked and let out another distressed sound. He appeared agitated, wincing with pain at the slightest movement.

"Don't try to speak or move. You're safe. Nod your head if you are cold." Sarah kept her voice low, and she felt helpless while his face contorted once more.

He nodded once, with obvious effort.

Although she knew she'd regret doing so, Sarah rested her hand on his bare arm, light as a feather so as not to startle him. When his face registered nothing, she began rubbing his arm to help his blood circulate. When the friction between their skins built up, a tingling awareness rippled through her body. A sensitized burning on her palm sparked with every stroke of the hard muscles beneath his clammy skin. An inexplicable awareness of his male body and her response to their close proximity compounded her confusion.

After a few minutes, she had to pry her hand away. It was too much, and the fact that she enjoyed it scared her.

Oh, you know you want it. Stop hiding from yourself. Have a little fun, the little uninvited and unwelcome voice said from deep within her.

Trying to ignore it, Sarah moved to take out a blanket. She had been taught to cool down post-surgical patients when fever was present. In this case, though, there was a risk of shock or becoming septic without the proper antibiotics and equipment, and that swayed her decision.

Taking a quick peek at the wound, she noted a few improvements. The stitches seemed to be holding up and the bleeding had abated, which was another good sign. After re-taping the bandage, she placed the blanket on him and tucked the edges around his body with care. That calmed the shivering a little.

Satisfied, she took his wrist and timed his respirations. Good, but not great.

Turning her mind to the next task, she leaned closer and whispered in his ear. "I will give you another shot of Demerol, which is all we have here for pain." She could see that he was trying to follow the sound of her voice with his head, but he stopped with a wince. Sarah quickened her movements and administered the last of the vial she had on hand.

The shot took effect within minutes, and the man faded into another restless slumber. Sarah again checked his vital signs, recording his body temperature and the appearance of the surgical site, and jotted them down. Everything looked as well as could be expected. She hoped that the bullet removal and the transfusion were well within the golden hour. If so, he would have a better chance of survival.

Weary, she returned to the desk to complete the remaining progress report. Her stomach growled, but since she couldn't leave him by himself, she concentrated on finishing her report.

A few minutes later, his teeth began chattering. Sarah watched him shiver underneath the layers of blankets. She was running out of options.

There were no other blankets left in the clinic, and his shaking began to turn into convulsive tremors. When he gave an agonized scream of pain, she thought, *Man, it never ends*. There was just one option left, and it was the one she had no right to do.

Everyone knew survival skill number one—body heat.

Not letting her doubts dissuade her, she climbed onto the little examination table, taking care to avoid his wound while she slid down next to him. *This should be easy.* Sarah expelled a deep breath and turned her body to face him, putting an arm across his chest and resting one leg around his. Simple enough, right?

It would have been, if the man's bloodshot eyes hadn't opened at her touch. Her body turned rigid at once, and she moved to lift her limbs off him.

Pink crept up her cheeks. Sarah lowered her eyes, afraid to look at him when their faces were almost touching. His eyes tilted in her direction.

"Do . . . it," his hoarse tone begged.

Sarah hesitated, but her innate healing sense would not let her refuse to do the right thing. She lowered her limbs onto his body again and inched closer. His slight movement suggested he was trying to snuggle against her, but whatever pain he'd been grappling with prevented him from doing so.

"Don't move. Just stay still if you can. You'll feel warmer in no time."

"Have you no respect for yourself, or even for me?"

The livid voice boomed across the room and tore away her cloud of lethargy. Sarah's eyes shot open, and she blinked, feeling disoriented. It took a moment to focus, but then she found herself staring up at a man who glowered back down at her. Her father. She bolted to a sitting position and glanced across the room to the empty bed. With a gasp, she realized that she had been dreaming all along.

It had felt so real. She shivered at the memory.

"You disgrace yourself." Her father's accusation made her cringe.

Sarah heard curious voices outside the clinic. There wasn't a doubt that the entire town was waiting for the verdict. Their small town's antenna was very good at learning about these types of situations. Reports must have already been spreading. Considering the inexplicable turn of events, this would have qualified for a front-page headline if they had a local newspaper.

Ahila glared at her with disapproval and walked out of the room. His anger was something she'd expected, and her one hope was that that he'd accept her explanation.

She closed her eyes and leaned on the desk for a brief moment before dutifully following her father outside the clinic. The scene outdoors was no surprise. Old and young alike had gathered, their expressions ranging from curiosity to outright accusation and blatant disappointment. Just a few people showed any signs of sympathy, Lily and Trimble among them.

"Do you have any idea what you have done?" Ahila's voice boomed. It was no wonder why words in Beaver traveled fast.

"I did what I thought was right. Surely you're not putting me through school so I can pick and choose who to help?" Sarah's rising voice questioned. Her usual reserved character was gone. Instead, she spewed the same venom with which her father was lashing her.

"You had no right to give away what little medicine we had left. Didn't you think about the possibility that if any one of us fell ill, there would be no chance of surviving because you gave away the few provisions we had?" Anger flashed in her father's eyes while he stared her down. He had a slight stature, but size didn't matter. Ahila was big in presence and command.

"I did the right thing, Papa," Sarah cried in response. She clenched and unclenched her fists. How could she make her father understand?

"You did not! You chose an outsider and made him your priority. They come here with full knowledge that we cannot give them much in terms of medical assistance. They sign their waivers. They know what to expect."

"I'm not going to become a doctor to make decisions about who deserves to be treated." Tears came down with a gush, and she couldn't help the quivering in her voice.

Lily took a step forward, but Trimble held her back.

"And you won't ever become one," Ahila thundered. "As of today, I'm washing my hands of you. Consider yourself expelled. You're no longer a part of this tribe. This community you turned your back on will no longer fund your training. You're on your own."

"Papa, you don't mean what you're saying." Pain squeezed in her chest. Sarah inched forward and dropped to her knees.

"I meant every word. Your blatant disrespect of my position and of the man you're promised to will be your shame to bear. You can leave now." Ahila turned on his heel and started to walk away.

“Papa, please . . .” Sarah scrambled to her feet and ran after him. She tried to pull on his arm to make him stop. Instead of even glancing in her direction, he shrugged off her hand and strode away in silence.

Banishment in the Gwich’in culture, though rare, was still practiced in current times. There was a degree of detachment from the American laws in rural areas such as Beaver. Tribal leaders were often called upon to decide on cases ranging from petty theft, domestic abuse, and disturbances to traffic mishaps and other crimes. That authority also included town business, which could take months for the local government to intervene in. Banishment had become a part of their policing structure, but it was a harsh decision that could only be handed down by the head of their tribe.

This was now Sarah’s reality. She would be banished from her father’s home and from the only place she’d ever known. Her crime? Saving a life.

Ahila considered his actions as stemming not from prejudice but from his responsibility to look out for the best interest of his people. Sarah had understood that goods and medications were hard to come by. Delivery occurred just once a month because transportation was both limited and expensive. Medicines cost money—money they didn’t have. For Sarah to decide the best course of action in the situation was deemed irresponsible.

With the banishment given, she couldn’t stay on the tribe’s land until the decree was lifted. The ban was now in force and must be carried out right away.

Turning around, Sarah saw a blur of faces that regarded her with the same fire she had seen in her father’s eyes. Only Lily and Trimble stepped forward to intervene when people began stalking in her direction, intent on carrying out her father’s judgment.

“There’s no need to do anything.” Trimble raised his hand, holding off the herd that would otherwise push her onto the next plane out of town. “I will personally see to her departure. Go on home.”

Speaking with the authority of a future leader, Trimble persuaded the throng of people to disperse. *Surreal* couldn’t even begin to describe the whole scene. Sarah wrapped her hands around her body to keep from falling apart. When Lily pulled her into her arms, Sarah knew that her exodus couldn’t be postponed.

She pulled away from Lily, whirled around, and ran home. Millions of confused thoughts were flying through her mind. Banished! Where would she go?

Packing was a fast chore when you owned close to nothing. She was out of the house within minutes, having packed a duffle bag filled with a few clothes, books, a family picture, and a couple hundred dollars she managed to scrape together.

Sarah walked to the plane depot and waited for Lily. With little money to her name, she wouldn't be able to go very far. Looking around, she saw few people in the immediate area. Most of them hadn't heard the verdict yet, but they gave her questioning looks nonetheless. Lily and Trimble arrived after a few minutes. Trimble wore a grim expression, while Lily looked like she was on the border of hysteria.

"I believe this happened for the best," Sarah said with false confidence. The smile she tried to muster for their sakes failed to reach her eyes.

"Hello? Sarah, just in case you don't realize this, you have been banished from your home. Now, tell me . . . when did that qualify as good?" Lily said incredulously.

Exasperated, confused, hurt, and scared, Sarah drew out a long and shaky sigh. "Don't you think this incident voids my arranged marriage to Trimble?"

A bittersweet expression flashed across Lily and Trimble's faces.

"This is not how it should be. Not at your expense. Not like this." Trimble shook his head. "This isn't right. You did an honorable thing."

"This is Father's way of showing me that I've crossed the line. Who knows? Maybe I deserved it. But don't think for even one minute that I regret my decision." Despite her tears, Sarah jutted out her chin in defiance.

"We have a little something for you." Lily fished inside her bag and produced a wad of bills. "Take the money—you'll need it. It's not much, but we think it should get you through the next few weeks while you're looking for a job and a place to stay."

Reluctantly, Sarah accepted the money Lily shoved in her pocket. She had little of her own and nowhere to go, and being proud wasn't going to get her anywhere.

"Thank you."

"Do you have any idea where you're headed?" Lily's eyes brimmed with tears.

Sarah shook her head.

The sound of the bush plane's little engine sounded—an alert that it was ready for commuters to come onboard. "Well, this is goodbye, for now." Sarah's heart grew heavier by the minute.

One thing she regretted was not having gotten the chance to find out what happened to that man. She hoped that he had survived his wound and would be able to get back to normal.

Glancing at the people boarding the aircraft, she waved for the driver to wait.

"I want to know if he made it through the night." Sarah gathered her duffel bag and slung the strap over her shoulder.

"I'll try to see what I can find out," Lily promised with a sniff.

A stab of worry lanced Sarah's heart. "I'll call soon, and you can tell me about him." The whistle sounded, signaling the plane's departure. "I must go."

"Keep in touch." Lily held Sarah's hands before pulling her into a fierce hug. They cried together.

"I have to go." She pulled away before Lily could say another word.

Sarah's actions had driven her to take a different route and go somewhere unexpected. With a snap of a finger, life had doled out a staggering and humbling hurdle to overcome, yet there was no regret on her part. She'd saved a life, and that was all that mattered. From this point on, she had other problems to worry about. The timing couldn't have been any worse, but she squared her shoulders. To lift her flagging resolve and reiterate her ability to face the unknown, she spoke aloud.

"Bring it on."

Chapter 5

In the past month, thoughts of her father and the fateful day that led to her expulsion from her town occupied most of Sarah's waking hours. Yeah, it hadn't been a walk in the park. She'd racked her brain for ways to get Ahila to lift the ban, but it wouldn't be easy. When he set his mind on things, he was almost impossible to budge. He refused to take her calls, which confirmed that he remained angry and unyielding.

It went without saying that the stranger had been on her mind, too. She often wondered what had happened to him after he was transported to Fairbanks. Did he survive his wound? Had any complications arisen from her impromptu, amateur operation?

Sarah had replayed the scene in her mind over and over. No matter how often her rational side assured her she'd done the right thing, the doubts lingered. She'd treaded the gray area of ethics. Talk about a sword dangling over her head.

"Do you have class today?" Cheryl came bounding into the room, a pesky, cheeky, honest-to-goodness fireball masquerading as a sweet, innocent-looking woman.

"Yeah, I'm leaving in half an hour."

In many ways, Cheryl Dobson had become Lily's Los Angeles counterpart when Sarah entered the university. They'd met during their first biology class together and had been inseparable ever since. Although their personalities were like night and day, Cheryl's bubbly attitude complemented Sarah's more withdrawn demeanor. Despite Cheryl's "speak your mind and think later" approach, the two women had hit it off right away. In fact, it was their differences that had paved the way to a unique friendship. They got along well, which had made it easier for Sarah to transition into her new environment.

Now, Cheryl gave her friend a long look-over before flopping down at the edge of the bed. Sarah knew what was coming. Cheryl wasn't one to mince words, and Sarah had gotten an earful already, especially now that they lived together. Upon her arrival, she'd called Cheryl from the airport, asking for a place to stay for one night. Her friend had jumped in with the offer to share a room in her home. Cheryl's parents were on board with the idea, inviting Sarah to stay with them for as long as she needed a roof over her head.

Every day Cheryl spotted her sulking, she'd throw out a barrage of smart-ass comments to get her to start talking about her feelings. Through all her scolding, Cheryl conceded she would have done the same thing in that situation.

"What's on your mind?" It wasn't a real question, but it was Cheryl's way of drawing Sarah out of her shell.

Frustration put an edge in her voice. "It's been a month, and my father doesn't sound like he'll budge."

Cheryl seemed to consider that and smiled. "Are you sure you're just thinking of your father?"

Relentless and borderline-annoying as she was, Cheryl had Sarah pegged. It was scary how easy it was for her friend to read her like an open book. Sarah chose to feign innocence. "What are you talking about?"

Narrowing her eyes, Cheryl peered at her closely. "You're not fooling me. Spill."

Sarah kept up with the pretense. "Spill what?"

"Don't tell me you haven't thought about that man whose life you saved. These were your exact words, and I quote, 'Cheryl, he's beautiful. A work of art. I haven't seen anyone as gorgeous as him up close.' " Cheryl laughed after mimicking her and ducked for cover, knowing full well that retaliation might be headed her way.

"What do you want me to say? I want to know what happened to him. You keep on bringing it up and blaming me for playing Mother Teresa. Now all I can think of is whether I messed things up more than I helped," Sarah objected, scrunching up a piece of paper into a ball and hurling it in Cheryl's direction. She missed, and Cheryl stuck her tongue out at her.

Sarah threw her hands up in frustration. That much was true—she'd crossed the line when she played doctor without a license. In her own defense, she had done it based on the urgency of the situation. She'd been second-guessing her decision ever since, but it had been a life or death call without the benefit of reconsideration or do-over.

Cheryl's expression softened. "For what it's worth, I believe you did the right thing."

"I know . . . I just can't help being curious."

"You spoke with Lily, right?"

Sarah nodded her head.

"What did she say happened after you left?"

"Lily said things happened real fast. When she came back to the clinic later, there was a helicopter, state troopers, and guys in suits asking questions. At one point, Lily said it got scary. The town had been thrown into one big crime scene. No one could leave until they were issued clearance."

"Wow." Cheryl chewed on her bottom lip. "Makes you wonder why he got shot and what's going on with that big entourage. You think he's an important man?"

Sarah considered that for a moment. The man had seemed nowhere near ordinary. Even in his sleep, he'd been intimidating, and she could easily imagine him being someone born to power. His clothes had spoken of fine craftsmanship and excellent taste—too bad she'd had to cut them off him. "Maybe. I really wouldn't know."

"Hmm . . . you did say you dreamt about keeping him warm that night, right?" Cheryl teased.

Sarah should be used to her by now. Still, color rose up her neck. Flipping over on the bed, she buried her face in a pillow. "Shut up!" The pillow muffled her response. She regretted ever telling her friend about that dream.

"Yeah, yeah." Cheryl giggled.

"Whatever." It was impossible to get Cheryl to take her seriously when she got into this teasing mood. It was Sarah's cue to leave for class. "I'm going. Don't wait up. There's a good chance I'll be late tonight."

Snatching her backpack off the desk, Sarah hurried out of the room before Cheryl could see how her teasing affected her. It was one of many things she wasn't ready to admit.

"Greg, the car's ready," Simon Moss called out from the doorway.

Gregory Andrews III glanced up from the mountain of papers on his desk—documents requiring his signature, approval, or review. He nodded at Simon, who left after scrutinizing him a bit longer than necessary. There were too many papers piling up around him, and Greg had no idea how fast he could get to everything. He'd been back in the city for two weeks following his long hospital confinement in Fairbanks. Since he couldn't make an appearance at work without clearance from the doctor, he opted to work from home. The trouble was his body hadn't been the same since he'd returned to the mainland.

Most days he felt better, and it seemed like he was inching back to normalcy. There were good days when he moved with ease, enjoying the absence of shooting pain from his abdomen or the recurrent nausea and dizziness. But some days, the only thing he could do was stay in bed or seated, or he'd have stumbled and hurt himself.

Greg planted his hands on the desk and hoisted his body up. Before taking a step, he plucked the cane perched on the side of his chair. The cane was a staple for him these days, an aid he needed in case his muscles decided to spasm without advance notice. It had happened many times earlier, and the results had been devastating. Busted lips, extreme fatigue, and a bruised ego were some of the side-effects he'd encountered after his surgery.

Clutching the cane, he hobbled toward the door, through the hallway and out of his Fifth Avenue penthouse to the elevator. The elevator attendant smiled at him when he approached.

"Good morning, Mr. Andrews. You're looking well today," the elderly gentleman greeted with sincerity.

"Thank you, Lewis. I'm feeling much better." Greg resisted the urge to snap back. Instead, he concentrated on the descending numbers encased in a metal display. His mood hadn't been the best and would remain sour until he heard from Trevor.

"Are you going for another appointment?" Lewis looked at Greg over his shoulder, his kind eyes crinkling at the corners.

Greg gave a silent sigh before answering. "Yes. It looks like it's never going to end." His tone sounded curt, despite his best efforts to keep his annoyance at bay.

At long last, the elevator saved him from the unwanted small talk. "See you later, Lewis. Say hi to the missus for me."

Greg waved to him before stepping out of the elevator. Pushing his sunglasses down to cover his eyes from the sun's glare, he headed to the glass door a doorman held open for him.

"G'morning, Mr. Andrews."

"Hey, Juan." Greg marched straight to the waiting limousine, and Simon closed the door after him. In the confines of his chauffeured car, Greg let out a ragged breath. *Here's to another day of tests, inconclusive results, and nothing solid to go on. How can doctors scratch their heads and repeatedly come up empty and still have jobs?*

Granted the woman, this Sarah, had successfully saved his life by removing the bullet and transfusing him with her blood. Although the surgery had been crude and performed under less than optimal circumstances, his test results showed no permanent damage in the affected area.

Greg's heart and fists clenched at the same time. Even though the doctors didn't understand the allergic reactions from the blood transfusion, there had to be medication to alleviate the nausea spells and the poor balance he'd been suffering from ever since. For heaven's sake, this was the twenty-first century. There had to be a corresponding treatment for every disease imaginable, and yet the doctors couldn't even come up with a name for his affliction. They just called them "side-effects."

He stared straight ahead and hoped no small talk would be necessary for the rest of the day. A wide range of concerns needed his attention, from work to his parents. And of course, there was Cade . . .

Now that was his top priority—as well as dealing with *her* . . .

Once Simon had taken the passenger seat next to him, the limousine purred and joined the city's morning rush hour. Out of the corner of his eye, Greg saw Simon regarding him with mild curiosity. As the head of the company's security, he had been one of the few people who knew the truth about what had gone down in Alaska. Simon had volunteered to act as Greg's bodyguard until he was back and up on his feet.

A reliable and loyal employee, Simon could always be counted on. In his late forties, Simon was as physically fit as a twenty-year-old, sporting a muscular physique underneath his everyday uniform of a leather jacket and denim pants. Since Greg stayed cooped up in his penthouse most of the time, this arrangement also gave his security man the much-needed vacation he deserved. As long as Simon understood his boss's need for privacy and quiet, they'd get along fine.

Greg had decided to keep everything on the down low for now, until Cade was found and apprehended. Until then, he'd continue to have his soon-to-be ex-wife followed. The more dirt the PI dug up on Cassandra, the better Greg's case against her would be.

Smirking, he settled on the plush leather seat. With his eyes closed, he focused his attention on the mark his mysterious savior had left on him—the heady scent of cedar and mint had been engrained in his brain.

After yet another disappointing meeting with Dr. Kemp, Greg walked out of the clinic still without a firm grasp on what was causing his frequent spasms and dizziness. His hemoglobin level had been tested several times and checked out okay. The doctor's latest absurd suggestion was to hire a personal caregiver to help him with basic chores. In short, Dr. Kemp wanted him to get a babysitter.

Just because Greg had money didn't mean he spent it irresponsibly. His doctor had come up with a list of recommended nurses who were available at the drop of a hat, but Greg had snorted at the idea and stormed back to the waiting car, ready to explode.

"Nothing again?" Simon pushed the button for the glass divider. The partition came up, ensuring their conversation would be private.

"No." Although he'd intended to say nothing more, Greg ended up blurting out the doctor's ludicrous idea. "Dr. Kemp wants me to get a nurse. A caregiver who can help me out while I regain my strength and remind me to take my medicine, like I'm a child."

Simon chuckled, as usual. He might have been a man of few words, but he was certainly not one to miss the humor in any given situation. "Did you tell him to go to hell?"

"Yes."

The ringing of his cell phone prevented him from replying further. Greg pulled his Blackberry from his trouser pocket and checked the caller ID, recognizing the number of a private investigation firm. "Trevor, I've been waiting for your call."

Greg listened to the head of the firm speak for several minutes.

"Are you sure that's what happened?"

Again, information came in a rapid-fire flood that included proof, names of witnesses, and sources.

"Then proceed as planned. I want it clean. Cover your bases." He paused and listened. "Yes, I know how much you're charging. Don't worry about the money. No trace, all right? And no one gets hurt. I'll handle the rest from my end. Thanks."

After he hung up, he smiled at Simon, who had been looking at him with a strange expression.

"There's been a change of plan. I'm going to listen to Dr. Kemp's advice and get someone to help me after all."

~

The autumn air was crisp when Sarah stepped out of the main building to head home after her last class. The days were shorter now, a far cry from the late sunsets she was used to in Beaver. She hugged her sweatshirt closer and braced herself for the two-mile walk back to Cheryl's house. Unlike Alaska, Los Angeles at nine in the evening still bustled with activities, cars continued to race by, and people littered the Westwood campus like the circus was in town. Back home, the only sounds she'd hear during her night walks were chirping crickets and the dense silence distinctive of their quiet town.

She missed home, and she missed her father. Regardless of what he had said, Sarah couldn't fault him for the decision he'd made. He had his people's best interests at heart. Being a leader came with big responsibilities, and that meant being an example to his people, even if it led to sacrificing his only child to prove his point. Her actions had come with a high price, and she was paying it.

Sarah turned left on Wilshire Boulevard, a busy thoroughfare, before she reached the section of houses a mile away. Cheryl's father had suggested she take the well-lit routes as much as possible, considering her lengthy walk to get home. The entire trek would take about thirty-five minutes, enough to get her mind all worked up.

Her main concern these days was her tuition fee. Ahila had made it clear that the tribe would stop paying for her schooling. With her hectic class schedule, all she could manage was twenty hours a week at the campus bookstore. If she was going to cover her food expenses and incidentals, she'd have to find a way to earn more.

Once she'd cleared the busy street, the lampposts illuminating the way were more spread out, giving just sporadic specks of light in the general vicinity. Sarah lengthened her steps, wanting to cut the walking time as much as possible. A nondescript car stopped a few feet away just as she was about to cross the street. She stepped back and waved, trying to allow the car to pass. Instead, the doors opened, and three men got out and moved in her direction.

Sarah clutched her backpack tighter, wishing more than ever that she had a cell phone. This would have been a perfect time to practice being a good citizen by reporting suspicious activities or run into an active member of the neighborhood watch. A few vital seconds passed before she realized she should run. She broke into a sprint, but she hadn't even gotten a few yards before strong hands gripped both her arms and yanked her back. Another hand was clamped over her mouth, making screaming impossible. A piece of cloth was tied over her mouth, and she was carried back to the car, kicking at her captors in a futile attempt to get free. They shoved her in the passenger seat, sandwiching her between two muscular men. That effectively squashed any hope of escape. Before she could take mental notes of her abductors' faces, a blindfold covered her eyes.

A deep voice came from the front of the car. "I will say this once. We're not going to hurt you if you sit still and stop fighting."

Sarah wanted to yell obscenities at the man trying to quiet her down, but the cloth covering her mouth muffled her angry protests.

Just when she'd thought her life was in the biggest mess possible, this happened. This experience tipped the scale from "mess" into "hopeless and shitty" territory. Tears burned her eyes, and she sent fervent, silent pleas to Dotson'Sa to make sure her suffering would be quick and painless. What were these goons going to do with her? Kill her? Rape her? The possibilities made her cry with terror and desperation.

Chapter 6

Sarah alternated crying with occasional attempts to beg for mercy around the gag, yet her captors stayed silent. They never relaxed their grip on her, either. They'd said she wouldn't get hurt if she stopped fighting. Could she trust her abductors' assurances?

Many scenarios raced through her head. Maybe this was some kind of payback. Or perhaps the Medical Board had found out about the unconventional surgery she'd performed in Beaver and decided to throw her in jail. If that was the case, though, how come these people didn't identify themselves before taking her? Nothing made sense, and her thoughts swam in a sea of fear and uncertainty.

In the enclosed space, the only distinguishable sound was the car's humming engine and the muted songs on the radio. The car had been cruising for about twenty-minutes, and she guessed from the swooshing sound of other cars that they were on the freeway. If they had been driving along residential roads, the traffic would have been more stop-and-go.

Forcing words past the gag, she tried again. "Where are you taking me?" Silence answered her once more. She could hear the annoying sound of someone chewing gum in the front passenger seat and the guy on her left drumming his finger on the glass window.

"Please, can someone answer me?" her muffled voice pleaded one more time. Her request fell on deaf ears.

After a few minutes, the car came to a stop, and Sarah jerked her head up, holding her breath and hoping the blindfold would be removed. It didn't happen. Instead, they ushered her out of the car without a word. Once her feet were planted on solid ground, the new sounds around her struck her as odd.

Most of the noise seemed to come from engines, propellers, gusts of wind, and the sound of planes taking off and landing nearby. Where in God's name had they taken her? Sarah stayed where she was until someone took her elbow, guiding her forward. She shook the hand off and refused to move.

Whispered conversation swirled around her, but the roar of engines and buzzing propellers made it difficult to understand anything. Growing more hopeless with each passing second, she made a final attempt to break free from her three-man entourage by turning back to the car. It was a bad decision on her part. Huge bodies surrounded her like a brick wall, and then one of them slung her over his shoulder.

At that point, Sarah lost her bearings altogether. Rage engulfed her, and she began pounding on the man's back with all the force she had. No matter how hard she struck and hit, no one hit her back. The only response she got was a grunt of pain and irritation from the man who held her like a sack of rice.

Before Sarah could strike out again, her arms were pinned to her back, rendering her helpless and disheartened. Without the ability to scream, she started to cry, feeling more scared now than ever.

When she was a child, her mother had made her memorize prayers in their native language, even if she'd barely understood their meaning. *"If you're ever in a dire situation, say this prayer and you shall feel comfort."* In her hysterical state, she began praying out loud in the words her mother had taught her. Her suspicion that they were putting her on a plane was confirmed when she heard a female voice welcoming them aboard. The woman was abruptly shushed by one of the men. Sarah was lowered into a seat, and then her wrists were bound in front of her, and a lap belt secured her.

Sarah continued to chant her prayer, although quieter this time. She kept repeating the words until exhaustion took its toll, sending her spiraling into a restless slumber after the plane took off to its unknown destination.

When Sarah awoke, it felt like she was resting on a bed of clouds, so soft and luxurious. She smiled, never imagining she'd ever get a chance to touch the fluffy cotton, ever. They've always been out of grasp, something she admired from afar. This time, she laid on them, not just enjoying the experience but also loving the glorious sensation.

If she were dead, then she must be in heaven. Her smile got bigger. At least Dotson'Sa had heeded her prayer for a quick and painless death.

Sarah recalled her mother saying that heaven was whatever you wanted it to be. It could be a bed of clouds, songs of happiness touching your heart, a remarkable scent of the most fragrant flower, and peacefulness unknown to man.

She must be in heaven. Her hand caressed the fluffy clouds again, and another grin spread across her face. When she opened her eyes to feed on the images of her own utopia and her vision adjusted, she noted light yellow walls with stenciled flowers. Among them were her favorites—forget-me-nots and stargazer lilies. She basked in the beauty surrounding her.

Her eyes traveled to the furniture. It was exactly what she would have envisioned for her perfect sanctuary. The toile upholstery had been paired with black, distressed wood tinged with gold specks, and the overall effect was breathtaking. It was the sort of room you would only see on television or in home decorating magazines. Sarah's gaze traveled upward to where a canopy spread across the expanse of the bed. Dainty and ethereal, its panels were also made of the same sublime toile material.

Sighing, her mind raced back to her father, wondering when they would meet again. Then she thought of her mother. Could their separate heavens ever cross paths? Did individual heavens find an intersecting point where happiness could flow freer? She marveled at the idea and let the comforting thought warm her.

Still basking in the scents and visions of happiness, she heard a tap coming from her heaven's door. She rolled her eyes at the errant humorous idea that crossed her mind. Someone wanted to see her—an angel perhaps?

With the grace of pleasure coursing through her, she replied, "Come in." Even her voice sounded dreamy, and that made her beam with radiance.

A short, plump woman with graying blond hair and dressed in a starched white uniform walked in. Her cautious expression was replaced with a welcoming smile the instant their eyes met. "Good morning, miss. I gather you slept well?"

Sarah's smile dimmed. It was as though a record had been playing a beautiful melody until someone scraped the needle across the vinyl. Her bubble burst.

She looked at the woman with a blank expression.

The face of the angel, or whoever she was, lit up. "You were mighty tired last night when you arrived, so Simon brought you here to your room." The woman stopped at the foot of the bed.

Well, wasn't that dandy? Sarah even had someone named Simon carrying her to bed. She lifted the clouds that were wrapped around her like a cocoon and pushed herself up into a sitting position.

"I was?"

This heaven was fast becoming more odd than divine. Sarah scrutinized the material she'd first thought was a bed of clouds. Scooting to one side of the bed, she ran her fingers on the goose down comforter and brought it to her nose to give it a sniff. It was luxurious, all right.

"Yes, miss." The woman moved toward the curtains and pressed a button. In an instant, the drapery receded from sight and the room was bathed in sunlight. She looked over her shoulder at Sarah. "Do you prefer breakfast in bed, or are you planning on joining Mr. Andrews?"

That was Sarah's cue to jump out of bed, panic returning to claw at her. This wasn't heaven, and the woman standing before her wasn't an angel. "Who are you? Where am I? And who is Mr. Andrews?" she screamed in terror while she backed away from the woman, finding herself next to the floor-to-ceiling window. She whipped her head to check for an escape route, just to discover that they were at least thirty floors from the ground.

"My name is Matilda. I'm Mr. Andrews' nanny. Well . . . I was a long time ago. I'm his housekeeper. I apologize that I can't answer your other question. I'd rather let Mr. Andrews answer that for you."

Matilda stayed in her spot and did not approach Sarah, who at that point felt like a scared cat after a cold shower.

So the heaven she'd been dreaming of was, in fact, some kind of hell? Would someone pinch her now and tell her she'd been punked?

"Matilda, did you know I was kidnapped?"

Astonishment crossed Matilda's face, and she scolded Sarah. "Mr. Andrews wouldn't ever do that. In fact, why don't you get dressed and join him in the dining room so you can set everything straight with him."

Sarah stared at the woman, dumbfounded.

The older lady strode to mirror-paneled double doors at the far end of the room and opened them. "Clothes in your size are all here, as well as shoes, which were ordered for you." She pointed to neat rows of outfits, which were arranged by color scheme, and another little closet within a closet, which held shoes of different colors, styles, and heels.

"I don't know who he is," Sarah croaked.

"He sure sounded like you kids were well acquainted. Now, why don't you wash up while I tidy your bed? Dress warm, just in case you two go for a walk. Bless his heart, he sure needs it."

Sarah took a step back, eyeing every exit point in the room. *It's obvious that Matilda adores Mr. Andrews,* Sarah thought. Because of that, she knew the woman wasn't someone she could rely on for help. Her brain started thinking a mile a minute. She'd have to plan her getaway once Matilda left the room.

"Fine, I'll meet Mr. Andrews for breakfast, but please leave me for now. I'd like a moment alone."

Matilda nodded her head in understanding, no doubt thinking Sarah had lost her mind. The woman walked to the door, but not before she gave Sarah a final, fleeting glance. "The dining room is down the hall to your left." She tilted her head before closing the door.

With her mind racing, Sarah ran back to the window and looked out. Given a different set of circumstances, she would have been gawking at the grandiose view which greeted her, but nothing in her current predicament could be considered grand. Not even the tall skyscrapers or the beautiful skyline dotting the magnificent tapestry could distract her.

Where am I? She had been kidnapped—taken against her will and held as a prisoner in this beautiful nightmare. *No exit here*, she thought after studying the seamless window.

Sarah scurried across the room, grabbed the golden doorknob, and twisted. Relief washed over her when it opened. She could slip out of the room and hide somewhere until the coast was clear, and then she'd run for the front door as fast as possible. With that small plan in place, she poked her head out. Discovering a man standing across the hallway from her door, she recoiled in an instant, slamming the door shut just as he looked up.

Dotson'Sa, why have you forsaken me? The question ran in her mind, but she was unable to utter the insolent words. Still, she was trapped. That pretty much summed up her situation.

She darted to another door and opened it with trembling hands. It wasn't another exit. Instead, she found herself staring into a bathroom straight from *Architectural Digest*. Fear crept up her spine, but she took a few tentative steps toward the marble sink.

I'm going to be sick! Panic made her stomach start roiling. Turning the brass spigot, she let the running water flow to drown her sobs.

After a few minutes of dry heaves, Sarah rinsed her mouth and glanced up. In the mirror's reflection, she could see the window behind her. It was small, too small to even fit a young child. There was no way out for her except the front door, and getting there would be tough with the guard standing outside.

Sarah walked back to the bedroom and slumped onto the bed. "At least I'm alive for now." She uttered the words aloud to convince herself how lucky she was. Alive and trapped in a nightmare.

Replaying what Matilda had said earlier, she knew she could get her answers from this Mr. Andrews. She would be happy to have breakfast with him if she'd get her freedom in return. It might have been naïve of her to think this way, but she had to believe her abductor possessed a good heart. Regardless, even if she had to grovel and beg, she'd do anything necessary to reclaim her liberty. But before she got ahead of herself, she still needed answers. Who and what was behind her abduction?

With her mind made up on how to approach the situation, she decided to get a quick shower. After the much-needed physical cleansing, which also cleared her mind and added an ounce of self-confidence, she proceeded to check on the clothes Matilda had shown her. When you had very little, choosing was easy. Presented now with a closet filled with name-brand outfits and gorgeous clothes, Sarah found that selecting what to wear had become an enormous task. Her limited knowledge of fashion trends made her cringe while she touched every fabric.

Whoever had selected these clothes had no idea what kind of person she was. Most of the items were dresses, which she never wore. In Beaver, all that was required were jeans, T-shirts, and thick jackets. The only times she wore dresses was for weddings and funerals. Scowling, she pulled on a lavender sweater with exquisite beading down the front, tan slacks, and brown sandals. She walked to the full-length mirror and stared at her reflection. Although she liked her appearance, she hated the sense of dread that now descended upon her. How convenient for her to be able to look good before she was fed to the wolves. Doubtless, Mr. Andrews was the head of the pack.

Sarah put her hair into a tight bun, and then took a tube of lip balm from the bathroom drawer, applying a little to her lips. Leaving her face untouched by make-up, she felt as ready as she'd ever be and opened the bedroom door.

"Good morning, Ms. Jones," the man in the hallway greeted her.

She stared at him, not knowing what to say.

"Ready for breakfast?"

He didn't wait for a response but gestured for her to follow him. The long hallway seemed to be where most of the bedrooms were situated. There had to be about five, including hers, if her observation was precise. Judging from the intricate moldings and expensive lighting fixtures, the place had been put together by someone with expensive taste and a boatload of money and resources.

Trying hard not to let the strange surroundings intimidate her, Sarah followed her tour guide closely. They walked toward an open space that could have spanned the size of a half basketball court. Big, tastefully decorated, and terribly daunting, this section included a formal dining room and adjoining living room. Sarah had never seen the likes of a house such as this one. When they turned to a smaller room, she saw Matilda again, standing by the corner and smiling in a maternal way. Her guide stopped next to the older woman, and she held out a cup for him.

"Good morning, Ms. Jones." Matilda dipped her head in a manner that seemed calculated to put Sarah at ease.

"Uh . . . hello." Sarah was tongue-tied, and articulating a response proved difficult. With a knot twisting inside her stomach, she focused on the man seated at the head of the table, whose back was turned to her.

Mr. Andrews.

Sarah stopped in her tracks a few feet behind him, vacillating between several things while she tried to decide what to do next. Should she sit down, smack Mr. Andrews in the head, or run for the door? She was still deliberating when Mr. Andrews threw down the newspaper he'd been reading and turned around to face her.

Gunshot wounds never deterred her and complicated exams failed to give her pause, but in that particular moment, she felt her heart jump straight out of her chest.

"You!" Blood rushed to her face from the sudden fury that engulfed her.

"Yes, and good morning to you, Ms. Sarah Jones. Let me introduce myself. I'm Greg Andrews." He didn't offer his hand nor did he get up from the chair. Instead, he regarded her with an amused expression while he raked his gaze over her from head to toe and back to her face. His tone was smooth, but his jaw clenched for a few seconds, making her think she'd imagined a smile in there somewhere. "Please have a seat and join me."

His noncommittal tone infuriated her. "Care to explain what this kidnapping is all about?" Her eyes flashed with anger.

Matilda gasped at the accusation. Greg signaled for privacy, and the other man hurried to escort the older woman out of the room. Greg watched them with a wry expression before turning his attention to Sarah.

"Sit." It sounded more like an order than a request.

Sarah couldn't help the fire burning inside her. "You don't kidnap someone and order them around," she snapped and trying to move back to the door.

"Don't leave." He hastily rose to his feet to follow her.

She didn't look back, breaking into a run. Concentrating on locating the exit, her steps halted when a loud crash sounded, followed by muttered curses. Sarah wheeled around and found Greg on the floor, clutching at his right leg.

Instinct told her this was the perfect chance to get away. She turned around again, eyeing the front door. Although she wanted to run, she just didn't have the heart to abandon a person who appeared hurt. "Darn it." She gritted her teeth and pivoted in time to see him struggling to stand. What was with the Florence Nightingale syndrome? Sarah hesitated, looking toward what she believed to be the door that would lead her to her freedom, and then back to Greg on the floor.

Her blasted inherent need to nurture got the best of her, and she ran back to his aid. By that point, Greg had already hoisted his body up with the help of a cane.

"Let me help you." Sarah took his free arm, but he shook her off.

"Don't touch me. God knows you've created enough problems for me."

Sarah stepped back, appalled by the allegation. "I created problems for *you*?" she repeated.

"You messed me up real bad." He took a few shaky steps, pulled up a chair, and lowered his body onto it.

"It seems to me that I saved your life," she spat, incredulous.

"And I'm going to thank you for that, but it doesn't change the fact that you had no idea what you were doing. *Playing doctor*." The last words were muttered as if he didn't want her to hear them, except she did.

"Playing doctor?"

"That's what you did. You removed the bullet, sewed me up like a doll, and exposed me to numerous conditions that allowed infection to set in. You also performed a blood transfusion that has created one side-effect after another." Greg pointed to his leg with disdain.

His words hit her like a ton of bricks, and Sarah slumped onto the chair across from him. She had done what she could. "I'm sorry." The quivering in her voice triggered a floodgate of tears. Sarah cupped her face in shame while tears poured out in a relentless burst.

Greg didn't move or say anything. Sarah sensed him shifting in his seat several times while the pressure of the past month came down on her—hard. She'd meant well. She had just wanted to help. Snatching a table napkin, she wiped her face. Greg remained quiet, and she realized he'd been watching her.

Sarah spoke again once she'd gotten her frazzled nerves in check. She looked up and met his gaze squarely. "Is this why you had me kidnapped? So you can rub my mistakes in my face? Punish me?"

He seemed to consider her question before answering. "It's one of my reasons."

She angled her body toward him. "What are the others? You want to throw me in jail?"

"I thought about it, but what good would it do me?" Greg's lips thinned, and without giving her a chance to answer, he added, "I have other things in mind as compensation for your poor judgment."

"This is blackmail. I can sue you for kidnapping, Mr. Andrews." She shook her fist at him, but he just shrugged his shoulders in response.

"Sue me? With what money, Sarah? Last I checked, you'd been driven away from your home. You have no money, no place to stay, and no other means to pull your life together." He cocked an eyebrow. "As far as I can tell, no one has even missed you yet."

That might have been true, but he had no right to sling the unfortunate details of her life at her. Sarah stood, refusing to listen anymore. "You have no right to talk to me this way, Mr. Andrews. If you want to put me in jail, go ahead." She brought her arms together and turned them around, her wrists facing him.

"No jail time for a girl like you. I have other things in mind." He smiled.

Right then, she hated everything about the man whose life she'd saved. Maybe Ahila had been right after all. She'd had no idea what she was doing.

Chapter 7

"You can't force me to do anything." Sarah glared at him. "If you want to sue me, go right ahead."

Greg smirked. "Aside from taking you from LA, all decisions from this point on will be yours to make." He regarded her intently, appreciating the girl's spirit and spunk. It didn't hurt that she looked much more beautiful in person than she had in the picture the private investigator had taken.

"How kind of you to consider my feelings." She raised her chin in defiance. "Although *taking* is a misleading term. You kidnapped me, Mr. Andrews. Just so we're clear on that particular subject."

"Call me Greg." He sighed, ignoring her scathing accusation. "Do you want to hear the terms?"

"Terms? How arrogant of you to offer me terms." The fire was back in her eyes, and they smoldered with unconcealed hatred.

"I will lay them out. It's up to you to accept, but I doubt you'll be able to resist. There are many things you need right now. If you ever want to graduate, you'll agree to my proposal. Saying no to my offer will delay"—he paused and smiled—"if not altogether derail, your plans."

He couldn't help adding that little threat. Sarah was a smart woman—academically, at least. Any simple-minded person would be certain to consider the terms first before declining. She must know how difficult it could get during the last year of med school, even if she'd had a boatload of money. Without financial support, the experience could be arduous, desperate, and frightening. He was about to offer the answer to all her troubles.

Greg stared at Sarah while she chewed her bottom lip, deep in thought. He observed her every movement—the comical way she gritted her teeth in frustration, and how her gorgeous eyes watched him while she weighed his words. The girl seemed fidgety, which added to his internal enjoyment. He chuckled to himself.

Sarah stood after a few moments and walked over to the big picture window in the adjoining living room. Greg gathered his cane and followed her, stopping a few feet away to wait. The tension emanating from her was palpable and almost electric. He stifled the urge to touch and soothe her.

She pivoted around. "What are the terms?"

"Why don't we sit down? I'm afraid my legs won't support me for a long time." Greg gestured to the leather sofa and, without waiting for her answer, plopped himself down.

Again, he waited for her to decide what she wanted to do. After a minute, she sat on the sofa across from him—as far away as possible, he noted.

Greg took that as permission to continue. "Okay. Since the rather rudimentary approach you took with the surgery, I've had recurring side-effects and pain in my stomach. The muscle spasms come and go, but most happen while I'm up and about. I also have aches and pains that inhibit my ability to engage in normal activities, such as going to work, attending my therapy sessions, and sometimes, even taking my medications."

"You need a nurse," she blurted.

"Those were the exact words my doctor used." Greg paused, making sure he said the right things that would bait her enough to agree. "This is where you come in. You'll be helping me get some work done when you're available, and going to my appoint—"

"Whoa! Whoa! Stop right there. I'm not a nurse. You're not thinking that I will agree to this." Her eyes morphed into slits, her anger blazing.

"You have no other choice. Plus, the pay and the other perks are going to be worth your trouble." Greg willed his voice to stay calm and even while he tried to make sure the prospect sounded as palatable as possible—an offer she'd find difficult to refuse.

"You're going to pay me?" Disbelief crossed her face. Sarah stood and began pacing.

"Yes, and I scheduled your classes around my own schedule. You'll attend school in the evening. And in the mornings, while I work, you can study if I don't need any help. You can earn your keep here by helping me out. Whatever else that's left will be your salary. You need not be concerned about your education being interrupted. Your tuition will be paid, and you will have a place to stay. It'll solve all your concerns, while paying me back for the mistakes you made."

Sarah stopped walking and raised her chin. It was obvious that she hated the word *mistake* as much as he did, but he'd never admit it. She narrowed her eyes. "Why are you doing this? There are better ways to spend your money and more competent people out there to help you."

"Perhaps I just want you close to me in case the doctors have questions regarding the incompetent emergency procedure you performed. Besides, I want your blood tested. It would be a big help in identifying the causes of my side-effects." He met her gaze without wavering.

"And if I say no?"

Greg replied without hesitation. "That's when I take you to jail and file charges against you."

Gray eyes grew wide, and her nostrils flared. Greg restrained himself from reacting to her amusing display of resentment. This was too much fun to let go. Though he hadn't intended to let things get this far, the girl was making it hard for him to take no for an answer. If anything, he wanted her close, but not for the reasons he'd given her.

He wanted to hate her for what she had done, but he couldn't. Greg owed her his life. She had risked the wrath of her father and faced banishment in order to save him. The least he could do was to try to help her out.

"You're not playing fair." She began to pace again.

"I told you. You're better off accepting my terms." He gave her a fleeting look. "You'll be able to finish school and get a license to practice *real* medicine."

"My friend Cheryl will be looking for me," Sarah proclaimed in triumph, not realizing this was something he'd already taken into consideration.

Greg smiled at her subtle warning. "I took care of that small detail, too."

Sarah crossed the room in a blink of an eye and loomed over him. Glaring down at him, her eyes flashed with deep rage. "What did you do?"

Unperturbed, his lips curved into a smile. "I sent a note, signed by you, stating your father had collected you from the university and was taking you back home to Beaver."

He watched Sarah's face turn crimson before she lunged at him.

"You're despicable!" she screamed and started hitting him on the chest.

With the limited movement he could make, he managed to avoid her next punch, grabbed one arm, and twisted enough for her to stop for a moment. Sarah fell next to him and shrieked before she began hitting him again. This time she did the deed with angry fervor.

"You rich people think you can just manipulate us, huh?"

"Sarah, stop it. I'm putting my money to good use here. Making sure a future doctor of America will learn what she needs to know."

"You dare insult me, too?" She kept hitting him.

He seized both her arms, despite the hits he'd been taking from her. No doubt blinded by anger, Sarah squirmed and jumped on him, using strength he didn't expect her to possess. She straddled his waist with her legs and started slapping him, tears pouring out of her eyes in torrents while she struck at him with undisputable fury.

He howled before she stopped.

"Greg, I'm sorry! I didn't mean to hit you." Sarah scrambled to her feet when he doubled over, clutching his stomach.

"For Christ's sake!" he cried when pain shot through his abdomen.

"I . . . I'm sorry." Sarah took one look at him before glancing down at his stomach area and spotting the fresh blood staining his shirt. She gasped and started pushing him against the sofa. “Lie down. Tell me where to find your first aid kit.”

“Cabinet . . . under the sink.” He cursed and pointed in the direction of his bedroom.

She disappeared into the hallway. Greg could hear a series of doors opening and closing before she reappeared. Sarah kneeled down next to him and snapped the white box open before pulling his hand away from the bleeding site.

“I’m going to lift your shirt so I can see what’s wrong.” Her voice was steady while she searched his face for approval.

Greg nodded. She lifted his shirt, and they discovered that his sutures had partially reopened. It had been just a month since the surgery, and the doctor had warned him not to engage in strenuous activities.

Sarah gasped. “I think we better get you to the emergency room.”

“Call Simon, and tell him to get the driver ready.” He tried to keep from crying like a baby, but the pain was back with a vengeance.

“Simon!” Sarah’s voice cracked and echoed across the room. It took several attempts before Simon came running into the living room. “Get the driver. We’re taking Mr. Andrews to the ER.”

“Greg . . . I said . . . call me Greg.” He thought he saw a brief flicker of amusement on Simon’s face before his security man pulled out his cell phone and punched in a number.

“Rudy, get the car up front. Two minutes,” Simon barked into the receiver. He shoved the phone inside his pocket and dropped to his knees next to Sarah. “Do you want me to carry you, Greg?”

“No! I’ll walk.” He might be hurt, but he wouldn’t allow let them carry him like an invalid. Greg pushed his body up, pausing when the pain became unbearable. Once he was up on his feet, Sarah looped his right arm across her shoulder, and Simon followed her lead and did the same.

Together, they moved toward the door that a sobbing Matilda was holding open for them.

“Matilda, don’t.” He shook his head at the woman when they passed her on their way to the elevator.

While they waited inside one of the cubicles in the emergency room, Sarah caught herself glancing in Greg's direction one too many times. His eyes were closed, and his hands protectively covered his stomach. Blood stains marked his once-immaculate white Henley, and she couldn't help the wave of regret that washed over her.

"I'm sorry, Greg," she mumbled once again.

Greg didn't respond.

Sarah had repeated her apology many times during their car ride to the hospital. Her impulsive tendencies often landed her in trouble, and she berated herself now for her actions.

Pacing back and forth, she was not sure what else to do with herself. She drew the curtain and poked her head out, checking to see if anyone was coming to help them soon.

"I will forgive you if you agree to my terms."

Sarah whipped her head in Greg's direction and pulled back the curtains. "Yes! Yes." Her acceptance came too fast. She didn't even give herself a chance to think of the details. All she cared about, in that particular moment, was taking his pain away, whatever it cost her.

The answer seemed to please him, because he smiled—one of those disarming smiles designed to melt her insides.

"Will you stick to your word?"

She hesitated for a moment. Was she really going to make this promise to a man who had kidnapped and flown her across the country to New York City?

Yes . . . Her inner voice had returned. You have nothing to lose but a lot to gain. Your father doesn't want you back. You might be overstaying your welcome at Cheryl's home pretty soon.

She nodded her head. "Yes." Why did it sound like she was giving him more than a simple promise?

Greg seemed to accept her answer. "As soon as we get home, I will give you the list of your class schedules. You'll be taking the same classes at Columbia as you were at UCLA. I had your transcript evaluated, and you've been accepted, no questions asked."

Although Greg had spoken softly, often gritting his teeth through the pain, Sarah heard him just fine. She shook her head in disbelief. "How did you manage to—" She paused. "Ah, I keep forgetting. Money talks."

Greg didn't answer, but he kept looking at her.

"Are you sure they're accepting me based on my grades and not because you bribed them?" she asked, suspicious again.

"Sarah, you're a straight-A student. Who wouldn't want you in their school? All I had to do was convince them to take you even though the semester had already started. When we get back, I'll have Rudy drive you there so you can sign some papers and familiarize yourself with the campus before you start attending classes."

The way Greg announced every detail made her cringe. She should be running for the hills. Everything about him screamed *weird*. He had taken matters into his own hands, believing he could predict what her answer would be. Greg had arranged for her to attend a top-notch university and . . . well . . . it was just weird.

"Why are you doing this?"

Greg looked at her with his piercing blue eyes. "Because I wanted to hate you, but I can't."

Taken aback by his response, she bristled and turned her back on him. She wanted to lash out at him, but she stopped herself. Not wanting to take the bait, she took a deep breath instead.

"When do I have to help you?"

"During the daytime. I have most of my work delivered to me, since I haven't been cleared to go back to work—"

"What do you do, Greg?" Sarah walked closer to the tiny exam table and glowered at him.

"I manage a shipping business."

"Who shot you?"

"What's with all these questions?" He glared her with sharp eyes.

"Who shot you?" she repeated.

"My best friend."

That halted the questions for a moment. She gave him a hard look before blowing out a long breath.

“Some best friend,” she announced in a profound understatement.

“You can say that again.”

Greg closed his eyes, and Sarah realized the topic was closed. There was no need to prod anymore. She’d find out sooner or later who this so-called best friend was.

“I want to make things clear. I will pay you back every cent you spent on me. If you’re going to pay me, keep the money toward my repayment. I will help around the house, so tell your nanny to give me some chores.”

Greg opened and closed his mouth, looking like he wanted to say something to dissuade her, but she shook her head.

“No. I don’t ever want to feel that I’m a burden to anyone. This arrangement is based on payback. So, I intend to pay every debt I owe you.”

“As you wish.”

Greg studied her one more time, but any further conversation was halted by the arrival of the doctor. Sarah stayed close to watch the whole process. After the doctor had given her instructions on how to cleanse Greg’s wound and left, they went home without further discussing the terms of their peculiar arrangement.

~

The first week had been a reasonable success. Sarah and he managed to get along without biting each other’s heads off.

Greg grinned while he shuffled papers across his desk. After a few days of limited movement, Sarah had at last given him clearance to do a few hours of work. She’d started her classes at Columbia right away and had kept her end of the bargain without instigating any more arguments between them. He kept having to remind himself that he hated her, but somehow, he always ended up forgetting about it all over again.

Sarah was seated on the sofa across the room in his study, engrossed in her first school report. Greg caught her glancing his way several times. This was what he’d wanted, right? To have her close to him.

"Is there anything I can get you?" She looked up, almost catching him staring at her.

"No, I'm fine. Finish your school stuff so we can maybe get some exercise."

That made Sarah get up and take quick strides to his desk. She gave him a disapproving look and perched her hands over her hips.

"You're not exercising today. I know you feel like you can do more, but we don't want to aggravate the stitches more than we already have."

"I'm going crazy inside this house," he lamented, pushing the papers aside. Greg clasped his hands behind his head and leaned back.

"I'll have Simon rent some DVDs," Sarah offered.

He chuckled. "No one rents DVDs these days. That's why we have cable and pay-per-view."

His teasing seemed to have embarrassed her, and Greg immediately wished he could take back his words. He kept forgetting this girl was not used to the luxuries of life. Nothing had come easy to her, he'd been told by his private investigator.

"Why don't we go out for dinner?" Greg threw the question with as much nonchalance as he could, not wanting her to think there was more to the invitation than there was.

"Why?"

"Because we need to eat, and I have to get out of this hole sometime. Anyway, you have no classes today."

Sarah considered his invitation for a moment.

"We're not going on a date, if that's what you're thinking."

Just when he thought she'd decline, she nodded her head. "Okay. What time should I be ready?"

"I'll make a reservation for seven o'clock. Be ready at six-thirty. Wear a dress?"

Sarah gawked at him as if he'd lost his mind, but she was quick to rearrange her expression. "O—kay." She chewed her upper lip before returning to her spot on the sofa.

At the agreed-upon time, Sarah appeared in the living room wearing an awesome number that made Greg stare longer than he'd intended. The white dress with its low-cut cowl neckline showed a modest amount of skin and complemented her brown skin just right. The contrast, in his opinion, made her delicate beauty stand out. Her hair had been swept into a loose, intricate ponytail, which made her long neck look more graceful. Her gold sandals complimented the dress perfectly.

"You clean up well." Greg meant it as a compliment, but the words came out wrong. God, you'd think he would have more finesse, given his years of experience with the opposite sex. Something about this girl made him say the dumbest things. He wanted to smack himself in the head the next moment. *Who says those things to a beautiful woman?*

She raised an eyebrow. "You don't look too bad yourself."

Now they were even.

"Shall we?"

Sarah nodded and turned for the door. Just before they cleared the doorway, she looked over her shoulder at him, her eyes calculating. "Just because I agreed to dinner doesn't mean I trust you, Gregory Andrews."

Greg tilted his head in acknowledgment and invited her to proceed with a sweep of his hand. She continued on her way, and he followed close behind, clutching his cane. He hoped for a stumble-free evening, both literally and figuratively.

Chapter 8

The moment they arrived at Le Bernardin, they were whisked to a reserved table for two. It was obvious the minute they walked in that Greg was a well-liked customer and a regular patron of the restaurant. They were treated like VIPs, and the deference the staff paid to Greg was over-the-top.

Sarah felt a bit out of her element. Well, make that *way* out of her element. She should've known Greg would choose an expensive and chic restaurant as opposed to what she'd been accustomed to in the past. Burger joints and fast food restaurants were her sole experience with dining out, being the only affordable option. Fine dining was never a possibility in the Jones household. So yeah, this was another first for her.

"Are you okay?" Greg eyed her, something akin to worry lacing his expression.

Sarah had often wondered if this was just an act. He had told her that he wanted to hate her. Now, he offered a tentative smile, and it seemed like he had no idea what to say. That made him more real and down-to-earth, rather than the rich snob she thought him to be. In all honesty, looking at him now in the soft glow of the candlelight, he was handsome in his dark blue blazer and ribbed, white cotton T-shirt, a perfect and very attractive Romeo.

It wouldn't be right to flirt with him, because as attractive as she might find him, they were nothing alike.

"Yes." Catching herself fidgeting, she clasped her hands together and rested them on her lap.

"Would you like something to drink? A bottle of wine, perhaps?"

Sarah hesitated. She'd been to a few sorority parties during her undergrad years, but they'd always served beer. The most exotic drink she'd had to date was rum and Coke. *How funny is that?*

"I . . . haven't . . . okay, wine is fine," she stammered and glanced around, feeling self-conscious.

Greg waved to a server and requested the wine list. When the man reappeared with a thick leather-bound book, Sarah's eyes widened. All she knew were red, white, and E. & J. Gallo, the latter being a brand she often saw on the shelf of their local grocery store.

Before Greg opened the bible of wine drinkers, he looked up. "Any preference? Bordeaux? Burgundy?"

Now he's talking gibberish. Sarah shook her head. "Anything you want is fine with me." That would be the safest answer from an ignoramus like her. She bet Lily would get a kick out of this story when she told her friend.

Greg flipped through the pages, and it appeared that he already knew what he wanted. In the faint light in the room, she caught him smiling while his eyes skimmed the list. "We'll have the Chateau Lafite Rothschild Cabernet Sauvignon." He closed the bible and handed it back to their server.

"Excellent choice, Mr. Andrews," the server commented, but instead of walking away to fill their order, he cleared his throat as if embarrassed. "I wonder if I may check your companion's identification, sir."

Greg was taking a drink of his water and spluttered at the unexpected question. Sarah busied herself, hiding her embarrassment by rummaging through the little gold clutch she'd decided to use for the evening. Her cheeks were burning by the time she pulled out her identification card.

"Here you go." She presented her driver's license with a smile.

The man glanced at her picture and back at her. He checked her birth date before returning her card with a grin. "I'm sorry, Miss Jones, but you look quite young. I had to check."

After their server left, Sarah replaced her card in her wallet and returned her attention to Greg. He appeared rather uncomfortable. She leaned closer and whispered, "Is everything okay?"

"Yes." Greg leaned forward. "Why do you ask?"

"I don't know. Did his question bother you?"

He hesitated. "A bit, I guess. I feel like a cradle robber coming here with a beautiful teenager."

She couldn't help herself from asking, "How old are you?"

"I'm thirty-five," he replied in a gruff tone, meeting her inquisition head-on. His blue eyes showed a mixture of anxiety and irritation.

Not too old, Sarah thought. She wondered which part made him uncomfortable. Was it that he was older or just that she'd asked? Greg must have known how old she was, considering he had taken the liberty of rearranging her life.

"You're not too old." She smiled at him.

"What does that mean?" He inclined his head. The blushing radiance of the candle's glow hit his face, highlighting the angular planes of his features.

"Nothing. You have accomplished quite a lot at a very young age," she commented, and he flushed. Good thing he wasn't wearing a tie—she imagined he'd be tugging at it by now.

Greg ignored her comment and picked up the menu. "Let's order."

Sarah decided not to press. If he found the statement offensive, he should've said so. She had nothing against honesty, but to each his own, right? Picking up the menu, she began to turn the pages. *French? Lord, what have I gotten myself into?*

Geoduck, Foie Gras, Skate. Her eyes widened at the prices. Nervous, she kept leafing through the menu until she found a less expensive option she could live with—pasta.

Sarah had never imagined ordering dinner could be a taxing experience until then. She glanced around and noted the crowd with unease.

The sommelier came back with their wine, a big grin on his face. A stout man with a big belly, he presented the bottle to Greg with a flourish. Greg, in turn, scrutinized the label and placed his hand on the bottle like he was caressing it. After the cork had been removed, the wine expert poured a small amount into Greg's glass through an odd-looking funnel. Greg lifted it to his face, and Sarah watched with open interest while he took his time to first inhale deeply and then take a sip, rolling it along his tongue.

He nodded to the sommelier, appearing pleased with his selection. The wine steward started pouring the thick, red liquid into her glass before adding more to Greg's. She picked up the wide-mouthed, round glass to take a sip, when Greg coughed a little and lifted his glass to her. Embarrassed, Sarah pretended to sniff the bouquet before tilting her glass in Greg's direction, just like she'd seen many times on television.

"Here's to a fabulous year for you at Columbia." He smiled and gave her glass a gentle tap with his.

The statement confused her, but she said nothing. Instead, she replied with a dazzling smile and brought the glass to her lips. The first swallow came as a shock. The foreign taste made her want to spit out the wine, but she held herself in check. There was no need to embarrass herself and Greg.

After their orders were taken, she began to relax, loving the warming effect of the wine in her system. It made her feel like she could chat all night.

"So, tell me about yourself," she said. If Greg knew everything concerning her life, then she needed to catch up and get some juicy tidbits about him, too.

"Can we not talk about me? Let's talk about you." He took a long and satisfying sip of his wine.

"You know everything about me already. You stalked me, remember?" She raised a brow, challenging him to deny it.

Greg shook his head, as if telling her not to go there. He sighed before offering a small amount of information about himself. "I'm an only child. I have an undergraduate degree from NYU, and I took my master's at Wharton's."

"Impressive." Wharton was one of the most prestigious business schools in the country. Sarah took another sip of wine. "Any other interesting information you want to share with me?"

"That's about it. As I said—"

"Gregory, honey!" A sultry, female voice cut him off mid-sentence.

They both looked in the direction of the interruption but not before Sarah caught a glimpse of Greg's grim expression.

The woman approaching them looked like someone who had just walked out of a fashion magazine. She was tall, leggy, glamorous, and gorgeous—the kind of woman who made women like Sarah seem insignificant.

The blonde bounded toward them with her straight, glorious hair bouncing on her shoulders. She stopped in front of Greg and held out her perfectly manicured hand. Sarah watched Greg's face turn murderous, his jaw clenching and his mouth curled into a vicious smile.

"Cassandra." He ignored her outstretched hand and leaned back on his chair, clutching his glass of wine.

"Oh, c'mon, honey. Haven't you got a kiss for me?" She pouted her plump lips at him.

Sarah watched the scene unfolding before her with curiosity. Who was this woman that could make him so uncomfortable and edgy?

Greg ignored the woman's request. "Cassandra, I have nothing to say to you." His voice had become chilling and detached.

"Oh, pooh. Why are you always so glum, darling?" She reached her hand out and tipped his chin upward.

"We have nothing to talk about." Greg angled his face away from Cassandra and sent an apologetic glance in Sarah's direction.

It was something he shouldn't have done, in Sarah's opinion. She'd rather the woman left without paying her any notice. She and Ms. Fashionista had nothing to say to each other.

"Oh . . ." The woman turned in Sarah's direction and gave her a quick visual check. "Who do we have here? Aren't you going to introduce your wife to the little girl?"

At that point, Greg stood and pulled the woman by the elbow, but his blue eyes remained on Sarah. "Sarah, I want you to meet my very-soon-to-be ex-wife, Cassandra." He turned his icy blue eyes to the woman while

Sarah tried to mask her shocked reaction. "Leave now before I call security and have you thrown out for being a public nuisance."

Cassandra laughed, a high-pitched melody filled with unconcealed pleasure. "I'm hardly that, my dear. Until the divorce is signed, sealed, and delivered, you and I are still married. I hope you didn't forget to tell your little friend about me." She glanced over her shoulder at Sarah's bewildered expression and laughed again. "Oh, you forgot, right? Pity."

"Leave now, Cassandra." Greg's tone brooked no contention. He had the look of a man about to explode.

"Okay, fine. It was nice seeing you, Greg and . . . Maria." Cassandra gave a dramatic wave of her delicate hand and walked away.

"I'm sorry about that." Greg flopped back into his chair and raked his fingers through his hair. His expression remained dark while he searched Sarah's face.

It took her a long time to respond. First, she took a big gulp of wine, finishing the contents of her glass, and poured another. When her nerves began to settle, she met his gaze.

"Is it true? You forgot to tell me you were married?" The accusation in her voice was evident, and something she couldn't control.

Greg met her allegation with a dead-set look in his eyes, challenging her to say more. When she stayed silent, he raised his glass to his mouth and took vicious pulls until it was emptied. After that, he poured another and watched her with a hooded expression.

"It's my business, and I don't want to talk about it," he said after a lengthy silence.

This pressed Sarah close to the edge of her patience, although the wine had helped her keep her cool. She doubted she would have remained calm otherwise upon finding out she'd been living in a married man's home. What did that make her? What would people think? Her father? Oh God, another shame she'd be tacking onto her piled-high blunders. To add to the indignity, Ms. Fashionista had succeeded in making her feel like a child, worthless and small.

Neither one of them spoke for a stretch. They took turns watching each other through heavy lids, and Sarah grew accustomed to listening to her internal ramblings. The room was busy, and their lack of conversation didn't matter to her. She watched the people around them cut their meat, fork succulent fish, and chew their delectable entrees.

Sarah lost count of how many times she'd refilled her glass. She took another swig, loving the warmth the luscious wine brought her. "Who thought wine could be so good?" She giggled and tilted her glass in Greg's direction. He seemed ill at ease, which emboldened her even more.

"Sarah, I think you've had enough." He lowered his voice.

"Aw, c'mon. I'm just getting started." She waved her empty glass around, and Greg did not hesitate to take it away from her.

He leaned closer and hissed in her ear. "You're drunk."

She giggled when his warm breath caressed her sensitive, flushed skin.

"No, I'm not. Where's the bottle? I love those Ernest and Julio guys, you know."

Perhaps it was the wine talking. Sarah became a foolish puppet who couldn't control her mouth at all. The dreadful thing seemed to have taken a life of its own, blurting every single thought that came to mind. She rested her chin on her hand and followed Greg's movements while he summoned their server, took care of the check, pulled his cell phone from his pocket, and made a quick call.

He spoke to her, but she only saw his mouth moving. Everything seemed to be muted and going in slow motion. Before she grasped what was happening, Simon was standing right next to her, and he scooped her up as if she weighed nothing.

"Wait, what about dessert?" was the last thing she remembered saying before being deposited into their waiting car and taken home.

Sarah woke up the next morning with a hangover that she swore was bigger than an elephant. Maybe it was an actual elephant sitting on her head, squeezing her skull with every intention of rendering her brain useless. She tried to get up, but the shooting pain in her temple made her sink back against the mattress.

That's what you get for guzzling wine like there's no tomorrow. That irritating voice was back again. Sarah covered her eyes with a pillow and groaned. She could just imagine what Greg must be thinking—she was cavewoman and had embarrassed him in front of high society. He would not take her out to dinner ever again.

Darn! She'd managed to avoid alcohol all her life with conscious effort. Many Gwich'ins had been lured by the modern world to sample the tempting taste and numbing effects of alcohol. Some of them died from alcohol-related diseases or liver problems, which stemmed from their ignorance and the boredom that was so prevalent in their community. What a shame. Sarah knew better than to allow herself to be caught, and during her undergrad years, she'd never had more than two beers, even with the mounting peer pressure. She remembered nursing the same drink at sorority parties all night long, making sure she stayed in control. What had she done last night?

A slight rapping on the door brought her head up and the pillow off her face. "Come in, Matilda." Her voice came out sounding like a croak.

It wasn't Matilda who entered but Greg, who shuffled in with a cup in one hand while leaning on his cane with the other. "Are you decent?" he asked before he hobbled closer to the bed.

Sarah wrapped the blanket tighter when she realized she wasn't wearing anything other than her undergarments. Unable to wrap her mind around the embarrassing situation, she blushed instead of answering.

"I can wait outside." Greg turned around and started walking to the door.

"No, it's okay. Just stay where you are until I tell you to turn back around." Despite her pounding headache, Sarah skittered to the closet and grabbed a robe. After putting it on, she called out, "I'm ready."

She walked to Greg and took the cup from him. "Why don't you sit down?" She eyed him with mild concern, knowing full well that his legs had been giving him problems again. Sarah blew the rising steam off the rim of the cup and inhaled, enjoying the smell of fresh-brewed coffee. She climbed back into bed, balancing the cup with one hand and pushing back the covers at the same time.

Greg hobbled to the chair next to the bed and sat down, spreading out his legs in front of him. "How are you feeling this morning?"

"Like someone bulldozed everything inside my head." She grimaced when another throbbing ache shot through her temples, a reminder of her stupidity the previous night. "How are you?"

"I'm fine." He shoved a hand through his wild morning hair, and his deep blue eyes gazed at her with intensity. "I came here because I wanted to apologize for Cassandra's behavior last night."

"No apologies necessary." Sarah paused to take a sip of her coffee, moaning as the warmth spread in her throat and trickled down to her stomach. "As you said, it's your business. I don't have the right to ask."

"It's complicated—"

"That's what everyone always says. It just got me thinking. If you are a married man, no matter what you're going through, I shouldn't be here in your home. What would other people think?" *What does that make me?* she wanted to add but didn't.

"No one will think anything. You're my employee," he insisted.

"I may be your employee, but it still isn't right. I wasn't brought up that way. I can't stay here any longer under the circumstances."

Greg leaned forward, resting his elbows on his thighs. "Sarah, listen to me. Cassandra and I are done. Been done. I'm just waiting for her to sign the stupid divorce papers, and it's all official."

He stood and hobbled over to the window, as if he were trying to hide his expression. Greg sighed before turning around to look at her. "Cassandra is a difficult person to please. I wasn't enough for her. That's why she screwed around."

Sarah stared at him with sympathy in her eyes. That had to have been very hard to admit. His wife screwing around must be a hard pill to swallow for any man.

"I'm sorry."

"Don't be. I'm not. I'm better off without her. She can have half of what I own. I don't care, so long as I can sleep in peace at night, knowing she won't make a fool of me anymore."

"But it still doesn't make it right for me to be here."

"You gave me your word." He shot her a pained expression, something that looked like loneliness. Sad, almost.

I did promise, didn't I? Oh Lord! What must I do?

Stay and finish what you've started. It's not like you have any other place to go, the tiny voice reminded her.

Sarah sighed and closed her eyes, vacillating between doing the right thing and staying . . . because she wanted to stay. She hadn't ever felt this free and alive. When she opened her eyes again, she found Greg staring at her, waiting for an answer.

"Fine." Her answer scared her. *How can you make important decisions so easily, as if you're buying candy at a store?* This time, it wasn't her life that could end up getting screwed, but her heart. At that moment, she didn't care.

Greg smiled. "I'll see you in my study in an hour?"

Chapter 9

There was just one thing Greg wanted and hadn't gotten in the past two months. Finding Cade was proving to be a task more difficult than he'd ever imagined, even with the help of the private investigators. Greg had retained the services of an investigation agency to track down Cade since the botched murder attempt, but somehow, his former friend had been able to evade them successfully.

After he returned from Alaska, Greg heard reports that Cade had moved out of the country. Others said he'd gotten another job out of state. They were nothing but unfounded rumors. He knew one thing for sure—according to the company's records, Cade had returned the rented aircraft to Fairbanks a few days earlier than anticipated. Greg had spoken directly with Cade's father, who was adamant that his son hadn't made contact with him or his mother.

Cassandra continued to be a thorn in his rear. She was a piece of work, all right, and a worthless one. Greg's anger rose to the surface. He still hadn't gotten over the rude way she had treated Sarah, talking down to her as though she were addressing a child. Cassandra would be shocked as hell once she found out that the girl she'd insulted had a promising future in the field of medicine.

Cade and Cassandra hadn't made contact with each other, of this much Greg was certain. When they did, he'd know the full the extent of their relationship and could build a solid case against them. One thing Greg was determined to accomplish: once they found Cade, he'd give him the justice he deserved. It was just a matter of time. All rats, one way or another, were bound to sneak out of their hiding place, and Cade, wasn't going to last long in hiding. Nothing would be sweeter than showing that bastard how he'd underestimated Greg.

He frowned at the mountain of paperwork on his desk. Although he'd made few appearances at work in the past weeks, Greg still preferred to stay home to be with Sarah. His father, the mastermind behind their successful business, had called repeatedly to inquire about his absence. Greg had come up with several excuses that had the added advantage of being true. His wound hadn't healed as expected, on top of which, he continued to experience dizzy spells and persistent allergies from time to time. All of his excuses were geared to protect Sarah from his father, because he knew from experience that the old man didn't want to be associated with people below his social status.

Pushing the unpleasant thoughts aside, he shifted to a more delightful subject. Sarah. He smiled at the sound of her voice echoing through the house. He had intentionally left the door ajar to listen to her singing while she ran around the house, feather duster in hand. At her insistence, he'd relented and let her help with chores in the house, much to Matilda's dismay. His nanny-turned-housekeeper extraordinaire governed a tight ship. She kept his home immaculate, cooked the best meals, and doted on him as if he were still a child. No matter how nosey and annoying she got, Matilda had been more of a mother figure to him than his real mother ever had.

His parents had been absent most of his life, so there wasn't any point in thinking about them now. Sliding his chair back, Greg took a moment to stretch his legs just as Sarah tried to hit a high note in her song and failed. Smiling to himself, he let his darker thoughts trail off.

After the first month of skirting around each other, they had managed to find a middle ground, a means to get along without reference to their arrangement, her life in Beaver that she missed so much, or their dinner-turned-disaster. She made no attempts to question him about Cade or anything relating to the shooting. Instead, they stayed close to safe topics, such as her courses at the university, his work, and, well . . . the New York weather. Every day with Sarah brought him immense satisfaction he hadn't felt before in his life. She often brought a smile to his face with her actions, her funny take on life, or the quiet times they'd spent together.

Knowing she was safe with him was more than he could hope for. He couldn't bear the thought of her running around Los Angeles, alone, penniless, and with a hazy future dangling on the horizon. After what she'd done for him, this was the least he could do for her. He'd orchestrated her abduction, made it seem like she owed him and like he needed more help than he did. Greg held no expectations except being able to be with her and enjoy the best time of his life.

He shook his head in disgust, angry at himself for not disclosing the real reason behind his efforts to get her to live with him. Maybe, he had approached the whole thing wrong. He shouldn't have had her kidnapped and forced her to stay with him under false pretenses. Sure, he had the side-effects of what she'd done, but he was alive. That was all that mattered. Each day that he spent with her made it impossible to feel any anger toward her. Now, all he had burning inside him was the need to take care of her. Was he wrong?

Closing his eyes, he let the image of Sarah drift in, her long, black hair flowing free on her shoulders and then falling to the small of her back. It was a picture he never grew tired of revisiting. Sarah's eyes were like magnets, the gentle shade of gray mesmerizing and urging him to get lost in them. Her full and robust lips kept teasing him to taste, to feel them against his mouth. Man, that woman had no idea how unraveled he got in her presence. Her body, though a bit on the thin side for his liking, still had curves in all the right places.

His heart rate increased with the vision, and he forced his eyes open. She held him captive, mind, body, and soul. The longer she stayed with him, the more the possibility of losing his self-control loomed on the horizon.

Sarah's marriage arrangement with Trimble was one of the first reports Greg had gotten from Trevor. Although such an arrangement was enough to give him a sharp pain in his chest, he had no right even to comment on it. He kept his opinion to himself, but why did it feel like he wanted to kill any bastard who came within several feet of her?

He remembered a conversation he'd had with Simon a week ago.

"Are you sure this is all about helping her?"

"What do you mean?"

"Aside from your generous nature, are there any noteworthy, um . . . emotions lurking somewhere deep inside?" Simon cocked his thick eyebrows.

He hated his bodyguard-slash-friend's intuitive nature. "What else is there?"

"I don't know . . . but I can guess."

Greg grunted in response. There was nothing to say. He wouldn't admit to something he found so hard to explain.

"Then why put on an act? Why can't you tell her you want to help her?"

"She comes from a long line of proud people. They don't take to strangers offering help."

"I don't understand. She seems to be a smart girl to me. She'll find out eventually that you haven't been upfront with her." Simon was too damned receptive for his own good.

"The only way she'll find out is if you tell her. And you're not going to do that, right?"

"Of course not. But I have to warn you, this has failure written all over it. I trust you'll do the right thing when the time comes."

End of discussion. He'd dismissed Simon before their conversation could turn into a full-blown confession.

Greg straightened in his chair and rubbed his back. He'd been working nonstop for hours, while Sarah continued to belt out songs without a care in the world. Sometimes he saw the little girl in her, one who hadn't had a chance to enjoy childhood before being thrust into a world of adult responsibility. He felt like her guardian almost, keeping vigil and making sure she retained a semblance of innocence.

"Hey, Greg, do you want your lunch here or in the dining room?" Sarah tapped the door and poked her head in.

"Doing work at lunch? Heck, no." He smirked and got up. Stretching his legs, a sudden twitching of his left leg alerted him to an oncoming spasm, and he sat down again to avoid falling.

Sarah ran to his side and knelt before him. "What's wrong?"

"Another spasm." Greg gritted his teeth and held his calf while he tried to stifle the involuntary shaking.

Sarah eyed him with mild alarm. "Here, let me help." She stretched his quaking leg across her thighs and began rubbing his calf, kneading and pressing her knuckles on the pressure point.

Her warm touch sent electric jolts through his skin, and he fought the urge to moan. Greg ground his molars to keep himself in check while Sarah continued to work her magic.

After a few minutes, the spasm ebbed, and she looked up at him. "How do you feel now?"

He gave her a relieved smile, but it was hard hide the fact that he'd enjoyed her touch. Man, he'd be happy to go through the pain again if she'd hold him again like she had just done. "Better. Thanks." Greg looked away, hoping she wouldn't notice the desire written all over his face.

"You're welcome. Shall we eat?"

Greg grabbed the cane from the floor before standing up and following her out the door. Once he was seated at the dining room table, Sarah went to the kitchen to grab their plates. Matilda's mild protest sounded from the kitchen when Sarah came back with two bowls. Greg's housekeeper hated the fact that Sarah had taken over most of the duties she'd enjoyed doing for him, leaving her with almost nothing else to do.

Sarah placed one bowl in front of Greg before taking a seat across the table. He hadn't seen the likes of this dish before. It looked like beef, with a pungent and distinctive aroma.

"What did Matilda cook this time?" He picked up his fork, ready to dig in.

Sarah smiled in a sheepish manner. Lord, if this woman kept looking at him like that with those big eyes, he'd soon come undone in front of her.

"I hope you don't mind. I ordered some Caribou meat online and made a stew." She was already spooning some meat from the bowl.

"Oh." He glanced down at the plateful of meat and back to her. "Not at all."

Greg had no idea what it tasted like or whether he would even like it, but he wasn't about to disappoint Sarah, especially when she had worked so hard on cooking the odd dish. He dug his fork into the chunky mix and caught one cube-sized piece of meat. Smiling despite his sudden apprehension, he took a bite.

"Hey, it tastes like beef," he exclaimed. He picked up the spoon and started digging in with enthusiasm. "It's good."

Sarah grinned, seeming pleased with his approval. Soon enough, their conversation stalled while they both worked on devouring their meal. Greg requested a second helping, which delighted Sarah even further.

"If you like it that much, I can cook other dishes for you."

"Does this mean Matilda's going to be disappointed because you're leaving her with nothing to do?" He laughed.

Sarah nodded. "Yeah, but I will show her how to make them, too, just in case I'm not around."

Wasn't that a buzz kill? Greg's smile faded, but he hid his emotion. "Sure, show her how to make the dishes."

The phone rang, halting any further conversation. Matilda walked into the dining room with an announcement. "A Mr. Jeremy Singer is calling for you, Miss Jones." Judging from the housekeeper's tone, she wasn't happy with the caller.

"Oh, thank you. Please excuse me." Sarah wiped her mouth with a napkin before disappearing to take the call on the hallway extension.

"Jeremy Singer?" Greg raised an eyebrow.

Matilda shrugged and answered his question with another query. "Why is a man calling her?" She shot him a questioning glance as if he should know the answer. Thanks to Sarah, her maternal instinct had gone into overdrive again. Without waiting for his response, she disappeared into the kitchen and left Greg to ponder the unexpected caller.

He didn't want to think about men calling Sarah, but he ended up with the same question: *Who the hell is Jeremy Singer?* While he waited for Sarah to return, he made a mental note to check the name later.

A few minutes later, Sarah came back. Instead of sitting down, she hovered over him. It reminded him of how kids acted when they wanted to ask their parents for permission for something, he thought sourly.

Greg looked up at her. "What's going on?"

Sarah fidgeted. He guessed what was coming.

"Jeremy asked if we can meet to discuss a term paper."

"When?" His tone came out flat, and he wasn't about to apologize for it.

She seemed oblivious to his cold, detached demeanor. "He wants to pick me up in an hour, but I wanted to ask you first if it's okay to leave. I don't know if you need me for the rest of the afternoon."

Greg clenched his jaw at the thought of another man picking her up and taking her to an unknown destination. He had forgotten how beautiful she was and that it would be natural for men to want to be with her. No, that was wrong. He hadn't forgotten. He had just hoped no one else would notice her the way he did.

"Why don't I have Simon take you instead?"

Sarah considered his suggestion and nodded. "Okay, I'll tell Jeremy. Are you sure you don't need me to do anything for you?"

"I'm sure," he replied, his voice bitter.

Greg spent the rest of the afternoon feeling disgusted with himself. What in the hell did it matter if Sarah went out to meet a man, or just a male classmate? He shook his head, dispelling the murderous mood washing over him. He'd been staring at the same document for over twenty minutes, and he couldn't concentrate enough to remember if it needed a signature or if he had to review the shipment details or what.

The sound of approaching footsteps brought his head up. Matilda tapped on the door before letting herself inside his study, carrying a tray.

"I'm sure you need this." She moved a few papers aside before setting the tray down. "Coffee or tea?"

"Coffee." He needed a jolt. This damn business with Jeremy had sent him spinning in a vortex of short temper and the wrong frame of mind.

Matilda poured a cup of coffee in silence.

"Thanks," he acknowledged without looking up.

Matilda was like an open book. He could read her emotional grid well. She didn't leave but stayed glued to her spot.

"Where did she go? Is this Mr. Singer trustworthy?"

He sighed, rested the pen on the desk, and leaned back. "Simon's with her, so we know she's safe."

"But I don't want her going out with strange men," Matilda insisted.

"I don't want her going out either, but she's not a prisoner here. She's free to come and go as she pleases. She's an attractive young woman, and she's bound to spread her wings. We're not going to stop her."

"No, Greg. I don't want her going out and doing the same thing Ms. Cassandra did to you." Matilda's tone reflected the disgust she always exhibited when Cassandra's name came up in conversation.

"She's neither my girlfriend nor my wife. I can't stop her from doing what she wants." His voice rose, and he hated himself for reacting in such a manner. Their years together had given the older woman a unique perspective on how he felt about everything, which left him feeling vulnerable under her observation.

Matilda snorted and leaned close enough that they could look eye to eye. "You like this girl, don't you?"

"Matilda, I'm not having this conversation with you. Go on. I have work to do."

The hurt that spread across Matilda's face made him ache. He hadn't talked to her in such a manner since Cassandra left him. She turned around and walked to the door.

"I'm sorry, Matilda," he called after her in a gentler tone. "I just can't talk about it."

Greg wanted to follow, but it'd be best to leave her be for a while. Besides, what would he tell her? He wasn't ready to admit to anything yet.

"Damn it." He pounded a fist on the desk and then raked his fingers through his hair, feeling sick to his stomach.

With his mood in a downward spiral and his concentration down to zero, Greg decided to ditch the mounds of paperwork and call it a day. He walked out of his study and headed straight to the wet bar. What else was there to do? He'd pretty much closed himself off from the rest of the world, even from his friends, since he had come back from Alaska. Calling someone this late in the afternoon and asking to hang out sounded pathetic. So, he scratched the idea. He'd rather drink by himself. Taking a bottle of Armagnac and pouring a generous amount in a glass, he took one quick pull, followed by another. Greg wasn't intending to drink a lot, just enough to loosen his tight muscles and relax his mind.

Man, he felt old.

Lying in bed that night, Sarah realized she hadn't seen Greg at all since her study session with Jeremy. It hadn't been late when she and Simon made it back—just half past eight—but Greg was nowhere to be found. She would've asked Matilda, but one look at the woman made her back off. She'd seemed upset. Had anything happened while Sarah was gone?

The afternoon meeting with Jeremy had been fun. She hadn't spent much time out with friends, much less in the company of the opposite sex, except for Greg. Sarah had caught herself several times imagining that it was Greg talking about cancer biology with her instead of Jeremy. She'd imagined Greg's blue eyes sparkling with animation while he discussed carcinogens and tumor virology. What was the world coming to? In the past weeks, she'd found it difficult to think of anything but Greg: Greg would love this; Greg preferred coffee to tea; Greg this, Greg that. Any more Greg, and she'd be a walking, talking Greg poster.

She tossed in bed and glared at the clock. Ten o'clock.

Sure, Jeremy was interesting enough. His wide shoulders rivaled that of a pro football player, and his brown, curly hair gave him a boyish charm, but she preferred mature men. Sarah liked a man who could take charge of situations and was able to say what he wanted and what he meant. She had even caught herself comparing Jeremy to Greg, which had been both unfair and unnecessary.

First, she wasn't attracted to either of them, and neither one had shown interest in her at all. Well, that might not be entirely true. She had noticed Jeremy's subtle movements and occasional attempts to start up conversation about whether she was involved with anyone. Second, she couldn't be looking for a relationship now, not when her arranged marriage to Trimble still hanging over her head. She'd be better off concentrating on her distant and still-hazy future.

Then the little voice appeared again. *Don't forget your feelings for Greg.*

She tossed again and again, before she gave up on sleeping. If it wouldn't come, she couldn't force it. Maybe some fresh air would help relax her mind. Sarah got up and pulled on the robe at the foot of her bed. She slipped out of the room barefoot, and the darkened and quiet hallway greeted her.

Knowing her way around the penthouse, she required no lights to get to where she wanted to go. Sarah tiptoed her way through the living room, making sure to avoid causing the slightest noise. She reached the patio, noticed the sliding door open a crack, and found a figure standing outside. Under the glow of the city lights, she recognized Greg's features illuminated by the radiant surroundings.

She turned to walk back but paused when she heard a sliver of the one-sided conversation that piqued her curiosity.

"If you're sure it's him you've located, I want you to tell me where to find him. I will personally see that he gets what is coming to him. It won't be pretty, but I won't be cruel. I don't think the bastard deserves to live a moment longer."

The weight of his threats slammed Sarah with a heavy dose of reality. Greg hadn't forgotten about the shooting and hadn't forgiven his friend, and he sounded like hell wouldn't stop him from getting his revenge. Her mouth gaped open at the burden of his statements, and she refused to listen any longer than she already had. Afraid he'd catch her eavesdropping, she ran back to her room, creating more noise than she'd intended.

When the door was safely closed and locked, Sarah leaned against the jamb and tried to catch her breath. Damn right, she was scared—scared of what Greg was capable of doing in a fit of rage. She had a vague idea of who he was referring to, and she'd be damned if she would allow him to take matters into his own hands. Was Greg the man he'd said he was? Could she trust the man who'd taken her against her will, or had she been living in a bed of lies all along?

After she regulated her breathing, Sarah climbed back into bed. All of a sudden, she felt impossibly tired. What could she do? In her confusion, she started reciting the prayers her mother had taught her. Gwich'in words flowed from her mouth like honey as she wished she could do something—*anything*—before things got out of hand.

Chapter 10

Sarah sat in the kitchen, eyeing the coffee maker with impatience, sometimes glancing over to the big picture window overlooking the twinkling skylines. At six o'clock in the morning, the city had yet to rise from its slumber to grace her with another day filled with forced solitude and boredom. Greg had been too distant.

She was up earlier than usual, just as she had been for the past week. Sleep had been rather evasive for several days now, which she attributed in part to the fact that she hadn't seen much of Greg, either.

Ever since she had come back from her study meeting with Jeremy and had overheard his conversation, she had barely seen Greg around the house. He'd refused every single one of her asinine attempts to draw him out, and he'd declined her invitations and subtle efforts with the justification that he was involved in long business conversations and satellite meetings. She had no reason to be in the same room with him under those circumstances, so she ended up moping in her room for lack of anything better to do.

From what she remembered of their arrangement, she was to help him out if necessary. All signals coming from him were that help from her was not needed. Why did it seem like he was avoiding her? The more disturbing outcome from this whole cat and mouse situation was that she missed him. It felt like she was experiencing withdrawal, and she'd be a hypocrite if she pretended Greg's absence didn't bother her.

She missed their conversations, their relaxed banter, and most of all, his companionship. With nothing else to fill her days, she'd gone out with Jeremy a couple of times, where they'd spent the better part of the day in the library buried in medical books. Sarah didn't think Greg would mind if she went out. She doubted he even realized she was gone. Simon accompanied her each time, but he would retreat to the sofa at the end of the room when her studying commenced.

The drip, drip, drip continued, and she tapped her anxious fingers on the granite counter. She kept the lights in the kitchen off, not wanting to wake up Matilda, who always fussed at her for performing even the simplest chore. The elderly lady often shooed her away, insisting that Sarah concentrate on her school-related work instead of helping around the house. Matilda had been sweet, but it was stifling at times. In a way, she reminded Sarah of her mother.

The coffee maker chimed at last, cutting off her flow of thoughts. The aroma of coffee wafted around the kitchen while she marched zombie-like to the cupboard. Sarah retrieved a big mug emblazoned with the Wharton School of Business logo. She smirked as she filled the mug to the brim and added a teaspoon of sugar. With the steaming mug in hand, she returned to the counter and sat on the barstool. While she waited for the coffee to cool a bit, she blew the rising steam away from her face, keeping tabs of any movement in the quiet household.

Greg, no doubt, would still be asleep. Before she'd gone to bed the night before, she had spotted him on the patio, engrossed in another phone conversation as he had been for the past few nights. Sarah thought of the conversation she'd overheard a week ago.

Several explanations flashed through her mind, and considering the possible outcomes made her cringe. Greg shouldn't take matters into his own hands; it would only lead to trouble. Sarah hugged her robe tighter around her body. The idea of Greg being involved with a heinous crime gave her chills, but they hadn't gotten the chance to talk in several days, not that she had any idea how to broach the subject. Still, it scared her to think of what Greg might end up doing. She had to help somehow—encourage him to talk to her. But how?

You'll have to engage him in a more meaningful conversation. Try harder, her tiny voice told her.

"And you think I haven't been trying?" she grumbled in the darkness.

"I didn't know you were in the habit of talking to yourself." Greg walked in, rubbing the sleep from his eyes.

She jumped, startled, and spilled some of her coffee on the countertop. "You scared me!" Hopping off the barstool, she hurried to the roll of paper towels, tore off one, and wiped the surface dry.

"I didn't mean to startle you. Didn't know someone else would be up this early. What are you doing talking to yourself in the dark?" Greg laughed, loud enough to wake the entire household.

He was garbed in nothing but a pair of basketball shorts, and Sarah, despite her embarrassment, couldn't tear her eyes away from him. Even in the darkness, she could see the contours of his chest muscles and his powerful back while he crossed the kitchen to switch the lights on.

Her blush always appeared at the worst time. Being caught talking to herself made her seem like a child, and worse, he must've seen her staring at him. Sarah felt the pink creep up her face when the lights blinked on. Mortified, she took a quick sip of her coffee and tried to ignore his teasing.

Greg stood in the center of the kitchen, looking rather smug and comfortable while he waited for her answer.

"Considering there isn't anyone else to talk to, I resorted to talking to myself," Sarah said, raising her chin. She blew out an irritated breath, hating the goose bumps rising on her skin with Greg's half-naked body staring back at her.

He folded his arms across his chest and gave her a long scrutiny before walking to the fridge. "You sound like you're sulking, little girl," he commented.

She picked up the laughter in his voice, even though she couldn't see his face. "I beg your pardon. I'm not a little girl, and I'm certainly not sulking." Sarah huffed and sat up straighter. *There you go—you just acted like one.*

"Hmm . . . that's not how it sounds to me." He turned his head in her direction for just a moment. "Whatever. I'm going to make an omelet.

Would you like some?" Greg took out four eggs, a green bell pepper, an onion, and fresh mushrooms and set them on the counter.

Sarah wanted to pursue his comment, but she let it slide. There was no point in getting into an argument with him over something silly. She nodded her acceptance when he raised an eyebrow. Taking another sip of her coffee and pulling her attention away from his bare chest, Sarah shifted in her chair uncomfortably. She could feel his eyes on her.

"Can I help?" She was hoping he'd say yes so she'd have something to distract her from the perfect male musculature in front of her.

He shook his head. "I've got it. I *can* cook, you know."

Greg took a cutting board from the cabinet and pulled out a Gunter Wilhelm knife from the wood block. It gave an ominous gleam when the overhead light hit the blade, and Sarah inhaled sharply. Greg settled across from her on the counter and started cutting the vegetables like one of those celebrated chefs on television, dicing and chopping and slicing with speed and confidence.

"You can make omelets?"

"Among other things." He lifted his eyes to her. "So, what have you been up to? I haven't seen much of you around the house."

His tone irked her for some reason. Greg made it sound like she was the one who had been unavailable. "You've been cooped up in your study from sunrise to sunset, so you wouldn't know if I'd died or what. If my guess is correct, I'd think you've been avoiding me."

Shocked with herself at her unprovoked outburst, Sarah jumped out of her chair and walked over to refill her cup, but not before she caught the look of what seemed like yearning and pain cross Greg's face. Just as fast, the expression disappeared.

Sarah had no idea how to interpret the heightened tension in the room. She kept her back to him while she tried to compose herself, drawing several deep breaths before returning to her seat. Greg kept slicing and dicing as if nothing had happened. She watched him in silence.

After a few minutes, he spoke again. "What made you say that? I've been around. You, on the other hand, had been in and out, studying with a *friend*."

It was so wrong for him to go there. He had no right to put her on the defensive. There was no way she was going to let him turn the tables on her. "In the absence of things to do around here while you're working, I had to use my time wisely. And don't tell me you just don't approve of Jeremy as a study buddy."

Greg's head jerked up at her caustic tone. His brows drew together, and he held her gaze for a good length of time before he broke away, walking to the cabinet to retrieve a bowl and a whisk from the drawer. It was just another one of those reactions she couldn't understand.

"I know Jeremy, all right. Son of Senator Singer, oldest of three boys, consistent on the Dean's List, and broke up with his model girlfriend not too long ago. I know him well enough."

"Have you been spying on my friend?"

"A senator's son graces the tabloids and newspapers once in a while. It's common knowledge among city folks." Greg didn't look up. He just continued to whisk the eggs.

The way he had recited all that information infuriated Sarah. "Look at me, Greg. Where is this coming from?" She leaned forward and tilted his chin up with her forefinger. When their eyes met, his expression surprised her. In his eyes, she found vulnerability she hadn't expected and a hint of jealousy, which made her heart soar.

Her finger burned where it touched his skin. Greg held her gaze for a moment before turning away. He walked over to the stove and turned the knob.

"Nowhere. It's going nowhere," he replied in a quiet voice.

That wasn't my question. Sarah eyes widened. Could Greg be jealous? Why? He hadn't given her a reason to believe he was interested in her in any way beyond the terms of their arrangement, which he was supposed to have concocted to benefit them both. As far as she was concerned, she was here to pay him back for what she'd done. So far, Greg hadn't benefited from their arrangement at all. She'd been doing the taking, while he seemed content to keep giving.

Sarah slid off the barstool, walked over to the stove, and stood next to him. "That's not what I asked. Tell me what's bothering you." She tugged at his arm.

"Nothing, Sarah. I'm looking after your best interests. Sharks are always out there, swimming around and looking for the prey to sink their teeth into. I'm just making sure you're protected and safe." He kept his eyes glued to the empty skillet, and Sarah itched for him to say more.

Minutes passed before he met her gaze. She held her breath. The way he angled his head made her think he wanted to kiss her. For a moment, she imagined his mouth on hers and what he'd taste like.

"Are you one of those sharks?" she couldn't help but ask.

His eyes flickered and he scowled. "I try not to be."

Once again, she'd managed to stumble and find another way to complicate everything in her life. Maybe it was a good thing Greg hadn't done what she thought he'd do. Instead, he trailed one finger along her arm.

"Be a good girl and pour me a cup of coffee, black."

Just like that, Greg turned his attention back to the omelet, leaving her standing there, embarrassed and on the verge of tears. Wheeling around, she made a feeble excuse about needing to use the bathroom and raced back to her room.

Once she was locked within the confines of her bathroom, she turned the spigot and left the water running to drown any sound she was bound to make. She blinked back the tears and stared at herself on the mirror. "What happened to you, Sarah? You're reading too much into this whole thing. The man is married, and there is no way he'd consider you his equal. He's rich, gorgeous, and well-bred, while you're nothing but a poor, little girl from a godforsaken town no one's ever heard of. What makes you think he'd give you the time of day?" Sarah stared at her unhappy reflection and frowned. Indulging in a pity party hadn't been something she would have done under normal circumstances. Somehow, being around Greg had short-circuited all her internal wiring, scrambling any rational thoughts and leaving her all tangled up inside.

After standing in front of the sink for what seemed like eternity, she splashed water on her face to remove the remnants of her tears and scrubbed her face until it felt raw. Sarah wasted several more minutes collecting herself until she felt brave enough to face Greg. By the time she walked back in the kitchen, he was sliding the last omelet onto a plate. She took a mug from the cabinet and poured coffee for him, placing it on the counter in front of him without a word.

They ate in silence. Sarah had a sinking feeling that she might just be falling for the man, which with all honesty had disaster written all over it.

~

"Tell me again why you're doing this?" Simon asked.

Greg threw an annoyed glance at his bodyguard, who sat across from him inside the limousine. They were on their way to Greg's Manhattan office. His father had called for an emergency meeting, and this meant Greg had to make an appearance.

"Doing what?" he asked, feigning innocence.

"You know what I'm talking about. Why don't you tell Sarah how you feel?"

Greg kept his tone cool, despite the knot beginning to tighten in his stomach. "Tell her what? That an old man wants her? That I'm going insane with jealousy because she's spending time with that Jeremy fellow? Think again, Simon. I'm not good husband material. Just ask Cassandra."

"Wait, who said anything about marriage?" Simon coughed out a laugh. "Cassandra is a piece of shit, if you'll excuse my colorful language. That woman didn't deserve you, and I would love the chance to wring her neck."

Simon always showed straight-up loyalty. Greg appreciated the devotion and would have said so if he wasn't so wound up over Sarah.

"She'll get her comeuppance, my friend. I'm looking forward to seeing the look on her face when she learns she's not going to get a single penny from me." The possibility was rather appealing. He'd hate to have her walk away with a large fortune that he'd worked hard to obtain. Rewarding the woman for her indiscretion seemed unfair when there were more deserving causes out there that could use the money. In fact, he had a perfect idea what to do.

"I'm going to say this once. Sweep the girl off her feet and get her out of the house once in a while. It's been months. Sarah may be free to move around as she pleases, but with the absence of family or friends, she can't do much. She's wasting her time sitting at home with just me and Matilda for company."

"You want me to take her out?"

Simon ignored his mocking tone. "You heard me. Like a date. You know, like the dinner you took her to? Just keep her away from the alcohol. I don't want to see a repeat of that night again."

Greg considered what Simon said. He didn't want to make Sarah's life miserable. Had he been holding her back? How could he let his desire blind him enough that he could ignore her needs? He let the questions sink in and stared out the car window.

~

The minute he walked into the conference room, he realized the meeting was just a ploy to get him to come into the office. There was no meeting and no one present but him and his parents. Greg would've refused to attend if he'd suspected anything beforehand.

His father, Gregory Jr., was in his late sixties and was eccentric by nature. He was a man of regal build, with ash-blond hair and very few wrinkles to give away his true age. Underneath the striking façade, he was a shrewd and ruthless businessman. Oftentimes Greg found himself trapped into playing middleman between his father and their business associates or doing damage control. Greg Jr. might have built their business empire, but it had been his son who was responsible for securing its continued prominence and longevity.

His mother, Chelsea, was a smart-looking woman five years his father's junior. She used her sweet and cheerful demeanor both as a tactic to win admirers and as a guise to sway people to do her bidding. Vain and shallow, just like his father, she was slick and cunning in her business dealings.

Greg sat at the very end of the long conference table, as far away as possible from his parents, who hadn't even bothered to visit their son when he'd returned from Alaska injured. He imagined how torn they must have been to take time away from their social calendar or forgo a game of racquetball at the country club to visit him at the hospital. His stomach clenched with recrimination, but he kept his composure even.

With a mock display of compassion, his mother rose from her chair and walked the length of the room, stopping to give her son a kiss on the forehead. "Greggy, how are you? Why haven't you returned my phone calls?" She pouted her thick collagen-infused lips.

"Mother, as you may have heard, I've been busy recuperating and running this business from home." Greg gritted his teeth to keep from saying more.

He might be detached at times, but he'd had enough of the feigned affection of his absentee parents. They had always preferred to spend money, travel, and attend social functions instead of spending time with him when he was growing up. They pushed him to become this way, and he wasn't about to go easy on them. It wasn't enough that he'd gotten all the material things they could offer. He needed more from his parents, like their love, time, and attention—the usual things children required to grow up happy and secure.

"All work and no play, my son?" Chelsea teased before giving him a dismissive shrug.

Greg ignored the barb and turned his gaze to his father. "What is this meeting about?"

Greg Jr. regarded him for some time, but instead of feeling uncomfortable, this treatment just made his son's old resentment rise to the surface. Maybe Greg was being unfair, but he was sick of the whole charade. How he wished he could drop the pretenses and just walk away.

"I've heard you're in heavy negotiation with Smith and Jackson. Those clowns are hardballing us and are trying to squeeze every single penny they can out of the deal. If I were you, I'd cross them off. I've been talking to Stallion Lines, and they're showing willingness to restructure the deal and give us more leeway as far as schedules and shipping ports. I say let's meet with them and see what they can offer us this time."

Greg was half listening and half-tuned out by the time his father finished talking. He looked at the older man and rose to his feet. "Why don't you have your secretary call me with the date and time?" He grabbed his cane and turned to leave. "If you'll excuse me, I have other pressing matters to attend to."

Yeah, that would be taking a beautiful girl to see a movie. The sudden inspiration gave him purpose, and he strode out of the conference room without sparing a glance in his parents' direction. His mother's plea for him to stay went ignored.

He couldn't wait to get home. If he hadn't been afraid of stumbling, he would've run to the elevator. It was more than coming home to a familiar, secure place—it was the excitement of seeing the woman who kept his heart racing like he was running the New York City marathon.

When he got home, Greg lost no time heading to Sarah's room. He pounded on her door with the eagerness of a child, anxious to get going and show her a good time.

Matilda's voice came from behind him, her words deflating his high spirits. "She's not home. She left an hour ago to take a walk."

Chapter 11

"Turn left on Forty-Ninth Street," Greg called out in time for Rudy to make a quick curve, earning furious honks from a car they cut off. He would have gone on foot if his legs had been up to the task, but this was the next-best option.

Greg scanned the foot traffic for Sarah's features. The mix of faces and figures revealed people with blond, red, sandy, and brown hair, when all he ached to find was long black hair. Where could she have gone?

"Simon, concentrate on the left side of the street. Rudy, stop here and let me out." Greg scooted to the edge of his seat while the limousine eased into a no-stopping zone.

"You're not planning on walking, are you?" Simon's hand clamped onto the door handle, hindering Greg from opening the car door.

"That's exactly what I'm going to do," Greg responded in a tone that did not invite arguments. He pushed the door open and stepped out of the car, cool wind whipping at his face. Once he'd made the curb, Simon spoke from behind him.

"You have no idea where to find her?"

"No."

He glanced left to right at the people milling around them. Rows of shops loomed on either side, their window displays enticing shoppers to gawk at the merchandise. Greg hadn't the slightest clue which would appeal to Sarah. What would hold the most interest for a small-town girl? Was she into clothes, jewelry, or shoes?

The two men walked in silence, glancing into every shop they passed, covering one block in just a few minutes. Greg sensed the increasing stiffness in his legs, but he ignored it. He swiveled his gaze around, sifting through the hordes of shops and people around him until his eyes fixed on a small café with a big red canopy and empty chairs outside. His heart thudded against his chest when he spotted Sarah seated in a corner, a cup of coffee in one hand and a book in the other. Breathing a sigh of relief, he crossed the alley, leaving Simon to keep an eye on them from a distance.

"Mind if I join you?" he asked, catching his breath.

Sarah looked up, her surprise at his sudden appearance rendering her speechless for a moment.

"Not at all," she stammered, scooting her chair over to make space for him. "Coffee?"

"No, thanks." Greg eased his body onto the chair and rested the cane across his lap. "Are you all right? I got worried when Matilda said you went out."

She knew that he could very well just be checking up on her activities. Yet she couldn't help the warm, fuzzy feeling that coursed through her with the knowledge that he had come looking for her.

"Anxious to know if I left and breached our agreement?" she inquired, her teasing tone taking the accusation out of her words.

"No." He blew a frustrated breath. "I wanted to ask if you would like to see a movie with me."

The invitation was so unexpected that she gaped in disbelief, unsure whether she'd heard him correctly. She stared at him in shock until he leaned forward and waved his hand in front of her face.

"Hey, what's up with you?" Greg's voice was playful and his expression light.

Sarah gave a nervous laugh, and she felt flustered all of a sudden. "What movie would you like to see?" It didn't matter to her. Just the fact that they'd be together gave her goose bumps.

"The last time I went to watch a movie was two or three years ago." He laughed, looking sheepish. "I was hoping you'd take the burden off my shoulders and choose for us. I'm good with anything." When she raised her eyebrow, he added, "Really."

"Where do I look for movie listings?"

Greg pulled out his sleek Blackberry and punched some keys before he presented the phone to her. "Choose from the list, and scroll down if you need to see more."

Just like that, she was going to see a movie with him. Sarah glanced at Greg before focusing her attention on the phone. She felt his eyes on her while she scanned through the list. She wasn't much into chick flicks, though she thought Zac Efron was cute. Feeling a little mischievous, she decided to see how Greg would react.

"How about *The Lucky One*?"

The Lucky One was a love story in which the main character, Logan Thibault, was a soldier who found a picture of a woman in the desert and set out to find her after his tour of duty was over.

If Greg hated the idea, he didn't show it. "Sure, if that's what you like."

She laughed. "Nah . . . I don't care for chick flicks, although I love looking at Zac."

"Keep looking, then." Greg shook his head.

Sarah scrolled down to the end of the list. "If you're okay with scary movies, I'd like to see *The Cabin in the Woods*. I've heard good things about it."

He nodded as a slow, wicked smile flashed across his face. "Whatever you like. I'm good to go. Shall we?" Greg stood and held out his hand to her.

She hesitated, staring up at him for a nanosecond before placing her hand in his.

In a way, it was a monumental step for her. She was placing her trust in him. As much as she tried to warn herself against it, she couldn't ignore that she wanted him to touch her.

He squeezed her hand before pulling her up to her feet.

When she noticed his office attire, she frowned. She felt a little sloppy in comparison, dressed as she was in just a sweater, jeans, and mukluks. "Aren't you going home to change first?"

"Hate to be seen with your father?" Greg laughed and feigned hurt by clasping a hand over his heart.

Sarah hit him on the shoulder. "You're not that old. You may be stiff at times, but I don't mind being seen with you."

"Stiff, huh?" He snorted before nudging her forward.

Greg tucked her hand into the crook of his arm and led her through the crowded sidewalk. They spotted the black limousine parked a hundred feet away, Simon leaning against the door. He straightened as soon as he spotted them.

"Where to?" Flashing a wide smile, Simon held the door open for them.

"The movie theater. It's three blocks down and on the right," Greg replied. He let her climb into the car first before following her.

They sat next to each other, and Greg nonchalantly took her hand. Funny, she didn't mind it one bit. In fact, she liked the sensation of his soft skin pressed against hers. One touch told her so much about him—the firmness of his steadfast confidence and the softness from his life of privilege.

His hands were so unlike her own calloused ones, which had been through all manual work imaginable. She had washed dishes, chopped firewood, hand-washed clothes, and tilled their vegetable garden. It seemed like she'd done it all.

The drive to the theater had been quick, despite the evening rush hour traffic. When they stepped out of the vehicle, the night air had already turned cold, and Sarah shivered in her flimsy sweater. Greg hurried to remove his coat and place it over her shoulders.

"Thanks." She gave him a grateful smile. "What about you?"

He beamed at her in response. "You're welcome. I'll be warm if you let me keep holding your hand."

The prospect of continuing to hold Greg's hand excited her. This evening was turning out better than she'd anticipated. What had started as another drawn-out afternoon of solitude was turning into an evening full of promise.

Sarah squeezed his hand in hers and nudged him to start walking. "I guess we can call it even, then."

"I will see you kids in a couple of hours." Simon grinned through the limousine window before it drove away. Greg turned and waved and then walked up to the theater booth. Without letting go of Sarah's hand, he managed to retrieve his wallet, pull out a credit card, and finish the transaction.

"Popcorn?"

"If we can share."

"Sure. I'm famished. I didn't get a chance to eat when I got home. Once I found out you were gone, we took off." Looking a bit self-conscious about this admission, Greg shrugged and leaned on the glass counter to place their orders.

Once seated inside the theater, Sarah chuckled at the amount of food Greg had bought. There were nachos, hotdogs, and pretzels in addition to the popcorn and sodas.

"Are we pigging out tonight?" She eyed the collection of goodies on their laps and shook her head. Greg took a big bite off his hotdog and chewed with enthusiasm, a trail of ketchup trickling down the side of his mouth. Sarah reached out and dabbed at it with a napkin without hesitation.

He laughed, but he kept on chewing. After he'd swallowed, he spoke. "Yes, and I expect you to finish half of everything."

Sarah wrinkled her nose, although deep down, she loved this easy-going Greg. It was a far cry from the detached man he'd been for the past weeks. Feeling more relaxed around him, she took a bite of her hotdog. Soon it became a silent contest to see who could finish their food first. True to his word, Greg proved that he was indeed hungry. He ate faster than anyone she'd ever seen. It was a wonder how a man who ate as much as he did could remain so slim and fit.

After a few more minutes, the lights dimmed and the trailers started. Greg stashed their garbage underneath his seat and resumed holding her hand. It seemed like a natural thing for him to do. Although he offered no words, the mere touch of his hand spoke volumes. Everything about it felt right to her.

The movie lasted a little less than two hours. Instead of walking out right after, they sat and watched the credits roll while the crowd piled toward the exit. Greg still held her hand, just like he had before the movie started.

"Hungry?" he asked, and she burst out laughing.

"Greg, you're killing me."

"I could never do that." He shook his head with vigor, his voice low.

Rising from his seat, Greg tugged on her hand, and she stood. When he pulled her to him, Sarah felt like she was having an out-of-body experience. His fingers trailed the contours of her jaw, electrifying her with the boldness of his action. She had no idea what possessed her, but she rose on her tiptoes and brushed her lips against his.

His hand encircled her waist, tugging her closer. When their bodies touched, it sent jolts of warmth along her skin. The hard plane of his thigh rubbed against hers, and her breath hitched with anticipation. In this moment, it was just the two of them, together. Nothing else mattered—not the circumstances that had brought them together, nor the uncertainty of their future and the vast differences that divided them.

His mouth claimed hers, soft and gentle. Greg probed and sucked, his tongue caressing hers. Sarah's response was more passionate than she would have thought possible. Her arms wound around his neck, and they deepened the kiss even more. With her limited experience with men, her belief that they worked, that they were good together, was based just on how wonderful his kiss felt. Greg's arms around her revealed sensitivities in parts of her body she never knew existed.

Just as soon as she allowed herself to let go and just feel, Sarah realized she had to end it. It could lead them nowhere except to trouble and heartache. He was married. The last thing she wanted to add to her increasing list of blunders was to be accused of being an adulterer. That wasn't something she could envision herself doing, even though it was clear that she liked him as much as he liked her. They were destined to share more than friendship—she was sure of it—but under the circumstances, nothing could happen, even if her body tried to betray her.

"You smell wonderful," Greg said, sounding dazed.

She didn't need this complication. "I'm sorry. I shouldn't have kissed you. I don't know what came over me." She pulled away and began walking toward the exit.

"I'm not sorry at all. I've always wanted to do that." Greg was right behind her, pulling her around to face him. His compelling gaze was enough to unravel her resolve, and she fought the urge to kiss him again.

"It's wrong, Greg. I promise it won't happen again. It was a lapse in judgment on my part."

"I won't make that promise."

With those words, he brought his mouth down on hers again. This time, his kiss was hurried, hungry. Time stood still, and she let out a long moan, surrendering herself to his long, needy, and urgent kiss. *Just this time*, she told herself. After they surfaced for air, she pushed him away. She had to.

"Let's go home. It's been a long day." She walked away without looking back. If she faltered now, there would be no guarantee she'd be able to make herself stop. Despite what her body wanted, she had to be strong, stay focused, and keep believing that none of this meant anything to him.

"Sarah!" Greg called out.

She kept walking until she spotted the limousine parked in front, giving Simon a weak smile before climbing in. Greg was soon settled in next to her, and they made the short drive back to his place in silence. Sarah stared unseeing out the window. If Simon noticed anything strange, he didn't mention it, although he sent occasional questioning glances Greg's way.

Greg walked Sarah from the car and into the penthouse. When they reached her bedroom door, she stopped to wish him a good night.

"Thanks for the movie." *And the kiss.*

She turned around without waiting for his response, but his arm wound around her waist and pulled her to face him.

Sarah raised her chin and looked up at him. "Greg, we can't . . ."

He stopped her. “And I still can’t promise I won’t do this.” His mouth came down on hers in one quick, fluid motion. He tasted her mouth again, and all she could do was hang on, too startled and dazed to resist.

As fast as the kiss came, it ended, leaving her flustered and confused. Greg walked to his door and, with a slight dip of his head in her direction, disappeared inside.

Sarah walked straight to the shower, hoping the warm spray would ease her tired muscles. A long one, perhaps, might do the trick.

Greg marched into the bathroom after he left Sarah in the hallway. Even though he’d wanted to stay and keep kissing her, the better part of him—the reasonable side—kept telling him that he was taking advantage of her. She was confused and alone, and no matter what it looked like, she trusted him. The first thing he’d done with that trust was to abuse it just because he couldn’t contain his urge to claim her.

He’d felt this way from the very first time he saw her. Even in the tense situation at the time, he had seen the passionate woman hidden underneath her quiet exterior.

Simon had warned him several times that this relationship, or whatever it was, had disaster written all over it. He could see the telltale signs, but he couldn’t stay away from her. The woman, with her beautiful face and her scent of mint and cedar, made his head spin.

Turning the shower valve all the way to cold, he walked under the spray. He wanted the icy blast to wash away the fevered thoughts he was experiencing, as well as his body’s reaction to his encounter with Sarah.

Making a mental note to try harder to keep his hands off her next time, Greg finished his shower. He promised himself he would stick to his resolve and resist her charms. It was a good start, just as long as his body would take heed and listen.

He was sitting in bed and halfway through one of Warren Buffett’s books when his phone rang. He put the volume down and checked his caller ID.

“What’s new, Trevor?”

“Mr. Andrews, we hit a little snag.” Trevor cut to the chase.

Greg liked the man. There was no beating around the bush with the guy—he'd call things what they were.

"What kind of snag?" Greg leaned forward and rested his elbows on his thighs.

"It's Mr. McPherson. We've been trailing him for several days to ascertain his permanent residence. He is now living in Los Angeles." Trevor coughed and continued with noticeable reluctance. "We found him meeting with Mrs. Andrews in a restaurant today."

Greg rolled his eyes. "Trevor, tell me something I don't know. We've been expecting this. It was just a matter of time before we caught those two together. So give me his address." Greg reached in his nightstand drawer for a Mont Blanc pen and was poised to write.

"Mr. Andrews . . . it's not your wife we found dining with Cade McPherson. It was your mother. She met wi—"

"What the hell are you talking about?" Greg's voice rose, and for once he didn't give a damn. He made no effort to mask his anger.

"It was your mother we saw with Mr. McPherson two nights ago, and we have pictures to prove it." Trevor's tone seemed apologetic, and Greg heard no more. He hurled the telephone across the room and watched it slam against the wall, snapping into several pieces before it hit the floor.

Chapter 12

The next day, Sarah left for the library as soon as Greg's footsteps crossed the hall to his study. After their encounter the evening before, she wasn't too crazy about seeing him. She left a note with Matilda, to be given to Greg whenever he emerged. Pulling her jacket close to her body, she braved the biting morning breeze and set out on the ten-minute walk to the library.

Her mind couldn't wrap itself around the idea of kissing Greg. She still couldn't understand what had possessed her to instigate it and to allow him to repeat it over and over. Well . . . she knew why—she had wanted it more than she dared admit. Her shock was caused by her willingness to let things happen rather than the act itself.

Sarah wasn't an expert in relationships or anything to do with male-female interaction. Even to her amateur eyes, she could see that what they had shared last night had been special. Greg was special.

The more she thought about it, the more she hated the way her body responded to Greg. She was afraid that her self-control was no defense against Greg's charm and presence. Although she wasn't a prude by any means, he was still a married man. That alone should send her packing, not acting like a crazed nymphomaniac. Nothing about Greg guaranteed she would come out unscathed after everything had been said and done. How many times would it take her to repeat these warnings in her head before she listened?

After gathering the materials she needed for the day, Sarah set out to try to study. She scattered books across the library table, intending to spend more time studying and less thinking about Greg.

With her concentration veering toward Gregory Andrews III several times, she still managed to cram in the necessary studying. Med school hadn't been easy, and Columbia was proving itself to be tough enough to keep her on her toes. It was a good thing that she was up to the task, and she intended to graduate with good grades on time, if not earlier.

Glancing around the quiet library, she noticed a few early patrons like her. Young and old, these people were intent on getting as much done as possible in the morning and beating the influx in the later hours.

The silent ticking of the clock at the far end of the room provided a steady cadence, which kept her going. She had six hours before her first class for the evening. If she read fast enough and got her work completed, she might have the chance to walk around and check for job openings.

Sarah wondered how long her arrangement with Greg would last. He couldn't have any intention of babysitting her for the duration of the school year. Why would he even care to waste time on her, anyway? New York City, although a small land mass compared to bigger cities like Los Angeles and Chicago, packed a punch as far as population. It should have something to offer her, despite her lack of professional experience.

Greg had mentioned he wanted her around because of the pathology testing to come. He wanted to find out where her inexperienced work had led them and which of the side-effects he'd been plagued with had stemmed from her improvised blood transfusion. Still, he seemed healthier each passing day. Although his spasms hadn't improved, the sutures were healing well. An overwhelming possibility struck her. Her stay in the Andrews household might no longer be welcomed by the end of the semester.

Sarah's nerves did a number on her at the thought of leaving everything she'd grown to appreciate in such a short time. It would be harder than she cared to consider. Greg . . . would she even dare to imagine beyond the kiss?

If she had to leave, where would she go? *Stay*, the little voice told her. After transferring from UCLA to Columbia, she had no reason to move back to Los Angeles. She'd have to come up with a means to earn a living—anything to sustain her until she finished school. She could take out the necessary student loans and hope scholarships were still available this far into the semester in her field of study.

In more ways than one, she was alone. Even if she had three people who cared for her here, everything she had was temporary. If her father continued to want nothing to do with her, she'd have to carve out a name for herself, one way or another. But of course, things were almost always easier said than done.

A nagging doubt strangled her. She couldn't leave until she knew for sure that Greg wouldn't do anything stupid in connection with that phone conversation she'd overheard. A big part of her refused to let him make that mistake.

Shaking away the sudden wave of paranoia, Sarah willed her mind to concentrate on the work lying before her, and she finished studying the material she'd intended to cover for the day. After the end of her study period, she returned the books to their proper shelves and set out to take the longer path back to the penthouse, hoping to snag a few employment applications along the way.

The day dragged on for Greg. After his conversation with Trevor the night before that had ended in the premature demise of his cell phone, he'd decided to purchase a new one from a store a few blocks down. He persuaded Simon to leave him alone and took the trek down Fifth Avenue with slow but steady steps.

He needed the time alone to think. The shock of Trevor's revelation left him in a tumult of emotions he found difficult to process. Finding out his mother had connections with Cade made his chest ache. The extent of their association was yet to be determined. Regardless, the small faith he'd still had in his mother had been crushed into nonexistence. Greg had always suspected that he was irrelevant in his parents' lives, but this latest betrayal took the hurt to a whole new level.

God, was the pain ever going to go away? Was he destined to be alone for the rest of his life? What made it so impossible for people to love him? His parents acted as though he didn't exist except when it was time to count their fortunes in the bank. Cassandra's affair made him think he'd failed at marriage, too. It was ridiculous, but he kept asking himself what had made her unhappy. What made the people around him hate the idea of his existence? It had to be his fault somehow. These people found his very presence loathsome and wanted nothing to do with him. To top it all off, Cade—his best friend—had tried to kill him.

Greg reached the store in a few minutes. For the next half hour, the enthusiasm of the sales representative ambushed his attention with the latest technology, and he came out of the store with both a new, state-of-the-art Android and a cell phone for Sarah.

Indeed, he was a sucker for her. Despite the tragedy that surrounded him, his mind kept going back to her. Sarah was his respite. She relieved his tired mind and aching heart. The passion of their kisses had sent jolts of tingling sensation from his spine down to his toes. For crying out loud, he'd not just acted like a delirious juvenile with her, but he'd done it in front of Simon, too. He couldn't help himself. Sarah had a way of making him forget his problems.

This much was true—being with her now would create heartache in the future. Greg shook his head, hating the very thought of giving her up. He had taken her under his wing with every intention of shielding her from the troubles he'd already caused for her. Instead of taking a burden from her, he had just confused her even more. It killed him to see the doubt in her eyes.

What had started as an audacious plan had now backfired. Greg kept telling himself he was just going to help her get over her own hurdles, and then he would let her go—it would be easy. But as the days went by, he became more and more uncertain that he could go on without her. It went without saying that he'd be damned before he would intentionally hurt her.

The kisses they had shared just made him want her more. He knew he had nothing more to offer her, but from this day forward, he'd have to make an effort to keep his hands to himself, even if it killed him.

Pulling out his new high-tech toy, he stopped short before crossing the intersection and dialed Trevor's number. Looking around himself while the phone rang, he caught a sight of that beautiful, long, black hair across the street. Greg had no idea how he could spot Sarah with such ease, but one thing was certain—he was drawn to her like a magnet.

He paid attention to her every move with keen interest, noting the way she examined her surroundings like a doe-eyed child, her fierce grasp on her books, and her curious glances at the flashing billboards overhead. She was going to cross the street in his direction, and he'd wait for her.

Moreover, he had a gift for her. In a way, it would be a peace offering for his stubborn refusal to stop kissing her. His outgoing call went straight to voice mail, and he left a hurried message. He punched the off button, slid the phone in his pocket, and walked forward to the curb to wait.

Greg waved at Sarah, hoping she'd see him right away, but it took several attempts before he could catch her attention. Her face was puzzled at first but then broke into a grin, and she waved back.

The pedestrian crosswalk sign flashed, and she was the first one to step off the curb. Greg heard the blaring warning of a taxicab running a red light and the screeching of the tires before his eyes witnessed the inevitable contact between the bumper and Sarah's body in grim slow motion. The nightmarish collision threw Sarah a few feet away like she was a ragdoll. Her body landed in a tangle of limbs with a loud thud on the cold pavement, followed by the sounds of shrieking brakes and loud screams.

Ignoring the pain in his legs, Greg bolted from his spot and ran across the street just as people started gathering around Sarah's body.

"Someone call 911!" a woman yelled.

He had no predetermined plan of action, but anger surged within his chest. He lunged at the driver just as he emerged from the cab. Greg had one thought in mind—*Make him pay!*

He threw a punch that landed straight on the man's nose. "I will kill you, bastard!" Greg yelled. Rage flowed through his veins like adrenaline, and he managed to land more punches on the horrified driver before several people pried him away. Cameras began to flash from every direction while the wails of sirens sounded in the distance.

"You're fucking crazy!" The cabbie spat blood on the ground.

Greg fought against the arms that restrained him. "I will kill you." He fought against the furious tears that rushed to his eyes. "If she doesn't make it out of this, I will kill you," he screamed once more at the stunned man before turning his attention to the group that had converged around Sarah. Like a madman, he shook off the restricting hands and squeezed his way through the maze of bodies, elbowing people aside without caring whether he plowed anyone over. When he made it to the front of the shocked crowd, he fell to his knees at the sight of Sarah's motionless body.

"Oh my God!" His cries echoed in his ears while he took stock of the awkward position of her body and the pool of blood underneath her head. As much as he wanted to touch her, he drew back, knowing that accident victims should not be moved in case the neck or back had been injured. Greg stayed where he was, aching to do something for her, until the medics got to the scene and shouted for space.

His vision blurred while he watched them prod and probe her body. He crossed the line of insanity, and his sobs shook him. "Sarah!" He wailed against the noise of shouts and screams surrounding him.

Soon enough, Sarah's body was hoisted onto a waiting gurney. Greg scrambled to his feet and raced to her side. "I'm a friend. Where are you taking her?"

One medic eyed him with sympathy. "Mt. Sinai ER," the man barked before the sound of the siren could drown out his voice with its incessant cry.

The ambulance pulled away, and Greg took his phone from his pocket while he turned to head in the direction of the hospital. Ten freaking blocks. He'd run it. "Simon, meet me at—"

A hand clamped on his arm, and he looked up to find a uniformed police officer. "Not so fast. I need for you to come to the precinct with me for questioning. The man right there claims you assaulted him," he said, pointing at the cab driver before lowering his hand back down to his gun holster.

It took a few seconds for the words to register. Another officer appeared, and Greg asked, "Where are you taking me?"

"Ninth Precinct." The first officer didn't let go of his arm.

"Simon, meet me at the Ninth Precinct." He dropped the phone into his pants pocket and scrambled to get a handle on what was happening. Yes, he had assaulted a man. Would temporary insanity be an acceptable excuse?

More camera flashes went off all around him while the cops escorted him to a waiting police car. Greg's life had gone from bad to terrible, and was now turning into a full-blown nightmare in a matter of minutes. All he wanted to do was flee the scene so he could see Sarah. God, if his damn legs had enough firepower in them to outrun everyone, he wouldn't be sitting in a damn police car on his way to the station for questioning.

Simon soon joined him there. Thanks to his quick thinking, he'd also summoned Greg's lawyer to meet them. Assault, Greg learned, had stiff penalties, and the police had a handful of witnesses pointing to him as the unprovoked aggressor. He was slapped with criminal intent to injure and had to put up bail, and the victim could file a lawsuit against him as well.

None of the things happening mattered. He listened to his attorney's litany of possible defenses while his bail was being arranged. All he cared about was getting to Sarah. Greg had Simon place a call to one of his friends who worked at Mt. Sinai Trauma Department for a special favor, asking him to find Sarah and make sure she had everything she needed.

"How long does it take to get all this damn paperwork done?" He pounded his fist on the desk in the holding room.

Tony Anton, his poor lawyer stared at him, no doubt startled by his display of impatience. An elderly gentleman, he shifted in his seat before rising to his feet. "Give me ten more minutes." He walked out of the room with brisk steps, leaving Greg to seethe in silence.

It took another hour before Greg was allowed to leave. He shot out of the chair and marched straight out of the place. He and Simon rushed to the waiting car, and Rudy whisked them to the door of the ER in a matter of minutes. Greg felt the burning pain in his legs, but he ignored the silent warning. While they ran through the double glass doors, he pulled out a bottle of muscle relaxants and popped two in his mouth.

The ER's waiting room was filled to capacity. Greg shoved past the long line, cutting to the front. "Sarah Jones. She was taken here via ambulance about two hours ago."

The triage nurse regarded him with an irritated scowl before checking the monitor. She tapped the keys, taking her time.

Greg felt his tension rise. "Can you hurry up, please?" he said between gritted teeth.

"Sir, you cut in line. I can send you back there if you don't hold your temper." The nurse continued tapping on the keyboard.

He bit his tongue before a nasty retort could pass his lips. Simon squeezed his shoulder in a silent plea for him to keep his cool.

"She's in surgery right now. There's a waiting area at the end of the hall. You can wait there." The nurse pointed in the direction of another hallway filled with people and turned her attention to the next person in line.

Greg couldn't prevent his hysteria from rising to the surface. He made a mad dash down the hallway, Simon rushing to keep up with him.

"Greg, I know how you feel, but it would help if could keep yourself calm. Nothing good will happen if you let that temper get the best of you again."

"I'm trying," he ground out.

The waiting area had a few vacant seats left. Greg took one, and Simon settled in next to him. There was nothing to do now except wait. God knew how long it would take.

Greg gave an absentminded glance at the muted television in an attempt to distract himself, but it didn't help. "Damn it," he muttered in frustration after just a few minutes.

"Is there anyone you should inform about Sarah's condition?"

Simon's tone was low, but Greg's head shot up nonetheless.

"Her father, but I have serious doubt he'd care."

Weren't he and Sarah two peas in a deplorable pod? They were two people with families who either didn't care for them or wanted nothing to do with them.

"That's not for you to decide. You should call and let him know."

Simon always acted like he had to be the voice of reason. Under normal circumstances, Greg would have teased his friend, but this time, he just glared at him.

Greg ran a hand through his hair, still trying to make sense of what had happened to Sarah. "I'll call as soon as I know what condition she's in." The concession was difficult to make, knowing what her father's cruel decision had done to her.

With nothing better to do, he focused on the television again. Repetitive new stories were being played until a breaking announcement flashed. He straightened on his seat when the first image flashed across the screen.

There he was, in the flesh, caught on camera striking the cab driver. Underneath his image was the caption: "Rich son of shipping magnate, Gregory Andrews III assaults cab driver."

Greg slumped in his chair. He had thought that his life couldn't get worse, but he'd been wrong.

Chapter 13

When it rains, it pours. Greg had remembered that quote many times during his life. If he didn't know any better, he'd think that someone had coined the phrase with him in mind.

Of all the things to happen to him and Sarah—and he included her because their fates had been intertwined when she saved his life—her accident was the hardest of all to accept. He would have done anything to prevent the accident from happening, but there was no predicting accidents—or avoiding them, for that matter. Still, this latest unfortunate event took the cake. Sarah, without a doubt, would suffer over the days to come while she recovered.

Simon stood and stretched. Just like Greg, he had been sitting there for the past four hours. He had given Greg his silent support each time the newsflash repeated, patted his back in encouragement when the doctor came out to give them a brief report on Sarah's condition, and continued to give him space to think without interruption. "I'm grabbing some coffee. Would you like some?"

"Yes, black," Greg replied in a clipped tone.

Even though the doctor had said Sarah was going to be all right, Greg couldn't make himself believe it without seeing her with his own two eyes. The doctor was a friend of his, and he had rushed for the surgery upon Simon's request to attend to Sarah's injuries himself. Thank God Greg had met Barry on one of his past hunting expeditions. They'd hit it off and had gone hunting upstate together several times since.

According to Barry, Sarah's injuries weren't life threatening. The back of her skull had sustained a hairline fracture upon hitting the pavement, and there was also a laceration that had caused profuse bleeding. So far, X-rays showed no internal bleeding, and although slight swelling had been noted, neurosurgery was not an option at this point. Barry promised nonstop vigilance until he could pronounce her "out of the woods."

After her head injury had been stabilized, Barry's primary concern had been her spinal fracture. A CT scan had established an unstable fracture in the thoracolumbar region, and Barry and another surgeon performed an immediate operation to fuse Sarah's affected vertebrae. According to Barry, the process of rehabilitation could take months, depending on her body's ability to heal. It might take even longer to create a solid fusion. Nonetheless, she would be off her feet for an indefinite time, and would experience back pain and weakness until she had completely recovered.

The hardest part to swallow was the pain and suffering Sarah would face when she woke up. Greg felt his chest constrict many times while Barry recounted the procedure Sarah had gone through. He hoped she hadn't felt a thing, and with any luck, the pain when she woke could be mitigated with painkillers.

Greg scrubbed his palms over his face, not knowing what else to do. They had told him to wait, and he'd been doing just that, even if it was killing him. Each second, each passing minute, felt like bricks, piling unbelievable weight onto his shoulders.

Simon came back with two foam cups filled with coffee. He handed one to Greg and sat down next to him.

"Thanks," Greg grunted, took a quick sip from the cup, and leaned back. Just like him, Simon was showing signs of fatigue. They had been sitting on the stiff chairs long enough. Greg's back began to ache and his legs were throbbing like hell, but walking outside to get some fresh air was not an option. He wouldn't leave this hospital until they called for him, even though Simon had suggested that he take a break a couple of times.

"About that phone call," Simon began. "I think it's a good time to contact Sarah's father now."

Greg flicked a quick glance in Simon's direction. He had been thinking of the same thing, but somehow, the prospect of talking to Sarah's father held no appeal for him, even if he'd never met the man.

"I think you're right. There's no need to prolong the inevitable." He checked the time before pulling his brand new phone from his pocket. Beaver would be four hours behind them, and there was a possibility he wouldn't be able to reach anyone at this time. It was improbable that anyone would still be at work at the town hall at seven in the evening.

He dialed for an operator. "I need assistance locating a number in Alaska."

It took the operator several minutes to locate the phone number for Beaver's town hall, where the office of the tribe leader was located. Greg waited, and after about five rings, voice mail picked up. Having no other option, he left a message.

"Hi. My name's Greg Andrews, and this message is for Mr. Jones. I'm calling on behalf of Sarah Jones. Sarah has been in an accident. She's fine and resting in a hospital here in New York City. If you would like more information, please call me at this number." After leaving his number, Greg hung up with a sigh.

What a way to break the news. He downed his remaining coffee and crushed the cup with his hand. It felt good to get a chance to release a little of his pent-up frustration.

"What now?" he muttered to no one in particular.

Simon shrugged his shoulders. "I guess we'll keep waiting?"

Greg responded by leaning forward to rest his elbows on his knees and dropping his head into his palms. "I know I will. Go home, Simon."

"Nah . . . I'll keep you company until they transfer her to a regular room."

Gratitude welled within him, but he was too tired to verbalize it. The day had turned into something from a horror film—one of those movies where the hits kept coming. Just when you thought you were done, another blow blasted from out of nowhere.

Greg kept his eyes closed in an attempt to relax. With all the buzzing conversations around him, it was impossible to find any peace.

His phone rang. Checking the caller ID, he groaned, hesitating before picking up the call. “Trevor, what’s up?”

“I have an interesting turn of events to report.” The PI announced on the other end.

Interesting is a good word to use right now. I could use something to distract me, Greg thought to himself. “Go on.”

“When I called the other night, we’d seen your . . . um . . . Mrs. Andrews walk in the restaurant to meet Cade.” At the mention of those two names, Greg’s blood began to boil. “I could tell from their body language that they were arguing, so I went into the restaurant to get closer. I overheard Mrs. Andrews accusing Cade of shooting you.”

Greg shot to his feet. “What else did you hear?”

“Well, it seems Mrs. Andrews produced some pictures. Soon after, Cade ran out of the restaurant. I couldn’t follow right away, for fear of recognition. Your mother called 911, but when the cops came and searched Cade’s place, he’d had a window in which to get away. I don’t think their investigation led them anywhere. He’s still at large, and we’re still trying to track him down.”

“What? So where does this leave us? And where does my mother fit into it?” Greg’s voice rose, and his mind began to race. There were a couple of scenarios running through his head. “Talk about a turn of events.”

“Well, it seems like your mother hired PIs, too. That’s how she found Cade. But now that the authorities are involved, you can expect them to contact you sometime soon. I don’t know if you still want to pursue Cade as planned.”

Muttering a curse under his breath, Greg began to pace, which earned him a few curious glances from the people seated across from him. His mother’s involvement was not part of the plan. What was she up to, anyway? If she was beginning to develop a conscience and had decided to be a mother to him, she was a tad bit late.

He cupped a palm over the phone and kept his voice low. “Keep at him.

Let's talk after a few days, and I'll decide which direction we'll take."

"Sure thing. Anything else?"

"Anything on Cassandra? I'm anxious to close that chapter already."

"She's been quiet. My leads are coming up empty, but my gut tells me she's just waiting for the right time."

"Then stay on her tail, too." Greg ended the call with a frustrated sigh.

"Is everything all right?" Simon whispered from behind.

Greg stopped pacing and turned to Simon. He pointed to the door. There were too many curious people surrounding them, which wasn't good at all. Although it was doubtful that anyone would recognize him as the man shown on TV earlier, he didn't need to run the risk of being overheard while plotting revenge.

Before they reached the door, a nurse came out of the surgery area and called his name. Greg pushed aside his other concerns and ran to the woman's side.

"I'm Greg Andrews."

"Dr. Darnell asked me to tell you that Ms. Jones will be transferred to a suite as you requested. She still cannot have visitors, but Dr. Darnell is willing to make an exception for you." The nurse offered a tentative smile, and after giving him the room number, proceeded to instruct him where to go.

If it hadn't been for the adrenaline pumping hard in his veins, Greg knew he'd have collapsed from anxiety by now.

"Go home, Simon, and wait for my call. I don't think I'll make it home tonight." Greg took a deep breath before walking to the elevator. The shadow of exhaustion loomed over him, a vicious reminder of the day he'd had, and an unwelcome portent of the future that loomed ahead.

Sarah had opened her eyes just a fraction when a wrecking ball of pain slammed into her skull with maddening fury. She heard a groan, which sounded distant and yet familiar. When she tried to turn her head, she found it was impossible. Her head appeared to be strapped to something solid and hard.

She closed her eyes, willing her mind to tell her what she'd missed. How on earth had she ended up in this strange-looking place? The beeping sounds of equipment made her think of a hospital, and that idea was the trigger that unleashed a flood of recent memories.

Greg. She stepped into the street. A taxicab barreled in her direction. Her screams before landing on the pavement. She remembered nothing after that. Now, here she was in the hospital room. Everything started to come into focus. Her once-dissociated thought process began piecing information back together.

How badly hurt was she? Unable to move her head to survey the rest of her body, she tried wriggling her toes. It gave her an odd prickling sensation, like her brain had transmitted the order but the receptors were slow to respond. She moved her hands, one at a time. Even if they felt like they weighed a ton, a rush of relief surged through her when they flexed at her command. And she could feel touch, she discovered. A hand gripped hers, and she squeezed it in response.

An overwhelming sense of happiness engulfed her. She could feel. She wasn't paralyzed as she'd first thought. The exhilarating relief brought tears to her eyes. Before she could blink them back, a rush of emotions consumed her, and she began sobbing uncontrollably.

Sarah held on to the hand in hers like it was her lifeline. She was shaken to the core. Then all of a sudden, Greg was leaning over her.

"You're awake," he whispered. His face came closer, and his eyes searched her face. He let out a sigh of relief when she offered a weak nod.

"Yes, I think I am," she sobbed.

Greg's expression flitted from surprise to utter happiness in an instant. Then he hugged her, careful not to jostle her and showered her with kisses over every inch of her face.

"God, I thought . . . I'd lost you." His voice was hoarse, as if he'd been crying. She must've given him quite a scare.

"You can't get rid of me yet." She smiled despite her tears.

A harsh laugh escaped his lips, and his eyes glistened with unshed tears. "I never want to get rid of you. I want to keep you, if I can. Promise me you'll be more careful next time." One tear dropped, and Greg tried to hide his face from her.

Overwhelmed by his display of affection, Sarah reached out to touch his arm. “Greg, don’t turn away. Please look at me.”

He obliged and turned back to her, and she saw the traces of tears on his cheeks. Sarah raised her hand to his face and ever so gently wiped the wetness away. They gazed at each other for a long time before he broke the connection.

“I have to tell the nurse you’re awake.” Greg pressed a button on the bed’s side rail and straightened up.

A female voice came from the bed speaker. “Yes?”

“Miss Jones is awake. Can you call Dr. Darnell and let him know, please?”

“Right away, Mr. Andrews.”

Sarah noticed the dark shadows underneath Greg’s eyes, and then recognized the clothes he’d been wearing before the accident. She frowned. “Greg, how long was I out?”

“About twenty hours. What do you remember?”

He started pacing, wandering out of her line of vision. Judging from the way his shuffling footsteps dragged across the tile flooring, she realized his legs must have been bothering him.

“Some of it. I remembered catching a glimpse of you before the cab hit me. After that, I can’t remember anything.” She lifted her head to follow his movement, but a shooting pain made her sink back down against the pillow. “I can’t see you. Sit next to me.”

This was the best way she could think of to get him off his feet. If she had been unconscious for that many hours, it meant he’d been without sleep for some time. She felt one side of the bed dip, and then his face came back into focus again.

Greg picked up her hand, brought it to his lips, and brushed a featherlight kiss against it. “Do you want something to eat?” His voice trembled.

The door swung open, and a cheerful male voice greeted them. “Well, well, my sleeping beauty is awake. Andrews, no food for the lady yet. Let’s go with clear liquids for the next twenty-four hours.” The newcomer stopped by the bed and leaned forward, giving Sarah a close up of her doctor. He was young, with the swagger of someone who knew his worth. Judging from his teasing tome, he had to be a friend of Greg's.

Greg coughed and narrowed his eyes, and the doctor laughed. She was sure she was missing something, perhaps an inside joke of some sort.

"I'm Dr. Barry Darnell. This is the part where I tell you how lucky you are that Greg asked for me to perform the surgery."

Sarah couldn't help but smile at his easygoing approach. "Is there going to be a part where you'll tell me I'm screwed?"

"Well . . . as a matter of fact, yeah. I've attached a rod in your back and screwed you back together." He grinned, looking very mischievous.

Sarah laughed harder than she'd intended and was rewarded with a zinging pain in her head.

"And that would be my cue to call the nurse so you can have a dose of painkillers."

Greg interrupted. "Darnell, can you turn down the charm a notch and tell Sarah what to expect?"

"God, Gregory, crack a smile, will you?" Barry laughed before he turned his attention back to Sarah. He picked up her hand and brought it to his lips—not what she'd expect a doctor to do, but given her unique situation, nothing surprised her anymore. "You fractured your skull. There was slight swelling earlier, but the last CT scan we took showed improvement. You'll feel nauseous for the first few days, but after that, I think you'll be fine. If you experience anything out of the ordinary, please let me know right away."

"Is walking going to be a problem?"

"Um . . . let's see." He scratched his chin as if in deep thought. "You're liable to have moments where some parts of your body will feel numb, but that will go away in time. So, if I were you, I'd let this gentleman right here carry you wherever you need to go. I wouldn't advise hiking or running the marathon for now, though."

Sarah, in spite of herself, giggled at the doctor's lighthearted approach to putting her concerns to rest.

Barry's green eyes sparkled. "There's also a laceration in the back of your head that is all stitched up. I shaved as little hair as possible, so I'm very happy to say most of your long, silky hair remained intact."

"You know, if you weren't such a great surgeon, I would've asked for someone else. I don't like your method of charming your patients," Greg teased.

Barry chuckled and slapped him on the back. "Greg tells me you're a medical student at Columbia, Ms. Jones."

"Well, it looks like this accident is going to set me back a semester. That is, if I can even manage to stay after this."

That was her greatest concern now. Recovering would mean that she'd have to lose precious time, and there was a possibility that her arrangement with Greg might come to an end, too. Sarah saw Greg stiffen out of the corner of her eye, and he took her hand again. He may have wanted to say something, but he held back for the time being.

"And that's where I come in again. If you must know, I'm an alumni and a member of the Board of Physicians and Surgeons at Columbia." Barry paused, waving his hand with a dramatic mock flourish, and smiled. "I can coax your professors into giving you all the lessons to take home until you're well enough to physically attend class discussions again."

"You can do that?" Sarah's breath hitched.

"Of course I can. If my projection for your healing is accurate, it'll be about two months before you'll be walking and skipping like Cinderella again. That's barring any setbacks, of course."

Sarah released a grateful sigh. "Thank you."

He winked. "Don't mention it. I'm always happy to help. Now, if you'll excuse me, I have to check on Mrs. Johnson next door. She's been having Barry withdrawals."

Greg stood and shook Barry's hand. "Man, thanks for coming through for me. I owe you more than my life here."

Sarah couldn't believe what she'd just heard. Tears brimmed in her eyes while she committed the sweet words to memory. She must've hit her head harder than she thought. For now, she was content to bask in the warmth and comfort of having Greg close to her.

"Not at all, Andrews." Barry turned to the door with a wave and paused. "Let me take that back. How about taking me on a hunting trip to Alaska?"

Greg just laughed and shook his head at Barry, who chortled in return before closing the door behind him.

Chapter 14

Later that night while Greg dozed off on the sofa bed across the room from Sarah, the phone rang. Reaching for his cell phone in the darkness, he fumbled several times before he found it.

The number flashing on the caller ID was vaguely familiar. It must have been someone he had called earlier. Answering on the fifth ring, a defensive instinct shot through him at the sound of man's rough voice. From what little information Trevor had given him about Sarah's father, Greg gathered that the man they called Ahila was uncompromising and iron-willed. He had the feeling this conversation wouldn't be a pleasant one.

"Hello." Greg tried masking the discomfort in his tone.

"You left a message about my daughter. Who are you, and what is she doing there?" The voice was stern, a clear indication the man meant business.

Greg straightened on the sofa. "Yes. My name's Greg Andrews. I'm the man your daughter saved."

There was nothing but silence from the other end of the line, so he proceeded to give the information he thought Ahila needed to know. "She's here in the hospital. She's doing fine. She had some rod and bolts attached to her spine to help with the—"

"What I want to know is what she's doing there with you. That child will stop at nothing to pile more shame on this family. I want to talk to her."

Greg knew he was about to cross a line, but he wasn't going to hold back now. "Aren't you even going to ask how your daughter is? Didn't you hear what I said? She was in an accident. She could've died, and all you're worried about is your goddamn reputation?" His voice rose, and he darted a quick glance at Sarah's sleeping form in time to see her eyes flutter open.

"My daughter is my concern. Don't tell me what I should be doing, Mr. Andrews. You've done enough damage in our lives. Let me talk to Sarah," Ahila all but shouted.

"You don't deserve such a loving and hardworking daughter, you piece of—"

"Greg, what's going on? Who are you talking to?" Sarah's sleepy voice stopped him from cursing the old man out.

Just in time, he thought. Greg cupped a palm over the phone and pivoted to face Sarah. He vacillated between lying to her and coming clean about Ahila wanting to speak to her. Somehow he knew this wasn't the type of situation he could hide from her for long. She was bound to find out, and besides, family dynamics weren't his forte—his relationship with his own parents was on the verge of falling apart, after all. He just hoped he could prepare her for the tongue-lashing he expected her to receive.

"I have your father on the phone. I had to call to let him know about your accident."

Despair flitted across Sarah's face before she reached out her hand. "Let me talk to him."

Greg walked toward the hospital bed and handed her the phone. He knew he should give her some privacy, but he couldn't bear the thought of leaving her alone, so he slinked back to the sofa and sat down.

"Papa," Sarah whispered into the phone.

"I'm not asking you to come back home. I'm *telling* you to return, but just because you've caused enough trouble already."

Her father's tone startled her. She had no expectations of him, but the lack of compassion in his voice hit her with startling clarity that his anger hadn't subsided. It didn't matter at this point that his daughter had missed death by a narrow margin. Sarah was embarrassed to have expected more than what she knew her father believed she deserved.

"I can't. I'm in no condition to travel." She choked back the sob, blinking back the tears that stung her eyes.

"I will send someone to get you. You're not to venture out of this town ever—"

Sarah refused to listen anymore. "Didn't you hear what I said, Papa? I can't leave."

"You're the one who's not listening! I want you home where I can keep an eye on you. You must stop this foolishness, Sarah. This rebellious behavior has gone far enough." Her father's clear disdain brooked no argument.

She shook her head in defiance even if he had no way of seeing her. "I heard what you said, Papa. Your threats won't make me come home. I will stay where I'm wanted. Can't you, for just once in your life, think of me as a person with a mind of her own?" she replied with uncharacteristic boldness. Even though it pained her to talk to her father this way, he needed to hear what she had to say. The angry tears she'd fought to restrain gushed out, and she wiped them away with trembling fingers.

Ahila laughed with scorn. "My daughter, you're going to regret your decision."

Sarah's stomach clenched.

"The day will come when you'll crawl back here and beg for forgiveness. It's just a matter of time, mark my words. I'll be waiting for you."

His rebuke stung, and Sarah felt like she had lost her father all over again. This conversation had created an even bigger rift between them, far wider than could ever be repaired. She knew she'd regret her decision one day, but she couldn't think that far ahead. Blinded by her emotions, all she wanted from Ahila was respect for her point of view and her decisions, not to be treated like child who was incapable of deciding for herself.

"I'm sorry, Papa." She hung up.

Greg walked in her direction with hesitant steps. With the brace wrapped around her neck and body, she couldn't move or turn her face away, but she didn't want him to see her anguish. She didn't want his pity, nor did she want to hear what he had to say.

Sarah closed her eyes and sobbed, breathing through her mouth to keep the nausea at bay. Greg sat on the bed next to her and said nothing. Instead, he held her hand in that comforting way he always did and let her deal with her misery. He offered her the sanctuary of his presence and the comfort of his silence. Gathering her up into his arms, he began to rock her in a gentle rhythm until she yielded to a restless sleep.

~

Following the week after her homecoming, Sarah felt much better and almost back to her old self. Aside from the occasional back pain and numbness in her legs and feet, her healing came along just as Dr. Darnell had predicted it would. Matilda fussed over her like a mother hen, refusing to let her even lift a finger and feeding her home-cooked meals to "fatten her up."

"You're too thin. You've lost a lot of weight. High winds will blow you away if you don't listen to me," Matilda uttered over and over while she pushed food into Sarah's mouth as if she were a child.

Walking to the bathroom had even become a big production. Even without Matilda hovering around her like a hawk, the few instances Sarah had attempted to get up on her own had been thwarted by Greg's inevitable presence. His legs had gotten stronger, allowing him to pick her up and take her to the bathroom before she even had time to protest. This treatment went on until she was about to scream.

When Sarah expressed her frustration, Greg just held her gaze and reminded her that he wouldn't allow anything to happen to her, in particular while she was living in his house. So for the next two weeks, she was held hostage by two impossible, overzealous, caring individuals. They regarded her like delicate china, which made the slightest flinch from pain an unbearable embarrassment.

The days fell into a regular pattern. Greg carried Sarah to his study, and they would spend the day together. He attended office meetings via satellite, answered important forwarded calls, and ran the business from his home office, while she poured over the materials Barry had arranged for the school to send. This routine started after breakfast and was followed by an hour of lunch. Then they went back for another two to three hours of quiet work before they quit for the day.

Although their time together had been spent doing their respective work, it had also given Sarah plenty of opportunity to observe Greg. She learned a lot of things about him in the process, but it was his compassion for others that touched her the most. While she worked nearby, she overheard him order flowers for an employee who had a baby and listened to him scold another to take a break.

Most interesting were Greg's facial expressions—the way he furrowed his eyebrows before making a big business decision, smiled with contentment after sealing a business deal, and pretended to read when she caught him staring at her. Those were times when confusion muddled her mind. Everything reminded Sarah of the strange, unspoken emotions that had arisen between them, growing as each day passed, implicit and larger than life.

Greg was reluctant to leave her side and almost never left the house. As much as Sarah had grown to love his company, she would have appreciated a respite from the nagging issues that surrounded them. It was just a matter of time before those matters demanded her attention. She often wondered what was going on with his wife and what that condescending woman would think if she found out about their living arrangement. He never once mentioned his parents or the shooting. Sarah sensed that these things weighed on him, but he clammed up whenever she brought up either subject.

There were instances when he took phone calls in the privacy of his bedroom, but not before she'd overheard him mention lawsuits, lawyers, and other things she knew nothing about. Sarah saw worry shoot across his face several times, but he always dismissed her inquiries. She surmised there was a group of related problems that he refused to talk about, but she respected his need for space, just as he did with her issues with her father.

Greg never brought up the phone conversation she'd had with her father in the hospital. For that, she was grateful. Despite her curiosity about Greg's life, she was content to live on the sideline and learn from the man who had given her so much.

One afternoon after an unscheduled nap, she found a note on her dresser from him. She hurried to open it, her heart beating hard against her chest.

I'm going to meet a colleague for a couple of hours. I hope you enjoyed your nap. Greg.

Sarah wound up deciding to take the rest of the afternoon off, dozing on and off for the next hour. Afterward, she wandered to the kitchen where Matilda was humming a tune and covering a casserole with aluminum foil. Sarah climbed on the barstool and grabbed the television remote.

"Good evening, sweet pea. How was your nap?" Matilda looked over her shoulder and smiled. The term of endearment had spawned from Sarah's dislike of peas, which the older lady persisted in feeding her despite her objections.

She teased back, "Hello, Nanny. It was great." Sarah flicked on the remote control and started channel surfing. Most of the basic channels were transmitting the evening news, so she kept flipping, but Sarah switched back when she heard one newscaster mention Greg's name. Matilda's mouth gaped open while they watched and listened in horror.

"Gregory Andrews III, with his lawyer, appeared before a judge today on assault charges filed by George Rickard." A segment of Greg and the lawyer flashed on the screen, and the newscaster continued. "The incident happened following an accident on Sixty-Ninth Street, in which Mr. Rickard's cab hit pedestrian Sarah Jones. According to several eyewitnesses, Mr. Andrews attacked Mr. Rickard, resulting in a broken nose and fractured jaw.

"According to our sources, Mr. Andrews appeared grief-stricken following the accident. We have no details regarding his relationship to the accident victim at this time. Mr. Andrews was named one of New York City's top twenty businessmen of 2011 and has been going through a long and messy divorce from estranged wife Cassandra Denver-Andrews." A picture of Greg and Cassandra during happier times was then plastered on the screen.

Matilda started sobbing. "Turn it off, turn it off!" she screeched. Her eyes filled with tears, and she grabbed the remote control from Sarah. "I don't want to hear it. They tell lies!"

"Is it true?" Sarah's heart pounded in deep, painful thuds. "Did Greg attack that man?"

"Yes . . . he thought the man killed you. He hit you, Sarah. Greg will fight this. He has the best lawyer in town." Matilda sniffled while she wiped the tears from her eyes.

Sarah's heart sank further. "I'm sure he'll be all right," she reassured the housekeeper and hoped to God it was true.

Matilda nodded and went back to her chores, leaving Sarah to dwell on the gravity of Greg's situation.

Sarah waited in the living room for Greg to return. It was past seven when the front door opened and closed. One set of footsteps proceeded to the kitchen, while the other continued in the direction of the bedrooms.

Sarah had left the lights off on purpose to give her the chance to watch Greg first without him knowing. Even in the darkness, his demanding presence was hard to miss. She recognized exhaustion in the heaviness of his footfalls. His powerful shoulders slumped, and the hard plane of his jaw was tight. Greg was an image of a man who carried a burden, alone and isolated. It was a pity that she couldn't ease his pain.

She listened to his dragging feet while he crossed the hallway to his bedroom. Hugging her knees to her chest, she waited, knowing what would happen next. Just as she'd predicted, Greg came gunning down the hallway.

"Sarah!"

"I'm here, Greg," she called out.

When he turned the lights on, she had to squint her eyes to see him. Traces of worry were evident in his weary expression, but he hid them as soon as their eyes connected. If there was one thing Sarah knew about Greg, it was this—he always tried to hide his feelings as much as possible. The times he faltered were rare, but they were enough to reveal his vulnerable side.

"You almost gave me a heart attack." He flopped on the sofa next to her.

"I was waiting for you." Sarah scooted closer, and she felt him tense.

He raked his fingers through his hair and then tugged his tie loose. "Why? Have you eaten dinner?"

"Yes. Have you? I can reheat the casserole." She shifted to get to her feet, but Greg's warm hand clamped on her arm and stopped her.

"I'm not hungry. Just sit here with me." There was unmistakable weariness in his voice, as well as the eyes that regarded her now.

"Sure . . ."

Satisfied with her answer, Greg leaned back on the leather sofa and closed his eyes.

After she'd settled back down in her seat, Sarah decided to come right out and say her piece. "Greg, I want you to tell me the truth, and please don't shut me out," she started, her voice quavering a bit.

Greg's eyes opened, and he turned his head in her direction. "What do you want to know?" he asked with a frown.

"Why did you attack Mr. Rickard?"

He flinched. "Because I thought the bastard had killed you."

"You overreacted, in other words."

"I may have, but I'm not sorry for doing what I did. He ran the red light and hit you. A broken nose and a fractured jaw weren't close to enough payback for what he did to you." There was no remorse in Greg's voice.

"But I'm okay. You, on the other hand, won't get off so easy. You're all over the news. People took pictures, and the media is having a field day. I'm just worried about you, Greg." Sarah slumped against the cushion.

He scooted closer and picked up her hand. "I want to apologize for dragging you into this mess. I realize that people will start asking about you."

"I don't care about that at all." She tightened her fingers on his hand. "What I want is for you to be happy. You seem to have so much on your mind. I could help if you would just trust me."

"My one regret about hitting that bastard was that by doing so I dragged your name under this goddamn microscope of a life I'm living. But I'm rectifying matters. I met with my lawyers today, and we're going to do some damage control."

"Just how much trouble are you in?" Greg, in Sarah's opinion, was making strides. This was the most information he'd ever offered her. Still, she cast him a worried glance.

"I'll be fine. I have a criminal lawyer, just in case that bastard wants to play hardball. I'll going to slap him with a vehicular assault lawsuit, and he won't have an easy time trying to get money out of me. I've also retained a divorce lawyer. I figured I'd better get my divorce from Cassandra finalized. I don't want anyone putting your name in a bad light." Agitation marred his handsome face.

Sarah suppressed a sigh. "I don't want you to concede to your wife's demands for my sake. If you believe you should fight her for everything, you have to do it."

Intent blue eyes regarded her with speculation. "It could get ugly. They might start digging up stuff about you that you're not ready to deal with."

"I don't think we have anything to hide. They can talk all they want, and we can tell them to do their worst. But don't settle on my account. You've done too much for me as it is." Sarah hoped her tone sounded as unconcerned as she'd intended. It didn't matter if her heart was hammering against her ribcage at the lie. How bad could it get, anyway?

"Are you sure about this?" Greg eyed her, his expression wary.

"Yes," she replied, trying to sound convincing.

Greg scooted much closer to her, tightening his grasp on her hand before kissing her palm. Sarah closed her eyes when his soft lips grazed her skin. Then he whispered into her ear, his breath a featherlight caress that sent shudders down to her toes.

"You're such a beautiful and brave woman, Sarah Jones."

Chapter 15

Greg replaced the phone back in its cradle. He'd been having an interesting conversation with his divorce lawyer when he'd been distracted by raised voices. He rose to his feet and hurried out of his study. Sarah bolted out of her bedroom door as well, wearing a robe over her pajamas. She halted her steps when they almost bumped into each other.

"Stay here." Greg placed one hand on her shoulder when he passed her.

He recognized his father's voice even before he reached the front door. Greg wondered what the old man wanted from him. There could be but one reason for showing up on his doorstep at this hour—money. That had been his father's main concern of late.

"I don't care what time it is. I want to talk to my son." Greg Jr.'s voice echoed through the entire house and spilled into the hallway outside, despite Matilda's pleas that he keep his voice down. He shoved past Matilda as soon as he spotted Greg. "There you are. I've been leaving you messages, but you haven't even had the decency to return my phone calls."

"I sent you the report for the last quarter. What more do you want from me?" Greg bit out, unable to control his increasing annoyance.

With his usual arrogance, Greg Jr. strode into the living room, and Greg followed him. He wasn't sure he appreciated this unannounced visit. There was too much animosity between them, and he had no idea how to act around his father anymore.

Greg Jr. stopped mid-stride when he caught sight of Sarah standing in the hallway. "Well . . . who do we have here?"

He eyed Sarah from head to toe with obvious interest akin to that of a spectator at a freak show. Greg gritted his teeth and clenched his fists.

"Sarah, this is my father, the great Gregory Andrews Jr.," he offered by way of introduction. Any astute bystander could have heard the underlying tension and sarcasm in his voice.

Sarah smiled and extended her hand in a polite greeting. "Hello, Mr. Andrews."

"Ah, so this is the woman." His father looked at him, and then back to Sarah. "I know who you are," he sneered without acknowledging Sarah's outstretched hand and turned to Greg. "I didn't know you were into ethnic beauties. This squaw is rather appealing, considering her red skin. I knew the rumors had some truth to them."

Sarah gasped at the derogatory implications and left the room at once. Greg felt a wave of anger engulf him, so thick that he started shaking. He'd always known his father considered himself better than most people, but his treatment of Sarah and his racist outburst were inexcusable. With a few quick strides, he went face-to-face with the older man.

"Get out of my house!" Greg shouted.

"Don't you dare talk to me in that manner. You're who you are because of me, remember that," Greg Jr. spat out. "I can't believe you'd sacrifice your reputation for someone like her. Don't you get it, Greg? The media is feasting on this little romp of yours. You're acting the part of a rebellious son, just as you've always done."

"What do you mean by 'someone like her'?" Greg's temper flared to dangerous levels.

"What do you see in that gold–digging Indian girl?"

"I see a woman who risked her future to save my life. But of course, you wouldn't understand that. You've never cared that much for anyone but yourself." Greg's lips turned into a grim line.

"You seem to have the idea that we don't care about you. Don't you think that sentiment goes both ways? But if you're trying to catch our attention by parading around with that . . . that . . . *woman*, then you'd better realize you're not hurting anyone but yourself. Can't you see? She's not like us!"

Greg moved closer. "Don't make me kick you out, *Father*," he answered, grinding out the last word.

"You wouldn't dare, young man. If you think you've got it made, you're mistaken. I can take all of this away with just a snap of my finger," his father challenged, meeting Greg's steady gaze with equal defiance.

"You can take your threats with you when you go." Greg placed a hand on his father's collar, pivoted him around, and started pushing him toward the door. "Instead of sticking your nose in my business, why don't you pay attention to your wife? Find out what she's doing while you're too busy counting your wealth. That should wipe that smirk off your face."

It did.

Without letting go of his father, Greg turned the knob, swung open the door, and pushed him out. "Stay out of my life. You'll get your money on time, so just leave me the hell alone!" Greg shouted before slamming the door.

Greg Jr. banged on the unforgiving surface for several minutes, cursing at the top of his lungs. At last, his footsteps faded away.

Greg walked straight to the wet bar. He needed a drink to calm his anger with his father. The older man's blatant display of arrogance had gone beyond rude. He'd attacked Sarah's integrity and insulted her. Picking the first bottle he could lay his hands on, Greg poured himself a glass of whiskey.

Downing the contents in one pull, he banged the glass on the counter. "Who does he think he is?" he muttered to himself.

God, he hoped Sarah hadn't heard everything his father had said. Greg poured another drink and slid open the glass door to the patio. He needed to calm down and think. Although he wanted to check on Sarah, he suspected it would be best to leave her alone tonight.

Greg shoved a hand through his hair and sat down on a patio chair. Still fuming, he glanced around him and muttered a curse. How in the hell could he fix this one? He prided himself on nailing together the toughest deals, but tackling this one wouldn't be easy. Not after the offensive things his father had said about Sarah.

All he'd ever wanted was to make her life better in general. Then this happened. *Is there anyone out there who isn't out to get me?*

Footsteps sounded, and Greg turned to see Simon watching him with concern. "I heard everything. I knew you could handle him, so I stayed out of sight."

"If you're planning on playing Dr. Phil with me, get a glass for yourself and grab the bottle on the counter." Greg sank back in his chair.

"Sure, might as well join you, my friend." Simon returned with the bottle and settled on the other patio chair next to him. "I'm sure you're aware I treat you like the son I never had. So I'm going to tell it like I see it."

Greg responded by reaching over to grab the bottle on the glass table. After pouring another shot for himself, he leaned back and waited for Simon to continue. His friend and employee, although pushing fifty, looked healthier than most people in their thirties. Simon had always been a private person and seldom talked about himself. All Greg knew was that he was an ex-marine, had never married, and had lived alone until this bodyguard arrangement began.

"I believe there's a connection between Cade and Cassandra. I could tell even before you guys went to Alaska, when your wife . . ." He stopped, seeming embarrassed by the word. "Cassandra visited you at work. I observed the obvious attraction between them. But I knew that Cassandra loved attention, so I shut my mouth because none of it was my business. When you got shot, it wasn't hard to connect the dots."

"How come Trevor still can't provide solid evidence?" This cat-and-mouse routine had gone on long enough, and Greg's patience was wearing thin. He glared at the city's twinkling lights.

"I think Cade and Cassandra are just waiting for the right time, or they plan to meet somewhere. They're going to crack soon. Thanks to your mother's involvement, I'm sure the cops are all over this. I'm just hoping you'll give up the revenge you've been plotting. Don't take matters in your own hands. Wash your hands of these people, and go on with your life."

They were both taking alternate swigs of their whiskey. This was what he'd wanted all along, someone to whom he could unload some of the weight he'd been carrying. Although Sarah had expressed willingness to listen several times, he shied away from airing his dirty laundry with her. Having a wife who had cheated on him had done a number on his ego and brought his confidence to an all-time low. Sarah had been his redemption, and scaring her away was a risk he would not take.

"You think my mother is screwing Cade?" That was the question of the year.

Simon's mouth fell open before he shook his head. "You can't think she's that bad."

"I don't know what to think anymore. Of course I want to believe she's incapable of cheating, but I don't know my mother well." Greg sighed and took another quick swig from his glass.

"I think some people are just not meant to be parents. Yours love you in their way, but they just don't know how to be parents to you."

"You and your meaningful insights," Greg said, continuing to glare at the luminous lights in front of them.

Simon chuckled but then sobered. "This girl, Sarah . . . I think she feels the same way about you, but the timing isn't right."

Greg nodded.

"You guys ought to straighten out your own lives before you try to be together, if that's your destiny. I'm concerned she's not built for life here in the big city. She's very simple. Her needs are minimal, and everything about you overwhelms her, although I can see she's been trying."

"What do you suggest I do?"

Simon shook his head. "I wish I had an answer for you. I'm just dissecting what I observe. I'm sure you know what your options are, but you're just too confused to see."

"Dr. Phil would've done better."

Simon shrugged. "But he'd charge you an arm and a leg."

"True, but I can afford him." Greg sighed.

"According to your father, he can take it all back."

That was an empty threat, in Greg's opinion. "That's what he's held over me all along, as far back as I can remember. At first, it scared me because this life of luxury is all I've ever known. But after a while, it got old. I didn't go to business school to be harassed into believing his lies. It's just too bad for him that I conduct business better than he does."

"What do you mean by that?" Simon eyed him with caution.

Greg chuckled, despite his misery. "Even if he does decide to pull the rug out from under me, I wouldn't be as destitute as he wants me to believe I'd be."

"Ha!" Simon laughed. "I knew you were too smart for your own good."

Greg's expression turned solemn, and he continued to stare at the view without seeing anything. "I want you to promise to look after Sarah if the time comes when I can't."

"Stop talking like that. I'm not going to do your job."

Greg tore his gaze away from the view. "I have a feeling this arrangement will blow up in my face soon. If Sarah decides not to keep her side of the bargain, I won't force her to stay. But she has nothing to go back to and no family to look after her. I've been making arrangements for her. There's a trust I've created in her name that will build a decent hospital in Beaver. Once she's done with school, she'll have a place she can work, if that's what she wants."

Simon gave this information a lot of thought. When he looked back at Greg, his face reflected deep sadness. "It sounds like you've fallen hard for this girl."

"I have," Greg said. "But I'm not the right man for her. I'm, what? Ten years older? And we're worlds apart—you said so yourself. I'd hate her to have to live a life of anger and hypocrisy; my baggage isn't something she should have to share. But I can't even bear to think of what will happen to me if I lose her."

"Does she have any idea how you feel about her?" Simon asked, patting Greg's shoulder.

Greg let out a deep sigh. "No."

"Your life, your call. I'm just here to listen." Simon leaned back, crossed his legs at the ankle, and closed his eyes, leaving Greg to dwell on the things he'd said.

~

Greg must've been asleep for a good hour when a sharp, agonized cry woke him. Disoriented, he reached for the clock on his bedside table and then sank back against the mattress with a groan. He thought he'd been dreaming, until the cry sounded again. Awake now, he bolted out of bed, stubbing a toe in the process. Cursing, he grabbed a shirt and managed to put it on while he rushed out of his room into the darkness of the hallway. He had no idea where the cry had come from until he heard it again—Sarah's bedroom.

Simon appeared in the hallway looking bedraggled. "You heard it, too?"

"Yeah," Greg whispered. "I got this. Go back to bed."

"Call me if you need anything," Simon said, looking over his shoulder while he walked back to his room.

Greg turned the knob on Sarah's door, trying his best not to make a noise. When Sarah cried again, he all but ran to her side. Kneeling on the side of the bed, he found her flailing but still asleep. "Sarah, wake up. You're having a bad dream." He kept his voice low and soothing.

He gave her shoulders a gentle shake. In the darkness, her beautiful face contorted into the picture of agonizing fear. He was almost grateful for the excuse to touch her.

"Sarah, wake up." He gave her another light shake.

Sarah woke up feeling like Armageddon had unleashed its fury on her. Her body shook, beads of sweat ran down her temples, and her last scream still lingered in her throat.

"Sarah . . ."

Greg's voice sounded near her head, and her eyes shot open. She stared at him, not knowing if this was still a part of her nightmare.

"Greg?" She reached out and touched his face. "Am I awake?"

"Yes, you are now." He took her hand in his.

She blinked and pulled her hand back. "I hate nightmares."

Sarah scrambled to sit up while Greg rose from his kneeling position at the side of her bed.

"I heard your screams, so I came in to check on you." He watched her with a worried expression. "What got you all scared?"

She tried to remember but came up empty. "How can dreams turn you upside-down, and then leave you wondering what got you all riled up in the first place?" Blinking, she tried to compose her thoughts. "I can't remember."

"Do you want a glass of water?" Greg asked without moving from his spot.

Sarah shook her head and shivered, still feeling the effects of the forgotten nightmare. "Lie down with me?"

Why did she always end up speaking without thinking first? This was so wrong on all levels, but she was giving in to her heart's desire. If it was a mistake, then she'd learn her lesson pretty soon.

Greg hesitated. She couldn't blame him. He must know how she felt about him, although she'd fought hard to keep her emotions hidden. Greg was far too beautiful for his own good, and she had been mesmerized by him from the first moment she'd laid eyes on him.

She closed her eyes, waiting for him to turn her down. He didn't say anything, but then she felt the mattress dip under his weight. "I'll hold you until you fall asleep."

Sarah nodded and then turned her body in his direction. Greg eased himself onto the bed, and face-to-face, they stared at each other in the darkness. No words were necessary. They were just two people struggling with their lives and everything around them, and they needed each other. *That much is evident*, Sarah thought.

"Greg, hold me now?"

He considered her for a moment before reaching out and circling an arm around her waist to pull her closer. She lifted her head and rested it on his shoulder, her face brushing the crook of his neck. He swept some errant hair away out of her eyes and planted a soft kiss on her forehead.

"Sleep, my little girl," Greg murmured.

Sarah felt a sudden urge to kiss him, and it was too strong to fight. With her heart in her throat, she lifted her head and caressed his lips with hers.

Greg stiffened, but then he returned her kiss with surprising passion. Applying pressure to her spine, he drew her closer. She closed her eyes, savoring the hardness of his body rubbing against hers.

Greg had never felt quite as shaken as he was by Sarah's kiss. "I like being close to you." He could hear the tremor in his voice when he spoke.

"Me, too." Her words were low and seductive.

Sarah threaded her fingers through his hair when he pushed his tongue between her parted lips. The warmth of her mouth was inviting, and it mixed with her cedar and mint scent, sending his mind into a whirlwind of desire. Sarah circled her tongue in his mouth, stroking, teasing, and making him ache to taste more of what she had to offer. He felt her shudder.

"God, Sarah, you have no idea how much I want you." His voice sounded strangled, mirroring the conflict inside him. He wanted her, and his body was crying out to take her.

Tracing his hand on her thigh, he worked his way up along the curve of her body. She arched to meet his slow fingertips.

She moaned. "Greg, make love to me."

Greg hesitated, not sure whether he'd just imagined her invitation. Searching her face, he saw the same urgency he felt reflected in her eyes. Making love with Sarah would be the epitome of perfection. Joy stole through his veins.

He wanted to give her everything she asked for. But would it be right to her moment of vulnerability? This was Sarah, not some woman he could just jerk around and forget.

"Greg, have I offended you?" Sarah was still breathless from their kisses, but he could feel her draw back.

"There's nothing else I would rather do than make love to you." His voice sounded pained and defeated. "I want it more than anything in this world, but I . . ." He stopped himself.

"Greg, I'm asking you to make love to me. I don't care about the consequences. I want you—right here and now." She kissed him again, this time on the tip of his nose, and smiled.

"I don't want to hurt you." How could he deny the request of the only woman he'd ever loved?

"You said you'd never hurt me."

Greg couldn't see her expression in the darkness, but she waited for him to accept her statement without any sign of doubt.

"Never."

It was a solemn promise, not just to her but also to himself. Emboldened by her assurance, Greg eased his body into a more comfortable position and snaked his arm back around her waist to pull her closer. He traced his fingertips along her face and at last crushed his mouth to hers.

"God, I never thought I'd taste heaven," he murmured when they surfaced for air. Hungry for more, he skimmed his mouth down her jawline and then caressed her neck with his tongue. Sarah's back arched again at the sensual motions on her neck.

She dug her fingers in the small of his back, scraping his skin with her nails. Her touch elicited a primeval hunger within him, throwing him into a frenzy of lust. Unwilling to wait any longer, he tugged at her pajama top.

"Sarah, I want to see you now." He was beyond rational thinking. All he knew was how much he wanted to take her right that moment. Sarah held her arms up, and he slid her pajama top over her head to expose her taut breasts. Excitement welled up within him, and he proceeded to strip away her pajama bottoms, revealing a black, lacy bikini that glorified her breathtaking curves. He devoured her almost-naked figure with his eyes, from her breasts and the curve of her waist, down to the juncture between her thighs, still hidden by her underwear.

Sarah panted in anticipation. "Don't make me wait a minute longer."

There is no turning back now, Greg thought while the last thread of his self-control began to slip away. He would take her now. There was no doubt about it. A low growl escaped his lips before he captured her nipple, caressing it with his tongue while he pleasured the other one with his finger.

A surge of desire manifested in Sarah's eyes while she curled underneath him, moaning in pure ecstasy. He glided his tongue down her chest toward her belly button, holding her with his hands at her waist and rubbing himself on her. He could feel her responding to every movement.

Sarah tugged on his shirt, which he discarded on the floor in one hurried motion. She tilted her head, probing the contours of his chest with her fingers and moving along his skin, bringing a delicious tingle wherever she touched.

The strong outline of Greg's half-naked body took Sarah's breath away. She rose to a sitting position to get a better look at him. His skin glistened with sweat in the glow of the city lights that streamed in from the big picture window.

He watched her trail her fingertips from his jaw line to his collarbone and down to his chest muscles, where her hand at last came to rest. The warmth of his skin sent rippling sensations through her body.

"I don't know how much longer I can hold on," he groaned in her ear.

Looking up at him, Sarah gathered her courage and pulled his shorts down to expose his boxers. Her gaze fell on the bulge underneath, the sight of which created a flurry of goose bumps on her skin. She watched Greg hungrily while he slid his boxers down to the floor, revealing muscular thighs and powerful legs.

Her heart started thumping hard, and her body begged for fulfillment. Greg had to satiate her need now. Reaching out for him, her gaze remained locked on the powerful man before her.

Greg studied her face while she drank in his appearance. He took a deep breath, and she knew he'd recognized in her expression the same desire he was feeling. He slid down on the bed next to her, and she got on top of him. Her legs brushed against his when she adjusted her body to the length of his strong frame.

"You're perfect, Greg."

"And so are you, Sarah."

"Let me do this," she breathed into his ear, and Greg nodded his understanding. Sarah realized he'd give her whatever she asked. They were on the edge and ready to plunge. She adjusted her body just so, and he moved to accommodate her.

Sarah's respiration quickened and heat sluiced within her at the feel of his body underneath her. *This is it.* The warning flashed in her head, but it was more to nudge herself into believing a beautiful thing was about to happen than fear of her first time. Greg didn't have to know she was a virgin. She didn't want to distract him now, when they were about to share something more magical and meaningful than her supposed virtue. She ached for him. She couldn't even think. All she knew was that she wanted him so much, she would scream if this stopped now.

She eased her throbbing center and moved her hips around him until she felt him inside her, all of him. Greg jerked when her warmth surrounded him. They both moaned at the contact, and Sarah stilled once Greg filled her. Tight and hurting where he'd penetrated her barrier, she ignored the pain and concentrated on the union of their bodies. She wanted his love, even the discomfort that came with it. She loved this man—it was the one thing she knew for sure.

"Sweet Jesus." He gasped and groaned in her hair.

Time was forgotten, their desire for each other reaching its ultimate intensity. They came almost at the same time, Greg's hand at her waist when his final thrust took Sarah to her own blissful high. She cried out when the pain gave way to a pleasure and happiness she'd never thought possible.

"Sarah, thank you." Greg had tears in his eyes when he cradled her face in his hands. "I'm humbled."

She blinked back her own tears. *I will never forget this moment*, she told herself. She responded with fervent kisses meant to communicate her feelings for him without words.

They continued to explore each other, experiencing every intricate pleasure they could throughout the night. Sarah marveled at the gentle way Greg held her, praising her with his hands, his eyes, and his mouth. This was how she had imagined love to be—sharing with the man she loved. The truth startled her, but now she knew deep inside that it had been the driving force behind everything she'd felt from the moment she'd first met Greg. This was all she'd ever wanted, something close to a fairytale. Something she would never have had with Trimble.

Neither one of them said anything after that. Contented, Sarah relaxed, letting the even beat of Greg's heart lull her to sleep. She pushed the hurtful words his father had hurled at her to the back of her mind. *Greg isn't his father*, she kept repeating to herself, and she crossed her fingers that, for once in her life, her belief wouldn't lead her astray. Instead, she basked in the afterglow of their lovemaking, enjoying the warmth Greg provided and loving every second that their bodies were entwined.

Chapter 16

Sarah's senses awoke to the lingering scent of Greg on her pillow, her body, and everywhere around the room. Thinking of the night they'd spent together made her tingle inside, and she blushed from her neck up to her face. She smiled at the memory of their shared passion and his kisses on her skin and all over her body. The thrilling sensation of his arms around her still burned, sending a delicious shiver through her body. His heady aroma was a beautiful reminder of the time he'd held her in his arms.

She turned and swept her arm across the bed, half expecting it to land on his solid body. The other half expected him to be gone, just like he'd said. *I'll hold you until you fall asleep.* And sure enough, he was gone.

The glow of the rising sun flowed through the glass window, a sharp contrast to the sinking sensation in the pit of her stomach. The unforgettable desire still hugged her like a clinging vine, but now it was time to face the dreary prospect of what lay ahead of her.

Pain, loss, and regret were bound to follow—she had known they would. But not so soon. She had hoped for more time to bask in the afterglow of the most wonderful night of her life.

Sarah frowned at herself. What had she expected from him, anyway? Did she imagine Greg would sweep her off her feet and whisk her to paradise? Those daydreams only came true in movies. Sarah knew better than to hold her breath for a happy-ever-after with her prince. She would forever be a girl from Beaver—a squaw, as Greg's father had called her.

Having been cloistered in Beaver all her life, she'd been sheltered from the harsh realities of racial divisiveness. As much as she believed that black, white, or brown were the same, people outside Beaver were much, much different, as she'd discovered for the first time last night. Sarah had recognized the cosmic divide between her and Greg from the very start. She had known this from the very first day. When she'd cut away his expensive clothes to operate on him, she could tell he was someone special. He was from far away world that was not meant to cross hers. Another planet, whose orbit was always out of reach.

Last night, their orbits had connected, and for a brief moment, she'd experienced ecstasy and starlight. But now, his axis had already moved away from her again. Had she been foolish enough to fall for Greg? Every fiber of her being screamed the undeniable answer.

He wanted her close—that much he'd told her. She'd forgotten the real reason he wanted her around. Medical necessity had pushed him to find her, together with the possibility that his doctors might need to ask her questions. She'd been living under his roof for over two months, and his doctors had yet to summon her. It didn't quite add up, but she'd been too comfortable to say anything and risk rocking the boat. If there was one thing that terrified her, it had to be the idea of not seeing Greg anymore.

She took the pillow and covered her face with his scent. Pathetic. Homeless. Unwanted and shunned by her father and the tribe. Reeling from the previous night's passion, wanting more, and so in love with Greg it hurt. How pathetic. After inhaling Greg's lingering scent, she tossed the pillow aside and got up just as her cell phone rang.

She recognized the number right away. Could it be? Holding her breath and wishing with offering up a fervent prayer that her father was coming around, she picked up on the second ring. "Hello?"

"Sarah, it's me."

"Lily? Lily! Oh my, how did you get my number?"

"Your father gave it to me so I could—and I'm quoting him on this —'talk some sense into that friend of yours.' " Lily's harsh tone surprised her.

"He told you about our phone conversation?" Sarah moved to sit on the edge of the bed.

"He did. I know your father can be stubborn, but he hasn't been the same since you left. Sometimes I think he regrets everything he said and did, but he's just too proud to admit it." Lily sighed.

"He kicked me out, Lily. He didn't even give me a chance to explain. He kept telling me to be true to myself while I was growing up, and I was. And this is what I get." Sarah gripped the phone tight in her hand while she experienced the pain of his rejection again. She missed her father. He was her only family, and it pained her to be away from him, no matter the circumstances.

"I know. I think he's suffering deep inside. It's just his pride getting in the way . . ." Lily paused before shifting to another subject. "You know, after you left, there were outcries from a few elders about what you did. Mr. Vittrekwa, who we thought would share your father's opinion, questioned your father's decision. And you know how Old man Vittrekwa gets when he speaks his mind."

Sarah laughed. She was well aware that Mr. Vittrekwa often opposed her father's views, despite their lifelong friendship. Even if Mr. V voiced his displeasure about the behavior of kids these days and the encroachment of modern technologies, she remembered him saying, "If we can't beat them, we might as well join them." She also recalled heated arguments between her father and his friend about where their little tribe was headed and the best way to accept the ever-changing tides.

"I know. I'm glad he stood up for me. But that's not going to help me at all. Father made his decision, so I'm where I am now." Sarah closed her eyes.

"So, where *are* you?" The old, curious Lily was back.

"I'm in New York City . . ." She left the words hanging, unable to decide how to begin telling Lily about her and Greg. *There's no Greg and you. There's just an arrangement . . . and last night.* She pulled herself up short, pushing back the slow ache building inside her.

"With *him*, right?" Lily dove straight to the crux of the matter.

Sarah groaned. "It's a long story, Lily."

"Well, I have nothing but time, so spill." Sarah imagined Lily placing her legs on the desk, crossing them at the ankles, and leaning back against the chair.

Without much coaxing from Lily, Sarah related the night of her abduction, their first meeting, Greg's threat, and the eventual arrangement he'd proposed. Then, she fast-forwarded to their dinner, his wife, the movie, and the accident. She left out his father's racist comment, as well as the special moment they'd shared last night. There were some things she'd rather not discuss with anyone, even with her best friend.

"Are you telling me this man you saved had you kidnapped and threatened to throw you in jail if you don't cooperate with him?

Sarah nodded before she remembered Lily couldn't see her. "Yes."

"And the same guy enrolled you in one of the most prestigious schools in the country?" Lily's voice now had a dreamy lilt to it.

"Yes." Sarah hated to admit it, but Greg's behavior had a tendency to give her whiplash. He could be pushy and overbearing one minute, and sweet and compassionate the next. Sometimes hot, sometimes cold. He was a man she had yet to figure out.

"Sounds like a fairytale to me," Lily commented.

Sarah sighed. It hadn't all been a girl's dream come true. "Not by a long stretch, and besides, he and I are like night and day. He's rich, I'm poor. He's popular, and I'm a fly on the wall nobody cares about. There's no way there's going to be a fairytale."

"You sound disappointed." Lily fell quiet, leaving Sarah to question what her friend was thinking. "Sarah . . . are you falling in love with him?"

"Of course not." Her denial sounded weak even to her own ears.

If she were honest with herself, this arrangement had spelled trouble from the get-go. Either she'd been too stubborn to heed the warnings or was just plain dumb. She had dug her own grave, knowing the stakes were high and the likelihood of making it out unscathed would be almost impossible. She shouldn't have accepted help from a man who could make her heart flutter and scare her all at the same time. Sure, she trusted him.

But could she trust him with her heart? Even after last night?

"I know you, Sarah—well enough to guess you're torn between following your heart and doing what's best for everyone else. Girl, I'm telling you right now. Follow your heart." Lily paused, no doubt letting her words sink in.

She was right. A long silence followed. Sarah was unable to deny her friend's observation.

Thank God Lily now decided to pursue another topic. "There is another reason why I called. There's massive construction happening here in Beaver."

"What construction?"

"Someone created a generous trust fund for the tribe. The governor mandated that the entire town attend a meeting at the town hall a few weeks ago. He instructed your father to build a bigger clinic and buy better medical equipment." Lily paused to catch her breath. "Would you believe the mayor asked for you? God, Sarah, you're popular."

"What? Are you kidding me?"

"Would I joke about something like this? And you wouldn't believe the look on your father's face. It was almost comical." Lily squealed in delight at the memory.

After they'd hung up, with a promise from Lily to call again, Sarah discovered that she felt vindicated. Her actions may have landed her in this wild, gray area of uncertainty, but she'd never regretted saving Greg's life. If given the chance, she'd do it again.

Greg shifted in the uncomfortable chair. He'd been in this room not too long ago, although under much different circumstances. He was more than happy it had nothing to do with Sarah.

Man, Sarah again. How could one woman manage to occupy his mind every waking moment? He shifted in his seat again, restless rather than uneasy about being at the police station again. The root of his discomfort was what had transpired the night before—not that he was complaining at all. He just wished he'd taken his time to enjoy every moment with her and hadn't run away like a scared puppy this morning.

Yeah, he was scared. Their night together had been too good to be true—it was unexpected and a big mistake. Why had he let it happen? Greg knew the answer. She had asked, and he couldn't resist giving her what she wanted. He'd wanted it, too.

With an exasperated sigh, he looked around the small room. A calendar with an autumn scene hung on the wall next to an imposing wall clock that made relentless ticking sounds. A tiny window provided entry for the blaring horns of morning rush-hour traffic. The stale scent of sweat hung in the air as a reminder of the numerous people who had waited in this office before him.

Sitting next to him was Tony Anton, his lawyer. They've been called in to answer a few questions about Cade McPherson. The bastard had been nabbed late the night before at an Amtrak station on his way to Arizona.

The door creaked opened, and Detective Ramirez walked in with a manila folder tucked under his arm. He gave a quick nod to Tony and smirked at the sight of Greg.

"Thanks for coming in on such short notice." He sat down and proceeded to open the folder, spreading the contents across the table.

"You're welcome." Tony smiled. "So what are we looking at?"

Greg remained stone-faced when Detective Ramirez glanced up and focused on him. "First of all, I can't say I'm glad to see you here again so soon, but at least, the circumstances are—"

"Just get to the point, Detective, will you?" Greg snapped. Short-fused and not in a good frame of mind, small talk wasn't up his alley at the moment. This turn of events had messed up his plans. Even with Simon's urging to drop it, Greg ached for revenge.

Ramirez looked at him with contempt. "You know, I'm curious why you didn't inform us of Mr. McPherson's attempt on your life."

"I'm just trying to move on," Greg responded. He leveled a steady gaze at Ramirez, hoping the detective wouldn't see right through him.

"Hmm . . . if I didn't know any better, I'd believe you had other things in mind." It was a simple statement, but Greg could tell the officer was fishing for information. No way would he fall for such amateurish coaxing.

"If you called me in here just to tell me that, you could have called and saved me the trip." Greg leaned forward and eyed the pictures on the desk.

Ramirez was quick to follow his gaze. "If it weren't for your mother, we wouldn't have any idea that an incident had happened at all. I'm amazed how easy to manipulate some of our law enforcement agencies are." The detective shook his head and watched Greg for any signs of guilt, but Greg kept his mouth shut. He wasn't planning to divulge the lengths he'd gone to in order to keep all pertinent information on the down-low.

Ramirez tacked on. "Although the crime happened in Alaska, you and Mr. McPherson are residents of this city, you can file a formal complaint. If you choose not to, we'll proceed with the complaint your mother filed."

Greg seethed in silence. He wasn't sure whether to be grateful to or upset with his mother for ruining his one chance for revenge. "What type of complaint did she file?" Deep down, he felt a small measure of relief wash over him. The mere fact that his mother wasn't involved with Cade had given him hope and a little more faith in her.

"Attempted murder . . . and she's naming your wife as a co-conspirator." Detective Ramirez leaned forward, watching him like he was waiting for Greg to explode.

"I'd like to speak to my client in private. Could you give us a moment?" Tony spoke at the perfect moment—Greg couldn't have picked a better time. He needed to regroup.

Ramirez nodded and stood. "I'll be waiting outside."

Greg rose from his chair, dying to stretch his aching legs. The muscle spasms were rare nowadays, but stress and fatigue seemed to trigger his attacks, so it was wise to listen to his body's warning signs.

"Greg, is there a reason to believe your wife is involved?" Tony stood, too, but instead of watching Greg, the lawyer walked over to the window and gazed outside.

Greg hadn't expected this to happen. He had to act fast before it was too late. "I think there's a chance she might be involved."

Tony turned around, leaned on the windowsill, and crossed his arms, deep in thought. After a few minutes, he spoke. "Would you rather proceed with your mother's complaint, or do you want to file a petition to supersede it? Either way, you must appear in court for this. Since Cade has already been taken into custody, he'll have to put up bail, and he won't be able to leave the city."

Greg toyed with the idea in his head. His new plan was quite daring and downright stupid, but it was doable. Then there were Simon's words running through his head: *Don't do it, Greg. You're better off washing your hands of these people.*

"Let's file a formal complaint against Cade."

"And what about your wife?" Tony coughed to clear his throat.

Greg laughed. "I had to remind myself you're not my divorce attorney. Let's leave her out of it for now. You can call Ramirez back in here. I bet the guy is salivating over the shot at such a high-profile case." Glancing at the scattered pictures on top of the folder, he smirked. Perhaps he should send some thank-you flowers to his mother one of these days. Greg went back to the aging chair and sat down to wait.

Tony chuckled before opening the door. He stuck his head out. "Detective Ramirez?"

Ramirez walked in after a few minutes, carrying a cup of coffee. "So, has your client made up his mind?"

"Mr. Andrews will file a formal complaint against Mr. McPherson," Tony stated, pulling a notepad from his briefcase.

Detective Ramirez cocked an eyebrow. "And?"

"That's it. If there's anything else you need, call Tony." Greg rose from his chair. "I'm sure we're done here. If you'll excuse me, I have some important matters to attend to." He gave Ramirez and Tony a curt nod and left the stifling room.

As soon as he'd walked out the door, he spotted Simon waiting in the lobby, looking quite uncomfortable around the questionable characters surrounding him.

"Everything all right?" Simon stood, giving Greg a thorough look-over.

Greg nodded. He racked his brain for a Plan B. Fishing out his cell phone from his pocket, he dialed Cassandra's number. After three rings, she picked up, and Greg felt the immediate urge to clamp his hands around her neck.

Not yet.

"Hey, Cassie, can you meet me at Café Bevier tonight?" He used his sweetest tone, a weapon guaranteed to render his *wife* helpless.

Simon threw him a questioning glance, but he waved him off.

Greg suppressed the urge to throw up when Cassandra purred a quick assent. *Perfect*, he thought. Plan B might work after all. Cade might have been out of reach, but Cassandra was well within his grasp. Greg would be a fool to let her off the hook easily.

Sarah heard Greg's voice in the hallway when she stepped off the treadmill. She grabbed the towel from the rack and wiped the sweat off her face and neck. Strengthening her back had been a slow and painful process, but the daily exercises Dr. Darnell had given her were proving beneficial.

She walked across the well-equipped home gym to the yoga mat and sat down. Glancing at her reflection in the floor-to-ceiling mirror, she longed to chop off her hair, which had grown quite long. The Gwich'in culture preferred women with long tresses, which in their beliefs connoted femininity. Sarah had been itching to defy that tradition since her teenage years, but she hadn't had the nerve to follow through. She blew out a rapid breath, noting her hollow cheeks. Despite Matilda's best efforts to fatten her up, Sarah's body seemed to have a mind of its own. Food just passed through her without leaving traces of any weight gain whatsoever.

She stretched her legs sideways into a tolerable arch. Then she bent her body while she attempted to reach the tip of her shoe with her fingers. This time, she managed to reach her ankle. *Not bad*, she thought. Tomorrow, she might even reach another half inch. 'Gradual improvement' had been Barry's mantra. There was no need to push her body to extremes.

She went through the repetitive exercises several times before calling it a day. Her next class would begin in an hour. If she intended to make it to campus on time, she had to move faster. Sarah walked out of the gym just as Greg was coming in.

"Hello." Greg paused at the doorway.

"Hi." Her voice sounded somewhat tentative. "You left early today."

"Had some stuff to do." He looked at her in a way that told her he had something on his mind. "I will be out tonight, so don't wait up."

"Where are you going?" The question slipped out of her mouth before she had the chance to stop herself. It was a question she had no business asking, despite what had happened between them last night. Sarah wanted to slap herself for sounding like desperate. What could he be thinking?

"I'm going to meet someone for dinner." He turned away and continued on into the room, letting the door slide closed between them.

Their brief exchange set the tone for the rest of her day. She went through her classes feeling cold and confuse. The fact that Greg had made no attempt to clue her in on his dinner plans made it impossible to concentrate during class. "Out tonight" could mean anything, but she had a nagging suspicion it involved a *she.* Her day dragged on long enough to make her want to cry, and still she was plagued by these thoughts.

To make matters worse, the weather turned dreary just when she walked out of the building. The wind picked up, and dark clouds loomed above. Soon the rain poured down, soaking her to the bone before she had a chance to get into the waiting car.

Chapter 17

Greg watched his soon-to-be ex-wife with a wary eye. Cassandra exemplified class and beauty, and she had manners befitting royalty. She was in her element in this elegant setting. He knew she loved being seen at important events and attending galas—anywhere the limelight would be focused on her even for a short time. Cassandra was vain, and she would always go where the rich and famous hobnobbed. She lived for times like that, when her beauty was all that mattered.

She smiled back at the appreciative glances thrown her way and moved toward him, looking like she'd just walked out of a fashion magazine. Not too long ago, he'd thought he loved her, but now the mere idea repulsed him. Greg had no idea why he'd ended up marrying her, but he couldn't wait to get her out of his life and out of his wallet.

How he'd fallen for her remained a mystery. He'd have to use the silly excuse of many fools before him—*love is blind.* Sure, she was beautiful, charming . . . but she was empty. It had taken him six years to realize that part. Pretty sad. He'd always thought he was smart enough to recognize the warning signs.

Cassandra stopped a foot away. Showing off her perfect figure and her graceful body, she seemed to be offering an argument as to why he'd been a fool to let her go.

"Hello, Greg." She gave him a dazzling smile, but instead of being dazzled, he found his thoughts turning back to Sarah.

He smiled and got to his feet. "Hey, Cassie, glad you could make it." He hit her back with an equally mesmerizing smile, enough to make her regret screwing other men when she'd already landed such a big catch.

She flashed her teeth when he pulled out a chair for her, and sat down with an elegant flair. Greg sighed, once more reminding himself to stop comparing the two women. Cassandra's vanity was quite different from Sarah's down-to-earth and pretense-free attitude.

"I wouldn't miss dining with a gorgeous man in my favorite restaurant." Cassandra turned the full power of her charm on him.

Greg grinned, trying to establish an amiable air between them. With luck, Cassandra would be dumb enough to miss the charade. He summoned the waiter to get the bottle of the chilling Cristal champagne he'd ordered ahead of time. Nothing but the best, just as Cassandra expected from him. Greg let the silence linger while they waited for the bottle. Stealing glances in Cassandra's direction, he found her studying him with open curiosity.

"What are we celebrating?"

When she batted her long eyelashes, Greg understood what "wrong time and wrong place" meant. Cassandra was so wrong—she had been wrong back then and was even more so now. There was just one place he wanted to be, and that was in Sarah's company, any time of the day. Yet he'd endure this meeting to achieve his goal. Cassandra seemed like she'd make it easy for him. This wouldn't take long.

The champagne came, and after their glasses were filled, Greg raised his flute. "Here's to closing another chapter in my life."

Watching Cassandra's expression change like a cartoon character in a matter of seconds made his night. Her face twitched before she cracked a smile and tilted her glass. "Another chapter?"

Greg drank half the champagne and placed his glass back on the damask-covered table. "Yes. It's all over the news. I'm surprised you haven't heard."

If Cassandra suspected anything, she tried to hide it. Her expression remained bewildered. She sipped her champagne and waited, although her smile wavered a fraction. It would have been unnoticeable if Greg weren't watching for the signs.

"No . . . I've been out of the loop."

"Well, let me fill you in on the latest gossip." He leaned forward and clasped his hands together, intending to observe Cassandra's reaction closely. "As you already know, Cade shot me during a hunting trip in Alaska."

She nodded, avoiding his gaze. "That's how you met Maria, isn't it? News about you two is driving me nuts." Cassandra made no attempt to hide her disdain.

"Her name's Sarah. "She saved my life after Cade left me for dead. But let's not talk about her. As I was saying, Cade was taken into custody and is now out on bail. I guess, in a way, I want to make sure you know this so you will take extra precautions to protect yourself."

"Oh my . . . it's true, then?" For good measure, Cassandra released a big sigh. If he hadn't known any better, he would have thought she cared about his well-being.

He nodded. "I don't want anything happening to you. Even if we're no longer, you know . . . living together"—he scrubbed his face, false worry lines creasing his forehead—"it doesn't mean we can't be friends."

Cassandra beamed. "I like that—friends. Perhaps, we can turn it into something more again? We used to have this great connection . . ." She let her voice trail off, but her hand picked up the slack. With deliberate seduction, her fingers traced an enticing pattern on his arm, which used to send Greg into a whirlwind of lust. Not anymore, but he chose not to show it, instead taking her hand and bringing it to his lips.

Cassandra squirmed under his touch, moaning a delicate sound that made him cringe inside. He was so off the Cassandra bandwagon.

Their food order came, breaking up the intimacy of the moment. Greg smiled to himself. Pleased with his progress, he dug into his steak with satisfaction. It didn't bother him one bit whether she misinterpreted the cause of his pleasure. If Cassandra believed they had something going on, he was more than willing to let her hang herself with her own rope.

During a rare moment when the professor had excused himself from the classroom, Jeremy hopped over a few empty seats and sat next to Sarah in the half-filled auditorium.

"It's nice to see you back in class. I would have visited you in the hospital, but your housekeeper insisted you weren't taking visitors."

Leave it to Matilda to run off her friends. Sarah sighed. "I'm sorry . . . but yeah, I was quite a mess after that."

"I want to make it up to you." Jeremy's mouth quirked into a smile.

"You don't have to do anything. I'm fine, and as you said, I'm back. So we're good, right?"

Jeremy nodded. "Right . . . um, I've been meaning to ask you this, but I guess tonight's as good a time as any. If you don't have anything planned after class, I'd like to invite you to dinner. Nothing heavy. Just two people enjoying an excellent meal and good company."

There was no thinking necessary. Her social calendar hadn't been buzzing with activities. She had nothing planned for that night or any other night, for that matter. Greg was out for the evening, and the last thing she wanted to do was sulk at home alone. Besides, their arrangement held no clauses restricting her from going wherever she wanted to go, whenever she wished. Jeremy did say it was just dinner between friends. The invitation sounded harmless, and Sarah craved a change of atmosphere—anything to get Greg out of her mind.

"I'm not dressed for going out to dinner." Her usual attire of jeans, sweater, and knee-high boots wouldn't fit the classy dinner scene, but a quick glance at Jeremy's similar attire put her mind at ease.

"You can go anywhere without having to worry about what you wear. Your smile alone places you in the well-dressed category." Jeremy's eyes lit up, and he smiled wider.

Her lips curled at his lame attempt at flattery. "Whatever."

"I'll meet you after class." Jeremy beamed before going back to his seat, sporting a big grin on his face.

The next two hours passed quickly. Afterward, Sarah found herself seated next to Jeremy while he wove his Mini Cooper through the city's snarling traffic.

He pulled up in front of a restaurant. Its entrance was guarded by two humongous topiaries covered with white, twinkling lights. Even with Jeremy's repeated assurances about their appearance, Sarah had the sinking feeling they'd be underdressed. When Jeremy handed his keys to the waiting valet, she got out of the car, the door held open by another parking attendant.

Sarah squinted in the dim lighting when they made their way into the restaurant. Little candelabras adorned the walls, and their lights flickered, sending a warm and cozy glow across the room. From her vantage point, Sarah could see little tables for two sprinkled across the room, each with candles on top, creating an intimate atmosphere. She knew right off the bat that she had been right to be worried. Most of the patrons were well dressed. It was too late to turn around and leave, so Sarah heaved a big sigh and braced herself for the expected stares. However, one look at the hostess and the smiling manager, who came to greet Jeremy like an old friend, told her to park her worries elsewhere.

"Shall we?" Jeremy took her elbow and guided her through the maze of tables, following the hostess. "Is everything all right?" Jeremy whispered in her ear before pulling a chair out for her.

"We're dressed for a burger joint, not a place like this." She sat down and a menu appeared as if by magic in front of her.

"Don't worry about how we look. All you have to do is enjoy my charming company. No one will even care."

She laughed at his easygoing manner. "Okay, I guess it doesn't matter."

"Anything to drink, folks?" Their server produced another one of those large libation bibles, similar to the one she'd seen when she and Greg—

Enough! Sarah scolded herself. *No thinking of Greg tonight.* She noticed their server's gaze lingering in her direction.

Sarah thought for a minute. *No bottle of wine this time. I'm not repeating that debacle.* "I'll have a cosmopolitan." That was safer. She'd seen it on television many times to know it was a cool drink that was preferred by many women. All she needed to do was nurse one drink for the duration of their dinner.

"I'll have your Oban 18, no ice."

Sarah leaned forward. "What is Oban?"

Jeremy leaned in, too, resting his hands close enough that his knuckles touched hers. In the faint glow of the candlelight, Sarah saw the gleam in his eyes at her question. "It's a single-malt scotch. I'll let you have a sip if you want. I like it. It's very smooth, and it goes down well."

Gibberish, Sarah thought. Why do people talk about alcohol as if it were alive and breathing, complete with personality? "Sure. I'll have to make sure you don't drive drunk."

"One drink over dinner isn't going to get me plastered. And even if it did, we can walk over to the café to grab coffee afterward. That way, we get to spend more time together." He touched her hand, and although Sarah's first instinct was to pull away, Jeremy seemed pretty harmless.

They started an easygoing conversation, discussing their shared classes and the brutal months ahead. Their drinks came, and after a few sips of her pink drink, Sarah felt more relaxed. Jeremy's laid-back manner put her at ease, and she began to forget her troubles. His pleasurable company and engaging personality got her talking about Beaver and her father, but she left out the uglier details. No need to let Jeremy in on her present struggles.

During a short lull in their conversation, Jeremy took her hand as if it was a natural thing to do. "I have little confession to make."

Caught off guard, Sarah stiffened. "Okay?"

"I find you engaging and very attractive, Sarah. I'm not going to lie and pretend I'm not interested." Jeremy continued to caress her fingers. "I guess what I'm trying to say here is, I want to see more of you."

"I see."

Sarah weighed his words. Jeremy wasn't bad at all. In fact, he was gorgeous. His green eyes sparkled like emeralds, and he had sandy hair and a boyish, winning smile. But something was missing.

"My one concern is Mr. Andrews."

Sarah frowned. "What about him?"

"Rumors are flying that you're staying with him and all." Jeremy looked rather uncomfortable. He dropped his gaze on their touching hands.

Sarah pulled away, feeling embarrassed. She had no idea why. It was inevitable that her living arrangement with Greg would come up. Glancing across the room to buy time, something—or rather, someone—caught her eye. She blinked and found Greg staring at her from the far end of the room, his expression grim. Her immediate reaction was to check out his company. Cassandra sat across from him, talking animatedly. They looked just like any couple going out for a nice dinner. A sharp ache stabbed Sarah in the chest.

Jeremy continued to talk, oblivious to the reason behind her sudden silence. "Sarah, I'm sorry. I didn't mean to pry, and I know it's none of my business. I like you a lot, and I'd hate for you to end up with a married man." He tugged at her arm, his expression apologetic.

She peeled her gaze from Greg and focused back on him with a monumental effort. Her chest felt constricted, cutting off oxygen. The room seemed to grow smaller and the air thinner . . . or was it just her?

Right on the money—his date was a *she*. Although her feelings were uncalled for, Sarah found it impossible to get rid of the nagging stab of betrayal and jealousy in the pit of her stomach.

Summoning a response, she mock-glared at Jeremy. "Shame on you for listening to rumors, Jeremy. Don't worry. I'm not involved with Greg in any way." *Liar!* the damn voice screamed at her.

Relief crossed his face. "Then is it okay if I ask you out again?"

"I don't see why not." Her response was automatic and wrong. She wasn't interested in Jeremy, yet here she was, accepting his invitation to distract herself from the pain caused by the man across the room. How fast her evening had turned into a nightmare.

"Then how about going to a concert with me tomorrow night?" He sprang the question like he'd been planning it all along.

"Concert?" she asked, distracted by the realization that Greg was headed their way.

"Yeah, the old man has friends who are giving away some front row tickets. It would be nice if you could join me."

Greg stopped next to their table, and Jeremy straightened in his seat.

"Tomorrow's fine. I'd be happy to go with you," Sarah answered before she lifted her eyes in Greg's direction, hoping he had heard what she'd said.

He exuded a quiet strength and a commanding presence, which she attributed to age and experience. Jeremy appeared inexperienced and in total awe in comparison.

"Sarah, what a surprise to see you here." Greg's tone was cool and devoid of emotion. He showed no embarrassment about being caught lying.

Lying? The man is married, and that's his wife with him. What in God's name are you thinking? Sarah faked a smile. "I'm not sure you've met Jeremy. Jeremy Singer, this is Greg Andrews, my employer."

Jeremy stood and, although she could very well see the surprise in his face, he extended his hand to Greg. "It's a pleasure to meet you, Mr. Andrews."

Greg took his outstretched hand and clasped it. "Mr. Singer, the pleasure is mine."

"I didn't realize Sarah was an employee," Jeremy commented, oblivious to the sudden tension rising between his companions.

Greg's jaw clenched. "Yes, she is."

"That's good." Jeremy swung his head in the direction of Cassandra, who was waving at Greg. "I see you are dining here with your wife."

"Yes." Greg had more color in his face than Sarah had ever seen before.

"Well, don't let us keep you from a delightful dinner with your wife, sir," she said before she lost her nerve. This wasn't right. She had no right to feel this way.

"I guess I'll see you at work." He gave a quick nod before striding away with confidence.

Sarah's heart sank, and her body sagged.

"Are you okay?" Jeremy sat down, watching her with an intent gaze.

"Yes, I'm fine," she lied. Out of sheer impulse, she waved at their server, who was waiting nearby. "Please, bring me another cosmo." She lifted her empty glass.

Jeremy chuckled. "I guess I'm driving this time."

Sarah listened with half an ear to Jeremy's chatter while they ate dinner. Her food tasted like plastic, and the only thing that held any appeal for her was alcohol. She liked its calming effect, and despite her better judgment, she downed one more glass before their meal was finished.

Although she tried to concentrate on Jeremy's stories of his exploits during his first year in med school, she couldn't help but sneak glances in Greg's direction. She noted that Cassandra did most of the talking, as well as the touching. Sarah gritted her teeth, feeling sicker by the minute.

When Jeremy announced they were ready to go, Sarah stood faster than she'd intended in her eagerness to leave and stumbled forward. Jeremy's hand caught her waist, preventing her fall.

"Hey, are you okay?"

She laughed and nodded. "I'm fine. I just had more to drink than I'm used to." *No kidding.*

His hands stayed around her waist while he led her to the exit. "If I didn't know any better, I'd think you were a woman on a mission," he whispered in her ear.

"On a mission" was right—she was on a mission to get Greg out of her mind. The sooner they got out of there, the better she'd feel. Once they had stepped out of the restaurant, she broke free from Jeremy's touch. The blast of icy wind did very little to help her muddled thoughts. Confused at the raging emotions inside her, she let Jeremy talk her into extending their night a bit longer. He led her next door to a café.

The coffee helped. The more caffeine she ingested, the clearer things became. She needed to step away from the situation—keep Greg at arm's length, fulfill their arrangement, and then walk away.

In the café, the nagging reality hit her. She'd agreed to dinner, coffee, and the concert tomorrow with Jeremy, all just to hide the fact she was hurting. Seeing Greg with Cassandra had made her realize her place in his life. She was nothing but a diversion; an easy lay for him. And here she was, about to make another mistake by leading Jeremy on.

"I can't go out with you anymore, Jeremy. It isn't right. I don't feel the same way, and I'm afraid I'll end up hurting you." The words, though spoken with restless energy, were the truth. Feeling a sliver of relief, she took Jeremy's hand. "I can only be a friend."

Jeremy watched her with an intense expression, as if he were dissecting the root cause of her sudden declaration. He smiled, despite the sadness that crept into his eyes. "It's him, isn't it?"

Sarah nodded. What was the point in lying? "Am I so transparent?"

"Don't worry about a thing—your secret's safe with me." He brought her hand to his lips and kissed it. "I can be a friend, too."

~

Cursing under his breath, Greg phoned Rudy to bring the car around. Cassandra stood beside him on the sidewalk, her arms hooked around his. Come to think of it, he'd achieved what he came here for. She was all over him again. Must be the expensive champagne's influence, but he was happy with the outcome.

Rudy came and pulled up to the curb.

"After you." He held the door for her.

Simon nodded to Greg from the front passenger seat and ordered the driver to proceed. The limousine moved forward, and Greg caught sight of Sarah and Jeremy inside the café. Jeremy's lips mouthed something before he kissed Sarah's hand. *How freakin' cozy!* Greg seethed while the car rolled forward and joined the traffic.

He gritted his teeth in frustration. Raging jealousy consumed him, and Cassandra's continuous flirtation was driving him mad. The woman was relentless, and each time she rubbed her hand on his arm, the more he realized what an idiot he'd been.

Greg walked her to her townhouse, wishing he could get information through normal means instead of what she had in mind. He would have preferred to ask her outright, but he knew better. Cassandra wouldn't ever admit to being involved with Cade. Not a chance. She wasn't the smartest tool in the shed, but the woman's tenacity couldn't be faulted. Greg knew she would go to any lengths to get at least half his money in the divorce. He would fight just as hard to keep it out of her greedy hands.

"You've been quiet," Cassandra remarked in the elevator, her hand snaking its way up to the nape of his neck. She nibbled on his ear playfully.

"I'm just tired," he lied, trying not to squirm under her touch.

"Was that Maria back there in the restaurant?" Cassandra asked when they stepped out the elevator and started walking through the well-lit corridor.

He nodded and bit his tongue to keep himself from lashing out at her.

The intended put-down was not lost to him. “Here we are.” They stopped in front of her door.

Cassandra took her sweet time in retrieving her key from her purse. “Why don’t you come in?” she asked, pulling him inside without waiting for his answer. Not bothering to turn on the lights, she leaned in and seized his mouth with hers.

No bells rang and no sparks flew with their kiss, and Greg all but shoved her away. “Cassandra, I don’t think this is a good idea.” He headed for the door.

“The hell it isn’t.” A voice coming from the far end of the room froze him in his tracks.

Chapter 18

Greg pivoted on his heels at the sound of the familiar voice, one he hadn't heard since Alaska. He took a few steps forward, feeling a burst of anger override his reasoning. An abrupt return to sanity made him hesitate.

A chilling memory of the shooting flashed in his mind. He needed to be careful—Cade had shot him once, and the bastard could do it again. Maybe this time, Greg might not be so lucky. He watched Cassandra backtrack, ready to flee.

"You." Greg's tone was low and dripping with antagonism.

"What are you doing here?" Cassandra asked while she inched toward the door.

Cade's silhouette advanced a few steps, away from the shadows. In the darkened room, the only light streamed in from a lamppost outside, and Greg couldn't see much. He had no idea if Cade was armed, so he decided it was best for him to stay where he was.

Unlike before, when Cade had caught him by surprise, Greg was on his guard and wouldn't be blindsided. His eyes darted left to right while he planned his next step and where to take cover in case the situation got ugly.

By the looks of things, it would.

"What kind of question is that, Cassie baby? Aren't you happy to see me?" Cade drawled. He stayed where he was, concealed from what little light there was in the room.

"I . . . I don't know what you're talking about." Her stammered answer cemented Greg's belief in her guilt. Those two were indeed involved.

Under different circumstances, Greg would've rolled his eyes and given Cassandra a standing ovation for her close-to-perfect acting.

"C'mon, baby—didn't you miss me? It's been a long time since we last saw each other. I'm sure you didn't think I'd be able to stay away for very long."

Greg measured the distance between him and Cade. He would have to cover about ten feet to get to him. If he were to lunge forward, Greg might catch the bastard by surprise, but with the array of furniture and his bad legs, there was a good chance he'd miss. He could end up getting hurt, or even dead.

He decided to settle into the role of spectator for the time being, watching Cade's silhouette and Cassandra's movement from the corner of his eye.

"Cade, if you're here looking for trouble, please leave us alone. You've caused enough damage already," Cassandra pleaded while she continued to inch back toward the door.

"If I were you, Cassie baby, I'd stay put, because I won't hesitate to take you down with Greg. And don't even act like you have no idea what's going on. You're in this just as deep as I am. So cut the bullshit and come to me." Cade's voice turned low and dangerous. "Come on now, sweetheart. Come and give me a kiss."

Cassandra hesitated and started sobbing. Greg found himself torn between pity and fury. He felt sorry for her, and yet he wanted a chance to wring her neck before she got away.

"Cade, you don't understand," she wailed. "Greg and I are going to work on our relationship. This is all a mistake. Let's talk about this."

Her tears may have been a ploy to soften Cade, but they just seemed to aggravate him even more. He stepped out of the shadows, walking forward with guarded steps. Greg studied his movements, taking particular note of the gun tucked into Cade's waistband. A faint glow of light touched Cade's face, and his mouth twitched into a wicked smile. His eyes were sharp and calculating, and his shoulders were rigid with tension.

"Come here, you bitch. I'm gone for a few months, and you're already moving back into his bed?" The accusation, despite its venom, was also laced with hurt. When Cassandra stayed glued to her spot, Cade shouted. "Come here now!"

As if she'd been struck by lightning, Cassandra jumped. She ran to Cade like an obedient—but scared—child.

"Cade, please, please, don't hurt me," she cried, hesitating a few feet from him. He reached over and grabbed a handful of her blond locks and yanked her to him. Her cries tore at Greg's heart, despite the anger he felt toward her.

Greg thought the distraction provided a good opportunity to make his move, but Cade seemed to have read his mind and glanced his way. "I think your wife likes to be kissed like this," he sneered before planting a savage kiss on Cassandra's lips.

No matter how he hated her, Greg flinched at the punishing treatment Cade gave her. Helpless to intervene, he watched Cassandra struggle against Cade's mouth. Damn—as long as Cade was armed, he was left without any options. Greg clenched and unclenched his fists, hating his inability to fight back.

After the long, drawn-out display, Cade lifted his head with a smirk of satisfaction and focused once more on Greg. "So you found a way to stay alive, my friend." He laughed.

Greg had to think fast. They'd been *talking* quite long enough. He kept his voice even. "Ah yes. I refuse to die, my friend."

"I wish you would so Cassandra can take your money and we can go on our merry way. You have a knack for taking everything I want." Cade's eyes flashed with pure loathing.

"If you want money, you have to work for it."

Greg's reply brought Cade's fury to the surface. He pulled out the gun from his waistband and aimed it in Greg's direction.

Cassandra gasped and covered her ears. "Stop it, Cade!" She tried to move away, but Cade's arm was a steel band around her waist.

Cade wasn't listening to her. His entire focus was on Greg. "You talk like you worked so hard for your wealth. If it weren't for your father, you wouldn't be so high-and-mighty. And come to think of it, that Indian whore is staying with you for the money, isn't she?"

Greg considered himself a levelheaded man who seldom acted on impulse, but hearing such an offensive label applied to Sarah triggered something feral in him. In an instant, he lunged forward, aiming to bring Cade down. He wanted to settle this once and for all.

Greg's action prompted an immediate response from Cade. He stepped back and pulled the trigger without hesitation. Dodging the bullet, Greg missed his mark and landed on the floor chest first. Cassandra's scream filled the room, and Greg struggled to his feet.

His chest burned from the impact with the hardwood floor, yet his instincts made him move faster. Ignoring the pain, Greg scrambled toward the nearest sofa for cover. Not an ideal hiding place, but it would have to do.

Cade aimed the gun again before Greg could get clear, but when he fired the next shot, Cassandra pulled at his wrist. The bullet went wide, missing its target and hitting the sofa instead.

Muttering an oath, Cade struck her in the head with the butt of the gun and added a hard slap across her face. "You made me miss, you stupid bitch." His tone was one of a man possessed by inner demons, one hundred percent focused on completing his mission.

Cassandra ended up unconscious in a heap of limbs on the floor, and Greg realized his chances of getting out alive were growing slimmer by the second. His mind raced while he tried to move away from Cade—the sofa wasn't going to protect him from gunfire.

Footsteps advanced, and another shot rang out. Greg only had a brief moment to register Cade's wild eyes looking down at him before he felt pain radiating in his lower limb. He'd been hit. His eyes traveled down to his injured leg and tried to assess his situation. The darkness made it difficult to discern the damage, but he knew he'd been struck in his right thigh. Greg cried out, feeling the same pain and experiencing the same fear he'd endured in Alaska.

With nothing he could use to fight back, he clutched at his thigh and tried to crawl away on what was now his "good" leg. Greg felt blood gushing from the wound, and more strength seeped out of him with every passing moment. He refused to die now, no matter how loud Death knocked on his door. If the Reaper did manage to claim him right here and now, his one regret would be not telling Sarah how he felt about her.

"I think this time I'll make sure you're dead." Cade's maniacal laugh rang out, and he walked closer, his footsteps pounding against the hardwood floor with every step.

Despite the pain every movement elicited, Greg turned his body around to meet Cade's gaze with determined resolve. If he were to die, it wouldn't be running away like a coward. The other man's expression held no remorse, no pity, and no awareness—just pure hatred.

"Why do you hate me so much?" Greg asked through gritted teeth. The question had been nagging at him since Cade's first attack.

His former best friend smirked and pointed the gun at his head. "I don't hate you. I just don't like people who get have everything just handed to them. Money, women—"

Without warning, the door blasted open, and a shot rang out. Cade fell face-first onto the floor, blood oozing from his head. Silence fell around them before Greg could even comprehend what had just happened. His vision blurred, and the next thing he knew, Simon was kneeling next to him, his expression grim.

The sound of sirens blared all around him, and everything moved in slow motion.

"Greg, buddy, how are you doing?" Simon searched his face before turning his attention to Greg's injured leg. "Damn it! I knew something was wrong when you didn't return right away. I shouldn't have listened to you and come sooner."

"Simon, I'm fine. Check on Cassandra." Unbearable pain shot through his Greg's leg, and he bit his lip hard to keep from crying out. Distant sounds of footsteps echoed, and he became aware of voices from people gathering outside the apartment.

"No." Simon had already started moving, cursing under his breath all the while. He removed his belt and cinched the leather on Greg's thigh with deft motions.

When the binding tightened around his leg, Greg cried in agony. He closed his eyes while the excruciating pain shot through his system like adrenaline. Nausea gripped him, but he opened his eyes and tried to lift his head to look at Cade's motionless body. His head started to spin, and blackness soon swallowed him with an overwhelming, sick familiarity.

~

Sarah let herself into the darkened penthouse a little before midnight. There was no telling if Greg had made it home yet, but she doubted it. From the look of things, Greg had been enjoying himself with his wife. They must have gone somewhere and—.

She reined her mind and pushed the vision away. She couldn't go there. Even so, nothing could stop the little voice from asking, *You think they're not doing what you're afraid they are, Sarah? You want Greg for yourself, don't you?* She wanted to shout her denial, but who was she kidding? The answer had been staring her in the face all along. As much as she'd tried to curb her feelings for Greg, her heart had refused to listen. She'd fallen in love with him.

Sarah tiptoed to her bedroom, making as little noise as possible so as not to wake the whole household. The thing she needed was Matilda's maternal questioning or another lecture on what a proper lady should do and why she shouldn't stay out late with a man she didn't know well.

Had Matilda meant to refer to Greg, too? Because sure as the sky was blue, Sarah didn't know the guy at all. No matter how much she made herself believe she did, she had no idea what the man was capable of. This evening had left her with so many unanswered questions. Why go out with the woman he'd sworn had broken his heart? Why had he made that large contribution to her tribe? She was certain it had been him—she just hadn't found the chance to confront him about it yet. Why had he gone to such extremes to pull her out of her life in Los Angeles?

As much as she wanted to believe Greg's assurances, Sarah had a nagging feeling that he was keeping something from her. She'd been living at his house, eating his food, using his provisions, and attending a prestigious medical school with his generous funding. Her acceptance of his proposal had been based solely on the information he had given her. It was her understanding that she would repay him by helping to find answers for his recurrent medical problems that stemmed from her radical blood transfusion and the surgery she'd performed on him.

It had been close to four months, and not once had she been summoned to answer questions from his doctor. She wasn't as stupid as Greg appeared to think. There was a hidden agenda behind their arrangement, and she'd be damned if she didn't get to the bottom of things soon.

Removing her clothes, Sarah tossed them into the hamper, grabbed her robe from the closet, and proceeded into the bathroom. She adjusted the water temperature before pulling her hair from its tie. Working her fingers through the tangled strands, she looked at herself long and hard in the mirror.

What had she become? Was she just a rebellious daughter trying to prove herself to the world, as her father had said? Thinking back, if it hadn't been for Greg, she wouldn't have been able to stand on her own two feet. Shame crept in when the realization hit her.

Greg's father had called her a gold digger. The words stung because they held some truth. She had been using him all along. She'd used his generosity to advance in a society that seemed to find her odd and different.

Maybe her father had been right. She should've just stayed in Beaver.

Sarah glanced over her shoulder and found the water in the tub had reached a good level. She dipped her toe in, testing the temperature. The water's warmth invited her in, and she lowered her body into the tub, hoping a long soak would relax her aching muscles. She let her head rest at the edge of the claw foot tub and closed her eyes.

For the next hour, Sarah soaked in the water and let her mind wander. Jeremy had been gracious enough to accept her poor excuse for her selfish behavior. Before they'd parted, she had made it clear to him that they could only ever be friends.

Her heart already belonged to someone else, and she was just not capable of reciprocating Jeremy's feelings. It was a good thing that he'd taken her explanation like the gentleman he was, accepting her apology with grace.

At least she had taken care of the issue before it could become a full-fledged problem. Leading Jeremy on would have been a big mistake, which could have blown up in her face. Sarah felt a bit better with that matter resolved, but she still had issues she needed to discuss with Greg. Once and for all, she'd find out the truth, and she would do it tonight.

She took a quick look at her prune-like skin and decided she'd soaked long enough. After drying herself off, she changed into sweats, grabbed a book, and walked toward the kitchen. She poured a glass of milk and proceeded to the living room, where she planned to wait for Greg's return. Sarah settled on the bigger of the two sofas and began reading. She hoped Greg would come home soon.

Matilda's frantic and hysterical voice seeped into Sarah's subconscious before she woke. It took her a few minutes to remember where she was and why. Opening her eyes, she found Matilda shaking her shoulders.

"Sarah . . . Sarah . . . wake up!"

She registered the older woman's tear-streaked face with deep concern. "What's wrong?" Sarah sat up, and the book on her lap slid forgotten to the floor. A quick check on the time told her it was now four in the morning.

"Get dressed. We're going to the hospital."

Matilda pulled Sarah to her feet. Still quite a bit disoriented, she almost stumbled.

"What's going on? Who's in the hospital?" Sarah braced her hands on the sofa, her instincts telling her to prepare for a shock.

"Greg. He was shot again last night!" Matilda cried and yanked her arm again.

"What?" Sarah's cry filled the room. Dotson'Sa . . . why do you let the troubles keep coming?

Sarah ran to her room to dress. She was caught in the same nightmare as before—except this time, she wasn't there to make sure Greg made it out alive.

Chapter 19

During the short cab ride from the penthouse to the hospital, Sarah shivered underneath her light sweater. In her haste to get to Greg, she'd torn out of the house without grabbing a jacket. During the autumn months in New York, a jacket was as necessary as shoes. The only sound during the miserable fifteen-minute ride had been Matilda's hoarse crying and the steady click of the taxicab's meter.

Sarah focused on breathing in and out, regulating her heartbeat, and trying to calm her mind. Chanting the words in her head, she repeated, *He's going to be okay, he's going to be okay.* She tried to stay positive, thinking about all the things that made Greg special. It was a long list.

Matilda wasn't able to shed light on what had happened, so Sarah was left to guess. She had a strong suspicion that Cassandra was involved somehow. Who else? Cassandra was the last person he'd been with before the shooting. Other than his wife, Sarah was ignorant of any potential suspects. After all, Greg kept most of his personal business private, clamming up when Sarah started asking questions. Come to think of it, she couldn't blame him. There were things in everyone's past that they would rather not dwell on.

When the cabbie pulled up outside the ER, Sarah realized she had been in such hurry that she'd left without her purse and her cell phone. She wouldn't be able to cover the cab fare. In response to her helpless glance, Matilda pulled out several bills from her wallet and paid the driver. Getting out of the cab and hurrying up the steps, they raced to the reception desk to inquire on Greg's condition. They were relieved to learn that Greg's surgery had gone well and that they could find him resting in his hospital suite.

Feeding off each other's remaining strength, the two women barreled through the double glass doors and hopped in an elevator to get to the main wing. Once the elevator opened, they took off again, winding through endless loops and turns in countless corridors before they found Greg's room. There were two uniformed officers stationed outside, and Sarah's heart leapt in fear upon seeing them. In her experience, cops came when someone was in trouble for doing something wrong. Was Greg in trouble?

Matilda almost ran past the checkpoint when one of the cops stood in her way, the other one blocking access to Greg's hospital door. "Ladies, I need your IDs, please, and your relation to Mr. Andrews," the taller officer said, eyeing each of them with contempt.

In an apparent daze, Matilda pulled out her chunky wallet from her purse and showed the man her identification. "Matilda Rector, Mr. Andrew's nanny and housekeeper," she stated in a clear and distinct tone that oozed maternal authority.

"Okay." The cop nodded and turned to Sarah. "And yours?"

She hesitated. "I was in such a hurry to get here, I forgot my purse. My name's Sarah Jones. I'm a friend of Greg—Mr. Andrews." Sarah looked at the officer, her eyes pleading. He must be able to understand that people had a tendency to forget things in moments of extreme stress. Matilda had already slipped in the door, so there was no one to vouch for Sarah.

"I'm sorry. We're under strict orders to check every single visitor's credentials." The man turned away, and Sarah grew frantic.

"Please . . . I have to see him." She began unraveling, unable to keep the raw emotions from surfacing.

The officer glanced over his shoulder at her. "I'm so sorry. I'm just following orders. Maybe you can run home and get your ID?"

At that moment, Greg's hospital door opened, and Simon walked out.

"Hey, Sergeant Ruiz, she's part of the family. Let her in." Simon nodded to the cops and waited for Sarah to join him.

The cop gave her a smile of permission, and Sarah walked forward, her tears unstoppable now. Simon opened his arms, and she walked right into them.

"Is he okay?" She sobbed against Simon's chest.

"Yes. They took the bullet out—the same thing you did in Beaver. It hit a major artery in his right thigh, so the extent of the damage won't be known until he starts rehabilitation. But that's not important. He's alive . . . he's going to be okay. That's all that matters to me."

"Thank you, Dotson'Sa," she whispered.

Simon held her until her tears ebbed and she'd calmed down enough to talk.

"You're good now?" He lifted her chin with his index finger, studying her tear-stained face.

Sarah nodded. "Yeah."

He took her hand and led her inside the suite. The room was similar to the one she'd had after her accident. *Nothing but the best for Greg and his family*, she thought. Then she remembered what Simon had said to the cop. *"She's part of the family."* Whatever that meant, she was in.

She focused on the unmoving figure on the bed. Though he was asleep, pain was etched deeply into Greg's face. The pasty pallor of his skin and his sunken cheeks worried her. She rushed to his bedside, where Matilda sat holding his hand.

"Oh my." Sarah buried her face in her hands. She wanted to hold him, but she knew that restraining herself would be best just now. Blinking back her tears, she lifted her head and ran her gaze over the white sheet that covered Greg's body. She lifted it with care, taking note of the heavy bandages covering his right thigh. The gauze ran from the juncture of his pelvis to the top of his right knee. Sarah had no idea what had happened or the full extent of Greg's injuries, but she doubted she'd have the stomach to listen to the whole story.

"Do you have any idea how long he's been sleeping?" she asked no one in particular, moving over to the sophisticated machines that were hooked up to him. She checked the readouts, heaving a relieved sigh when she noted his stable vital signs.

"He was in surgery for almost two hours. Dr. Darnell extracted the bullet and did whatever he could to save Greg's leg and his life. He's been asleep ever since he was transferred here." Simon's voice was heavy with remorse.

Sarah turned around to face him. "Who did this, Simon?"

"Cade. I should have come sooner, but Greg asked me to wait in the car." Regret and frustration intermingled in his eyes, and Sarah felt her heart go out to the man.

Taking Simon's hand without a word, she led him to the collection of sofas on the other side of the room. Matilda watched them through her tears, still holding Greg's hand as if her life depended on it.

Sarah sat and patted the spot next to her. "Tell me what happened." Her reluctance to hear the story gave way to her need to find out what had happened to Greg.

Simon joined her on the sofa with a sigh, but hesitated before speaking. "There are things I'm not at liberty to discuss. It's Greg's business."

"I don't want you to betray Greg's confidence. All I want to know are the details surrounding the shooting." Sarah kept her composure. Breaking down was not an option. She needed to be strong if she was going to be of any help to anyone.

Simon grew quiet while he chose his words. He leaned back and stared out the window before he recounted what information he could divulge. "After dinner, Rudy and I drove Greg and Cassandra back to her townhouse. Greg told me to wait in the car with Rudy. I wanted to defy his order, but I couldn't."

Sarah knew what Greg had wanted from his wife. Why else would he ask Simon to stay behind? It took her a few moments to respond while she swallowed back the bitterness this thought gave her.

"I had a bad feeling, so I followed him in after fifteen minutes. As soon as I cleared the elevator, I heard a gunshot, followed by another, and then screaming. If I hadn't kicked in the door, Greg wouldn't have made it. Cade was aiming his gun at Greg, and he was going for the kill."

Sarah gasped, shivers riding up and down her spine. “Oh my God.” It was too painful to think of how close they’d come to losing Greg.

“I had no time to think. I shot Cade in the head.”

Simon’s voice was flat and emotionless, but Sarah sensed his distress and wrapped an arm around his shoulder.

“Simon . . . you did the right thing,” she whispered.

“That’s what the cops told me, but it’s hard to get over killing someone.” Simon’s body tensed, and he buried his face in his palms.

“It was either Greg or Cade. You had a second to decide.”

“Yeah. I found Greg bleeding on the floor. It was surreal. He was lying in a pool of blood, but instead of thinking of himself, he told me to help Cassandra.”

“She was hurt, too?” Sarah wasn’t sure what to think about this news.

“She’s been admitted here, as well. I don’t know the extent of her injuries, but I doubt they’re life threatening.” Simon paused. “I didn’t listen to Greg, of course. I plugged my fist into his wound after applying a tourniquet with my belt to slow the bleeding until the paramedics got there.”

“You have done more than was expected of you, Simon. You’re his family. I’m glad Greg had you watching his back.” Sarah glanced in Greg’s direction, and her heart shattered to pieces.

“I know, but I should’ve gone in sooner. He shouldn’t have been shot in the first place. Look at him, Sarah. The man has gone through so much already.”

“We’ll never know what would have happened if you hadn’t waited. The most important thing is that he’s alive. You saved him, Simon.”

Matilda stood and walked over to sit next to Simon. “You listen to me, Simon. You did what you had to do. Greg is still here with us, and that’s all I care about. We’re going to help him in any way we can to recover and move on. Whether he walks or not, we’ll be there for him.”

Sarah nodded her head in agreement. As much as it pained her to imagine what life could be for Greg after this latest incident, she could only be thankful he’d made it out alive.

We're going to make sure he gets through this, she told herself.

Sarah urged Matilda to take Simon home so he could get some sleep, against his protests. They were able to reason with him in the end, because Greg was safe now, and there were cops outside his room who'd make sure of it.

Once Matilda and Simon had left, Sarah moved to sit on the chair next to Greg's bed. With nothing else to do but wait, she took his hand and started chanting a prayer in her head. After a while, Sarah stood and fixed the sheet covering his body. She walked around the bed, making sure he was well covered and comfortable, and then she pulled a comb from the drawer and ran it through his hair.

Sarah was in the process of tucking tendrils of his longish hair behind Greg's ear when the door swung open. She turned her head to meet Dr. Barry Darnell's gaze. He offered a feeble smile, but it didn't reach his eyes.

"How are you, Sarah?" Barry stopped by the foot of the bed and pulled out a chart from under his arm.

"I'm good," Sarah lied. She walked to his side, and together they watched Greg in silence.

"This man of yours has nine lives." He shook his head and gave a shaky laugh.

"He is not my man, and you know it, Barry. I'm just an employee. But you're right—he's very lucky." Sarah was beginning to doubt the luck part, but kept that to herself. "What are we looking at?"

Barry didn't answer right away. He raked a weary hand through his hair. "I don't know at this point. Simon's quick thinking helped prevent a massive loss of blood—it could've been so much worse. Greg could've bled to death in minutes without Simon's quick thinking. I extracted the bullet. Now it's just a matter of how well he recovers from this."

Barry's voice lacked the conviction she would have expected from the confident surgeon. "Barry, what is it?"

He seemed to be caught in an internal battle. Sarah saw him flinch at her question, his jaw clenching when he spoke. "He refused a blood transfusion earlier."

Sarah knew what she'd heard, but she couldn't believe it. "Why would he do that?"

Being doctors often put them in a tight spot. They had to advocate for their patients. Therefore, they couldn't debate their patients' healthcare choices except in life-threatening situations or in cases of mental incompetence. Greg's refusal to agree to a transfusion, Sarah knew, had to be difficult for Barry to accept.

"He didn't want anyone's blood but yours. I'm telling you, the man is crazy. He'd lost a massive amount of blood, and still, he refused." Barry shook his head. "And in the absence of next of kin, we couldn't bypass his decision."

"He was awake before the surgery?" Sarah couldn't believe her ears. Greg had refused the transfusion unless the blood came from her? What a contradiction to what he'd led her to believe—he'd said her blood had messed him up. This whole thing sounded too bizarre for words.

"At one point, he was lucid, and I had to get his permission." Barry picked up the chart and began jotting down some notes.

Sarah looked at him before turning back to Greg's sleeping form. "Then what are we waiting for?"

"You were in an accident not too long ago. I don't think it's a risk I want to take."

Barry's tone told her that he wouldn't give in without a fight. They were already crossing all kinds of ethical lines here, but she'd made up her mind. Greg needed her more than ever.

"Barry, your hands are tied, and you know it! I'm going to sign a consent form. How long will it take to type and cross for the blood transfusion?"

He surrendered with a sigh. "If we start now, the lab can do the necessary safety screening and have the processed blood ready for him as early as this afternoon."

"Then we'd better not waste any time." Sarah nudged Barry toward the door. "I can't believe he'd do something like this."

They walked down the corridor, Barry slowing his pace to match hers. "It's weird how some people react to having someone else's blood in their system. It's more of a psychological thing for them. And you know damn well how my friend is. He's mental." Barry's tone was grim.

Sarah wished she could shake Greg for being an idiot and gambling with his well-being, but she probably would have done the same thing if she were in his shoes. In this regard, they were indeed similar—more than she cared to admit.

Much to her relief, the sentinels guarding Greg's room allowed her back in without any further questioning. As soon as she walked in, Greg stirred, and she almost ran to his bedside.

"Greg?"

His head turned at the sound of her voice, his smile immediate and brilliant even if his eyes stayed closed.

"Sarah."

"You gave us quite a scare." Happiness welled inside her chest, and she took his hand.

"I'm sorry." He opened his eyes and focused on her face. "God, you're beautiful."

"Flattery won't get you anywhere, Mr. Andrews." She leaned forward to kiss his forehead, lingering a few seconds longer than she'd intended, and whispered, "I'm glad you're okay."

He gave a weak smile and patted the side of his bed. Sarah sat down next to him and leaned closer. She recognized the effort it took for him to shift even a slight amount in the bed.

"Do you need pain medication? I can call the nurse."

"No . . . it'll knock me out again. There are things I have to do that can't wait."

"Greg, you just came out of surgery from a gunshot wound. I think whatever it is you need to do can wait."

For a split second, Greg looked like he wanted to argue, but he closed his eyes instead. "God, I hope Cassandra is fine. She took a nasty hit on the head."

Of all the things to say, it had to be that. A breathtaking ache seared her heart, but she masked her emotions well. "Barry came by earlier. He said you'll be okay."

"Liar," he bit out.

"What do you mean?" Sarah stiffened, baffled by his accusation.

"They didn't amputate because they were able to remove the bullet before it shattered my bone. The bullet hit a major artery, and God knows if I'll ever walk without a limp again." Greg sounded more resigned than angry.

"It doesn't matter. What's important to all of us is that you're alive."

Chapter 20

"I think you should go home to the penthouse to get some sleep," Greg said again. He'd been urging Sarah to go for several minutes, but true to form, she shook her head, obstinate as ever.

"I'm staying here with you. I'll leave in the morning when Matilda and Simon get here." She crossed her arms underneath her breasts and glared back at him. They'd been going at it for a while now, and she wasn't going to let him talk her into leaving him alone. Plus, she wasn't willing to be away from him just yet.

"You need sleep. You have classes tomorrow."

"I can sleep on the sofa bed. It looks comfortable enough." Besides, she needed to make sure he was okay. Sarah may have trusted the doctors and the nurses, but she'd feel much better if she were around to observe him herself—kind of an extra pair of eyes in case something came up. She began moving pieces of furniture around, shoving the coffee table and ottoman against the wall. The sofa bed was a bit harder. What she'd thought would be a breeze to set up was proving tough to budge.

"And they say this thing unfolds in less than a minute," she grumbled, using one foot to upend the cushion, but it just snapped back into place. With mounting frustration, she muttered a rare oath, and Greg let out a soft chuckle. After attempting half a dozen times with the same result, Sarah threw her hands up in exasperation.

Greg grinned, despite the exhaustion that marked his face. "I think that means you can go home now."

Sarah frowned, placing her hands on her hips. "No. You need someone here with you. I don't have to be very comfortable." The look she gave him meant she was as unwilling to budge as the sofa. She walked over to the closet and retrieved a pillow and blanket.

"Fine. You can sleep here, but I want you on the bed with me." He patted the space to his right and smiled.

"Wow . . . that was smooth."

"What?" Greg looked at her questioningly.

"I think that's the smoothest line I've ever heard to get a woman in bed."

"Well, either you sleep here on the bed with me, or I call Rudy to pick you up."

She tilted her head and narrowed her eyes. "Just this once, I'll relent."

He smiled at her small concession, seeming content with his victory. "I'll be a perfect gentleman, so you need not worry about me."

Sarah excused herself and ran to the bathroom, where she spent the next thirty minutes washing her face and raking her fingers through her hair. For some insane reason, her hands trembled, and she gripped the edge of the sink to stare at her reflection in the mirror. *Get a grip, Sarah. The man is incapacitated. There's nothing he can do to you, and for Christ sake, this isn't the first time you've been in bed with him,* she scolded herself in silence.

The moment she came out of the bathroom, Greg turned his head in her direction. It was obvious that he was having trouble keeping his eyes open. "I thought you'd never come out." His words were meant to tease, but Sarah's nervous anxiety made her stumble at the sound of his voice.

Greg reached out to catch her, even though she was still several feet away. His face contorted, and he bellowed in agonized pain.

Sarah rushed forward, not sure what help he'd allow her to give. "Greg, are you all right?" He nodded, gritting his teeth. She pushed the call button. "I'm calling for pain meds. I think you need some right now."

"I think so." His answer came out in a gasp. Sarah rubbed his arms to soothe him.

A soft tap on the door announced the nurse's arrival. "Can I help you?" the young man asked when he stood by the side of the bed to turn off the call light.

"Yes, Mr. Andrews is in pain. Is he scheduled for pain medication now?" Sarah spoke for Greg after glancing at his face and realizing he was in too much discomfort to speak.

The nurse glanced at Greg and nodded in understanding. "Let me check his chart, and I'll be right back." However, instead of leaving at once, he paused and stared at Sarah, almost as though he had gotten distracted.

Greg, despite the immense discomfort and the throbbing from his leg, must have caught a glimpse of the nurse's apparent fascination with Sarah, although his voice was calm when he said, "Will you go and check *now*?"

Like someone had cracked a bullwhip, the nurse snapped out of his ogling and rushed toward the door. Greg muttered a curse.

"What's wrong?"

"I don't like men who eyeball women like they're food to eat." He straightened his body on the bed, both to get comfortable and to create a bigger space for Sarah, but moving his leg seemed to be a monumental undertaking. "I need help."

"Are you jealous?" Sarah smiled before reaching forward to encircle her arms around Greg under his armpits, hoisting him up to a semi-sitting position.

"How do you do that? Lift me like I don't weigh a thing?" Greg fluffed the extra pillow and placed it next to his. He patted the cushion in invitation.

She hid a smile. His diversionary tactic wouldn't work, but she answered his question. "Everyone in the medical field is taught how to lift a patient without compromising their backs . . . but I don't want to talk about lifting procedures. Tell me why you're jealous."

Well aware she was treading dangerous waters, she climbed onto the bed. Sarah managed to position herself in a way that left a wide space between them. Greg tried scooting over, too, but the weight of his injured leg prevented him. She settled next to him and waited for his answer.

He took a deep, long breath before responding. "Because I want you for myself, okay?" His voice was so low that if she hadn't been holding her breath, she would've missed it.

"You want me? Like a child clamoring for a toy? To keep, possess, and own?" Somehow, the way he'd said it sparked anger in her that she hadn't realized she harbored. Sure, she wanted him, too, but there was more—there had always been more. From the first time she'd seen him, she had felt something stronger than mere attraction.

Greg stiffened at her accusation. He turned to look at her, his expression a mix of hurt and confusion. "Have I ever made you feel like a possession?"

Stunned at his question, Sarah aimed a challenging gaze at him. "That was never in question. What I want to know is if this arrangement we have is a way for you to set me up as your mistress."

Greg lowered his eyes, breaking their connection, and she had the sinking feeling that there was a chance he might admit to doing just that.

But then Greg shook his head. "No, that was never my intention. All I wanted to do was take care of you."

"Take care of me?" Sarah jumped off the bed, her eyes flashing with disbelief. "Take care of me? I'm not a child that needs looking after. I could always take care of myself just fine, even before you came along."

His hand clamped down on her arm. "Sit still, please. You're giving me a headache." When she had sat back on the mattress, he continued. "Sarah, I want you to understand where I'm coming from. I wanted you from the moment I laid eyes on you, in my penthouse—"

"Want? What's with the *want* word?" There it was again. Sarah glared at him, unable to tear her eyes away from his face.

"Damn it, will you let me *finish*?" His eyes blazed back at her, and he refused to let go of her arm, no matter how hard she tried to shake his hand loose. She kept struggling, and his hand went to the small of her back to pull her closer to him. "I've wanted you and more. The other night, you let me taste heaven . . . I don't think I'll want any other woman ever again."

Sarah stared at him, but before she had a chance to ask what he meant, there was a knock on the door, and the same male nurse came in. Greg took one look at him, turned his head to Sarah, and his mouth descended on hers. The kiss wasn't something she'd experienced before. This was hot, fierce, authoritative, and almost territorial. With so many thoughts whirling in her head, Sarah resisted at first before she found herself succumbing to the delicious flavor he offered.

The nurse's footsteps hesitated before approaching the bed. "I'll put your pain pill here on your bedside table," he announced, and Sarah soon heard the sound of the door closing.

When they surfaced for air, Greg kept his arms looped around Sarah's waist. He wore a satisfied smirk on his face, and Sarah blinked several times, speechless. Her fingers touched her mouth where he'd kissed her, tracing the tingling skin.

"What was that for?" She tried to push him away, but his arm still held her body against his, making it impossible to move away.

"You asked me what's with my wanting you. That's one of the reasons why I want you. Because you taste good, and I love the way you smell. I've craved you for so long." His eyes darkened. "And I love the way you respond to my kisses."

Sarah bit her lower lip. He was right. She had responded to his kisses with undeniable passion, even though she had known it would just lead to more trouble. She wanted to taste him again. Throwing her reservations away, she reached out and traced the planes of his face, his jawline, and along his neck. The attraction between them scared her, but she couldn't stop touching him.

"I . . . I want more from you, Greg." There, the words were out. In particular, that word *want* again.

Greg shuddered at her declaration. He caressed her back, rubbing soothing circles, his warmth burning her skin. "Tell me what you want from me," he whispered.

"I want what I can't have." How could she explain how she felt when she couldn't even grasp it herself?

"What do you mean?"

How could she think straight when they were this close and his touch was wreaking havoc in her mind? "Greg . . . we're from two different worlds. I knew that from the very beginning. I agreed to our arrangement because it would give me a chance to be with you, even if I knew you and I can never be." That knowledge might well kill her. "I like simple things, I lead a simple life, and . . . I want marriage to a man that I love."

"I'm doing everything I can so that we can be together."

She sensed his conviction was real. There was no doubt he meant what he said, but the memory from the night before gnawed at her—Greg with Cassandra, and whatever may have happened between them.

"You and your wife . . . why didn't you tell me? How can you pretend there's nothing between you and her? I saw you in the restaurant." A small cry escaped her at the memory.

"Oh, Sarah. I didn't mean to hide things from you." He tipped her chin so she was looking up at him. His eyes were pools of kindness when he spoke. "I called Cassandra so we could meet. To be honest, I don't know why I did. A big part of me wanted the divorce to be finalized, but another part of me couldn't accept defeat. I'd let her get away too easy. I hated the idea of her living off me, when I was certain all this time that she's been involved with Cade. Still, when I got to her place, I was ready to forget about it, to let her get what she wanted so I could have my freedom back. Then Cade was there . . ."

Sarah had to ask. "Are you trying to tell me that you and Cassandra aren't getting back together? But when I saw you at the rest—" Greg's fingers silenced her next words.

"For someone who's smart, you're not using your brain, or even just your eyes."

When she attempted to say something, Greg silenced her again, this time with his mouth, and Sarah shuddered with intense delight. When they broke apart for air, Greg continued his explanation.

"Cassandra and I shouldn't have happened in the first place. You were wrong in your assumptions. But I know what I saw in the restaurant. You and Jeremy . . ." Shades of dark clouds lingered in his expression, and he turned his head toward the window.

"No, Greg. Last night was a mistake. I shouldn't have gone to dinner with Jeremy. I only went because I couldn't go back to the penthouse, knowing you were somewhere else. And then I saw you there with your wife. I got carried away . . ."

"What do you mean?" Tension crept in his face.

"I drank more than I should," she admitted, feeling mortified for acting on impulse. "I accepted his invitation to go out again."

"Does that mean I'm too late?" His shoulders slumped.

Chapter 21

Sarah shook her head and grabbed Greg's hand in haste, more to tell herself this wasn't the time to think of herself and her foolish pride than to comfort him. With unaccustomed bravery, she brought it to her lips and kissed it.

Hope sprang up in Greg's eyes. "Sarah . . ."

"After we left the restaurant, Jeremy and I went to the café next door. We talked, and he told me how he felt. As much as I wanted to get you out of my mind and try to move on, it wasn't fair to string him along just because I couldn't be with the man I wanted."

Greg watched her, his eyes intent. He continued to hold her hand while she spoke, often squeezing it, which encouraged her to keep going.

"We parted as friends, although Jeremy asked me to look him up if things didn't work out between the two of us." She flashed Greg a rueful smile.

"He said that?" When she nodded, he smiled. "He'll be waiting forever because I won't screw up. Now, I want to know how you really feel about me, Sarah."

That was a tough question. She felt like she needed a day to compose her thoughts. With all the emotions he'd stirred up within her, a day might not even be enough. Where to start? How to tell him she wanted him as much as he wanted her? That she craved the feel of his body like he was the center of her universe? She wanted to tell him of her fears, too—in particular, her fear of losing him.

Greg must have seen the hesitation in her face, because he bridged the small gap between their bodies, inching toward her despite his physical pain. His hand went around her waist and braced her against his chest so she could feel his heartbeat thudding against her skin.

"Tell me . . . I don't care where you start. Just tell me what you're thinking."

Where to start? She breathed in and out. "When you were brought to my operating table, bleeding and fighting for your life . . ." She paused while the memories flooded back. "I knew I had to save you. Even if I had to improvise, I wanted you alive."

"Thank you for saving my life. I don't think I ever told you how grateful I am for what you did. " Greg buried his face in her hair.

"Now that Cade is gone, is the danger over?"

"I'm sorry for putting you through hell again." He grimaced, and his breathing increased.

"What is it?" Sarah's mind shifted at once to his medical needs. "Let me get your pain pill." She turned to get up from the bed, but he restrained her.

"Let me say this first. I want you, Sarah, more than I've ever wanted any other woman. I married Cassandra thinking I loved her. I know now that what I was attracted to was the idea of landing a trophy wife, not Cassandra herself. I made a big mistake. Now, you're in my life, and I want to make things right between you and me. I tried to shield you from my problems, but that just made them worse. I won't make that mistake again."

"What do you mean?"

"Your father and I had some words the day after you were admitted to the hospital. He pretty much accused me of tainting your purity. Maybe not those exact words." Greg shook his head.

"My father said that? Somehow it doesn't surprise me anymore."

He nodded. "Then I uprooted you from LA and transplanted you here. At first I thought I was making a sound decision. I would get to see you every day because you believed you owed me."

Sarah's head shot up, and she punched him in the arm. "Are you telling me that you made that up? You're not experiencing those side effects?"

He gave her an apologetic smile. "I may have stretched the truth a little bit."

"Which part?" She tilted her head, her eyes narrowed.

"Well, the spasms are real, as you already know. The blood, well . . . I did experience some allergic reactions early on, but a lot of it was an exaggeration."

"And I bought your lies—all of them. I swear, you rich people are so manipulative."

Greg's solemn expression told her that she'd struck a chord.

"I may have gone a little overboard, but I had your best interests at heart. Besides, I didn't believe you'd ever be interested in an old guy like me."

"You're just nine years older than I am," she protested.

He continued as if she hadn't spoken. "Then you had the accident. I blamed myself for it. I realized I plucked you from your comfort zone because I was thinking more of myself. It wasn't fair to you. And then I started falling for you. The possibility scared me, so I tucked tail and ran."

Sarah searched his face. "Tell me, is it so bad to find yourself attracted to me?"

Greg's eyebrows furrowed, and he shook his head. "No, except I have nothing to offer you except a tangled life. I can't even protect you from my father's verbal attacks. I have nothing to give you right now—not a name, not even a safe environment in which to thrive. All I have to give is my word that I will do my best to make it work between us."

The tenderness of the moment and his heartfelt admission brought tears to Sarah's eyes. Lifting her hand to his face, she brushed her fingers against his cheeks and smiled. "Maybe I should tell you how I feel about you, too. I have nothing to give you. Even my father doesn't want me around. I'm not trophy-wife material for you to introduce to your parents and to society."

Greg kissed the palm of her hand. "I don't need a trophy wife. But I'll be damned if I don't know your worth. You mean more to me than anything. Even more than my own life—"

She silenced him with her mouth. Despite their awkward position, she kissed him hard, intent on reiterating her feelings for him, but realized after a moment how tired he must be. Greg needed his rest. He'd have a long day tomorrow, including more poking and probing from the doctor. She hoped he'd agree to the transfusion after he found out that she'd donated her own blood. Greg had a lot to live for, and she'd be damned if she'd let him give up on making a full recovery.

"I want to keep talking, but you need sleep. You have a long day ahead of you, and I wasn't able to sleep well while waiting for you to come home." She gave a wide yawn.

"Home—I like the sound of that. I will pretend to believe you're tired, but we'll talk more about this tomorrow." Greg smiled and kissed her lips once more. His weary eyes twinkled a bit. "I want to hold you while we sleep."

Sarah wasn't about to argue against holding, embracing, and feeling his warm body against hers all night. She flicked off the light, and the room plunged into darkness. Greg twisted and shifted into a more comfortable position, tugging on her arm so she'd join him. She kissed him good night before she turned her back to him, fitting her body into the curve of his like a puzzle piece. It was a perfect fit.

Her head rested on his arm, while his other hand relaxed around her body, cradling her close to him. She could get used to this. They were quiet, neither one choosing to break the silence with words.

Once she heard Greg's breathing even out, Sarah smiled in the darkness, feeling a mix of relief and worry. Although she was glad they'd admitted their feelings for each other, she couldn't help but wish their situation weren't so damn complicated. Still, this wasn't the time to dwell on the negatives facing them. They would figure those out together once Greg had healed.

With a sigh, Sarah let her mind relax. The steady tempo of Greg's heart against her spine invited her to give in to the oblivion sleep offered, safe in the arms of the man she loved.

"I love you," she whispered. Sarah closed her eyes and savored her words for a moment, feeling liberated and light. She'd been dying to share them with him for so long.

"I love you more, Sarah."

She smiled, and the last thing she remembered before sinking into sleep was the overwhelming feeling of bliss and contentment. He'd said it. What more could a girl ask for?

Sometime during the night, throbbing in the lower part of his injured limb woke Greg from a sound sleep. The pain was so great that his sweat soaked his flimsy hospital gown. Despite the discomfort, he refused to move, fearing he'd wake up Sarah. He suffered in silence, hoping it would soon pass. His breathing shallow, he willed his mind to focus on pleasant thoughts to combat the pounding in his leg and the persistent nausea.

Barry had begged him to reconsider his decision not to accept a transfusion, but Greg had remained adamant. Now he was paying the price for his obstinacy. He didn't care—Sarah had given him her blood, and accepting blood from another now seemed like a blatant betrayal of that bond. It was a bond—whether she liked it or not—that would forever connect them. He gazed down at her once more. Her eyelids were twitching and her lips were parted. She was beautiful when she slept. He could lay there forever just watching her.

Another surge of pain racked through his body, and Greg remembered the pill the male nurse had left for him. Man, wasn't he a bastard for putting on that little show? But the guy had deserved it. No one ogled his woman. He liked the sound of that—*his woman*. The display might not have been one of his shining moments, but he had been powerless to contain the green-eyed monster.

He tried to figure out the best way to grab the little cup containing the pill without disturbing the woman in his arms. Forget the water. He'd chew on the tablet if it meant not waking up Sarah. He didn't want to move, but the damn pain made it impossible for him to go back to sleep.

Torn, he lifted her head in the gentlest way possible to free his arm. The minor flexing of his muscles sent a searing pain shooting through his thighs and radiating through the rest of his lower limb. He tried to stifle his involuntary cry but without success.

Sarah's eyes flew open, and she jerked up. "Greg, what's wrong?" Her voice, still laced with sleep, cracked in the darkness.

So much for not waking her up. "It's nothing. Go back to sleep." Greg gritted his teeth and swallowed back a groan.

She sat up on her haunches. "Don't tell me it's nothing. What's wrong?" He could see her trying to read his expression in the darkness.

"Damn!" Another wave of pain shot down his leg. Greg looked at her through unshed tears and closed his eyes.

"You're in pain, aren't you?"

He nodded and ground his molars. The bed dipped when Sarah stood, and Greg listened to her footsteps rounding the bed before her hand touched his arm.

"Here's your pain pill. You should've taken it before we went to sleep." She pressed the little paper cup into his hand. Despite her reprimanding tone, Greg caught the concern etched in her face when she helped him up.

"Thanks." He accepted the medicine and popped it in his mouth, hating himself for crying like a big baby.

"Here's a glass of water."

Sarah handed him a glass, and he drank in quick, greedy gulps.

"Do you want more?"

He shook his head. "If I drink more, I don't think my bladder will hold out 'til morning." Greg shifted his position, hating the perspiration-drenched material he wore.

Without a word, Sarah padded into the bathroom and returned with a urinal. "I will leave the lights off. I'm sure you won't have any trouble at all." She handed him the plastic container and pivoted around. He detected laughter in her voice.

"You're too smart for your own good." He took the handy urinal and worked on relieving himself. Mortified or not, he had to go, or he'd be crossing his legs until the morning. Once finished, he hung the urinal on the bedrail. "Thank you."

"You're welcome."

Sarah turned around, and he caught the smile on her face. Feeling embarrassed about her waiting on him, he closed his eyes while Sarah took the urinal from the rail and went to the bathroom. The sound of the toilet flushing followed. She came back a moment later holding out some baby wipes and a change of clothes for him.

"Can you sit up?"

Greg struggled to lift his body into a sitting position, but the pain continued to hit him in spurts. The damn medication still hadn't taken effect yet. "I can't." He flopped back down against the pillow. A feeling of dread washed over him. If this was how the rest of his life was going to pan out, it would be a pity if Sarah were reduced to being his babysitter. He'd wanted to give her more—this wasn't quite the route he'd wanted to take.

It was a good thing that she couldn't see the look of disgust etched in his face. He grunted, despising himself more with each passing second.

"Support your body with your arms, and I'll do the rest." Climbing onto the bed, she waited for him to hoist his body up before she propped several pillows behind his back. Without effort, she lifted his arms one at a time to slide off the sleeves of his gown. Using a towel, Sarah wiped the sweat from his back and slid a fresh gown onto him, tying the ribbon at the back of his neck. "Better?"

"Yeah." Embarrassment and gratitude warred inside him.

After she'd put the dirty linen away, Sarah climbed back into bed and snuggled up to him once more without skipping a beat. "The pain meds should start working any time now." Her arms circled his waist, and her face rested in the crook of his neck.

"I love you."

She looked up at him, her eyes tender. "I love you more," she replied, repeating the same words he'd used earlier.

How could he be in two places at the same time? It was heaven to cradle her in his arms, but it was also hell. Yeah . . . the pain had to go away. He'd had enough of *that* to last a lifetime.

The minutes ticked by, and relief came at last. The pain began to subside, replaced by the promise of sleep. "That's my line, you know . . . I own the words—*I love you more*," he heard himself say before the warmth of slumber embraced him.

Chapter 22

Sarah awoke to the tail end of what sounded like a shriek. Loud, rude voices interrupted her glorious time in dreamland. Her eyes popped open, and still disoriented, her sleepy gaze settled on the faces of a couple peering down at her. The man's face was somewhat familiar, but the aristocratic, blond woman standing next to him wasn't. Sarah glanced around, pulling the sheets up to her chin, feeling vulnerable. After a moment, she was able to focus and remember where she was. She tried sitting up, but Greg's arm was splayed across her body, making it impossible to move without waking him.

"Who is this girl?" the woman asked. Her tone even had an expensive lilt to it.

The instant she realized who Greg's visitors were, she jumped. Embarrassed and confused, she turned to check on Greg, wriggling out from underneath his arm. He stirred at the slight movement, and his eyes fluttered open to look up at her.

"Hey," he whispered.

"*That's* the one I told you about." Greg's father made no attempt to hide his disapproval. "The prairie nigger."

Sarah heard it and so did Greg. They both stiffened, and in one quick movement, Greg's arms circled her waist and drew her closer to him. He kissed her on the forehead before turning his attention to his parents.

"As much as I appreciate this visit, I don't think it's a good idea for you to be here." Greg's tone expressed clear disdain at his father's treatment of Sarah.

He shifted his position and cursed. At his painful shudder, Sarah scrambled off the bed. Instead of pressing the call button, she moved to go to the door, planning to leave without a word. As much as she hated to abandon Greg, the last thing she needed was to be the target of another racial slur. She refused to be caught in the head-on collision that was waiting to happen.

"I'll get your nurse to give you a pain pill."

She turned to go, but Greg's voice stopped her. "Please, stay here with me."

Sarah hesitated. She was dying to get away from the ignorant and hurtful words Greg Jr. would fling at her. This was not the place for her. The animosity between father and son was obvious, and she'd hate to be in the room when one of them exploded.

Chelsea rushed forward to fuss over Greg, but his father held her back.

"Leave him be. He's been looking for trouble all his life. I'm beginning to think he deserves everything coming his way."

She hesitated, her face crumpling.

Greg motioned to the door. "I don't care what you think. Just go."

Greg Jr.'s expression hardened. "Don't make a habit of throwing people out."

"Then don't make a habit of insulting Sarah. You know damn well I won't hesitate to throw you out again." Greg's voice rose. With one careless sweep, he went to hoist up his body, but his fresh leg wound made itself known. He sank back down, howling in pain.

"Greg don't—"

Sarah's caution was cut off when Greg Jr. crossed to the side of Greg's bed and glared at him. "You, bastard, had better get your life in order." Before any on them could react, Greg Jr. grabbed his son's neck and aimed a fist at his face.

With no time to think and her protective instinct kicking in, Sarah ran toward Greg's dad. "No!" she shouted, slamming herself against his body and knocking him backward.

Greg fell back against the mattress, hollering in pain. His cries jolted Chelsea into action, and she ran to Greg's bedside, crying, "Stop it! Stop it!" Her pleas were drowned out by Greg's piercing howls.

"Young lady, if I were you, I'd walk out of here right now." Greg Jr. appraised Sarah with contempt. "Just because my son decided he'd take you in, it doesn't mean you've been welcomed into the family. You're not free to meddle in our lives."

Shocked, his father's words lanced through her heart worse than any dagger. *You're not welcome.* The statement stung, and it was a definite cue to leave. "I'm sorry. I didn't mean to intrude into your business."

"Yeah, go back to where you came from, and don't come back!" Greg's father stalked Sarah until her back was pressed against the wall. His eyes narrowed into angry slits, and his mouth tightened into an unforgiving, grim line.

The sharp and distinct words hit her like she'd been doused with cold water, waking her to the impossibility of a future with Greg. Was this what being with him would entail? Insult after insult? With her own problems to bear, being called names just added to the weight she'd been carrying on her shoulders. Sarah hadn't signed up for this, and she wouldn't leave herself vulnerable to continued verbal attacks, whether he was the father of the man she loved or not.

"Enough. Stay away from her!" Greg shouted.

Poised to flee, she took one look at Greg, who was getting out of bed with his mother's help. Sarah knew the extent of his injuries, and the sight of him struggling to stand made her want to cry.

Torn between staying to help him and fleeing for self-preservation, she inched toward the door. Greg Jr. continued to glare at her, although he took a step back upon Greg's warning call.

"Don't go, Sarah." Greg's tone echoed in her head even if he couldn't manage more than a whisper. He hobbled to get to her, his eyes pleading for her to stay. Chelsea had her arms around him, but his weight seemed too much for her slight build to support.

"Greg, I'm sorry. I have to go. I will call you when I get home." Sarah turned for the door and left without looking back. The last thing she heard before the door closed after her was Greg Jr.'s scathing remark.

"Home? For Christ's sake, you're still married, you dumb bastard. You're just like your mother. Playing house with that little girl?"

She'd kept her composure inside Greg's hospital room, but the moment she'd cleared the hallway, she let the tears flow. Breaking into a run, she didn't stop until she'd reached the elevator.

Sarah stumbled when she bumped into a man coming out of the elevator. "I'm sorry." She dared not look up and show the world her anguish, but a set of strong arms steadied her.

"Sarah, what's wrong?"

She recognized Simon's voice and tried to wipe her unseen tears away. "Nothing. I'm on my way home."

Stepping inside the elevator, she hoped to get away before being subjected to a round of questions and answers. All she wanted now was to crawl into bed and cry. She punched the button, but Simon wedged his hand in between the steel doors and stepped in with her.

The elevator descended, the steady whirring sound pounding in her head, and she bit her lip to hold back a sob.

"Sarah, what's going on? You know you can talk to me." Simon's solemn voice echoed in the enclosed space.

His kindness and concern made the dam explode. The words rushed out of her mouth in a flood. "Greg is way out of my league. We're worlds apart. This life I'm leading with him is wrong. I knew it from the start, but I can't stay away from him. I wanted to protect myself from getting hurt, but it seems like I'm headed that way, no matter what. And I'm so scared. So scared of losing him."

Sarah threw her hands up in frustration. "All this craziness is scary. And to top it all off, his father hates me and thinks I'm just hanging around because of Greg's money. The things Mr. Andrews called me . . . how can people be so ignorant and cruel? Simon, I don't care about those things. I want Greg alive and happy." Torment clogged her veins, a sick reminder of how wrong her life had been. It hadn't been her plan to fall in love with Greg.

Simon's muscular arms enveloped her, and she sagged into him like a battered flower during a storm. "Whatever happened in there, don't let it get in between you and Greg. You have to trust your instincts . . . and him."

Sarah gazed up at him through her tears, unable to grasp the meaning behind his words. Her first inclination was to believe him, but her better sense argued against it. Doing as he suggested would only lead her to further heartache. She and Greg had nothing much in common except their love for each other. Was that enough? Sarah didn't belong here, and no matter how hard she tried, she'd never fit in. Their worlds weren't meant to align.

"I don't know, Simon. This isn't real. I've been living in a dream."

"It is real, Sarah. You can't fight it, and you mustn't. You and Greg have something special. I can see it." Simon's gentle tone touched her, and his smile provided the strength she needed.

"I need time to think."

"Go home, take a long shower, and think about what I've said. Don't let vile words of a boorish and bitter man lead you to believe you don't deserve to be with Greg."

The elevator stopped, and the doors opened. Sarah nodded, still unconvinced. The scent of the hospital scene wafted around her while they walked through the busy lobby, keeping her nerves frayed and her mood jumpy.

Within minutes, she sat in the back passenger seat of the limousine, and a silent Rudy drove her home. He gave her a sympathetic look when he held the door open for her. No words were necessary. Once Sarah reached the top floor, she let herself into the quiet penthouse.

No Matilda anywhere. At times, the woman was like a mother to her, a presence in Sarah's life she'd missed, but today, she didn't want to talk. She needed to regroup and collect her thoughts.

Shutting the door to her bedroom, Sarah leaned back and took a deep breath. Looking at the big picture, any outsider would tell her to stay away.

Greg was out of her league. What in the hell was she doing here?

You're in love with Greg.

"Yes, I am." Her answer came out without hesitation; defensive, yet certain.

Then you'll wait for him and talk about it, her inner voice asserted. You will make this work.

The ringing of her cell phone shook her out her thoughts. Wiping the tears from her face, she rushed to her nightstand where her purse sat. Sarah fished out her cell phone, and her eyes popped. There were ten missed calls and eight voice mails.

Lily! What could have happened to make her friend call and leave so many messages? Sarah's mind raced. Had something happened between Lily and Trimble? She quickly dialed the number and was relieved when her friend answered.

"Lily? What's wrong?"

"Oh, Sarah! Where have you been? I've been calling you since last night." Lily's frantic voice sounded breathless.

"Lily, what's going on? Did something happen to Trimble? Is that why you called?"

There was a pause, and it sounded like Lily was crying. "Sarah, your father suffered a heart attack yesterday afternoon."

This was not what Sarah had expected to hear. Her father was as strong as an ox. He was healthy. There wasn't any history of heart disease in his family. Why him? Why now?

"Dotson'Sa is sure pouring it thick." Sarah's hand gripped the phone until her knuckles turned white.

"Sarah, he is asking for you. I don't know what's going on, but I don't think he's doing very well." Lily hiccupped, and Sarah's heart plummeted to her toes. "You have to come home, now."

"Of course. I'll catch the first flight I can find." She hung up and hesitated, not knowing where to begin. It took her several seconds before she collected herself enough to run to Greg's study and power up the laptop.

While she waited for the computer to come to life, an overwhelming sensation hit her. How could all these things be happening to her and the people she loved? Was this her punishment for refusing to serve her people? She'd heard of Karma and had often scoffed at its implications, but now it seemed real. Too real. The law of give and take was infallible. For every action, there was an equal and opposite reaction.

The merry chime of the operating system booting up dragged her out of her miserable self-reproach. Drumming her fingers on the desk, she thought of Greg. What would she tell him? How would he take her abrupt departure?

Without hesitation, she dialed his number, but his voice mail answered. She tried several more times before giving up. Leaving a message wasn't an option—she needed to speak with him directly.

Within minutes, she found and purchased a transcontinental flight, which would get her to Alaska in seven hours. Add another thirty minutes for the bush-plane ride from Fairbanks to Beaver, and she'd be home.

Sarah packed her things in a nervous frenzy before she ran around the house searching for Matilda. The woman must have left for the hospital. In a hurried daze, Sarah wrote a short note explaining the reason behind her abrupt departure. Sadness blanketed her when she rushed out of the place she'd called home for several months. Although she hated to leave without saying goodbye, she had less than two hours to get to the airport. With the traffic looming ahead, she'd need luck to make it to the airport in time for her flight.

In the cab, she dialed Greg's number again and reached the recording once more. Time was running out—once she got on the plane, God knew how long it would be before she could talk to him again.

Traffic had been as bad as she'd expected, moving at a snail's pace until her nerves were ready to shatter. After clearing airport security, she had just ten minutes left to board the plane. With sweaty palms, she dialed Greg's number once again, hoping that this time he would answer.

Voice mail again.

Despite her aversion to leaving voice messages, she had no other choice. Sarah owed Greg an explanation for her abrupt departure. She hated for him to think she'd left because of what his father had said. Hurtful as the words had been, she had bigger problems facing her. Leaving town now while Greg was still flat on his back at the hospital might be construed as abandonment, and she didn't want him to think that was what she was doing.

As soon as his warm tenor finished, she spoke. "Greg, I'm at the airport right now, and my flight is departing in a few minutes. I'm on my way to back to Beaver. My father suffered a heart attack, and they say it's bad." Her voice hitched as raw emotions engulfed her. "I was hoping to get a chance to talk to you before I left, but I guess your phone is off. I'll try calling again the first chance I get. Take good care of yourself. Bye."

Sarah struggled to hold herself together and think rationally while she boarded the plane. Once seated, she could allow herself to dwell on her misgivings.

She was headed back home. It wasn't on her own terms—destiny had chosen for her. Was she leaving Greg behind for good?

Chapter 23

Seven hours later, Sarah arrived in Fairbanks, exhausted, anxious, and unhappy. The sun's departing glow lit the edge of the horizon, leaving a dreary cast of muted red. The cold, whipping breeze shot through to her spine while she gripped her jacket closer around her body. She glanced around, noting several passengers braving the cold and waiting for the last scheduled bush plane to arrive. Sarah pulled her cell phone from her pocket, powered up the little gadget, and waited for the announcement of missed calls or voice messages to flash.

Nothing. No calls from Greg.

Her heart sank. Had he gotten her message at all? Maybe he had but, after she left, had decided that she wasn't worth the trouble. She watched as the plane approached. Mr. V stepped out of the plane once his outbound commuters started unloading, and he headed in Sarah's direction. He tipped his baseball cap to her, his expression unreadable.

"Glad you came back," he whispered, mindful of the people around them, most of whom would know any news relating to the tribe.

Sarah felt their eyes on her. Some expressed sympathy without words, and the others glance her way with indifference. This treatment would be something she'd have to get used to now that she was back. A dark cloud settled above them while Mr. V searched her face.

She heaved a long sigh. "I never wanted to leave." That pretty much summed up her whole dilemma. Leaving had never crossed her mind until circumstances forced her to go.

"Let's get going so you can see your father." Mr. V gave her shoulders a squeeze before turning around to head back to the plane.

Instead of following, Sarah grabbed his arm. "It's good to be back." Contrary to what people might think, Beaver was her home. No matter what had happened to her in the past months—living in a fancy high-rise building, dining in fancy restaurants, and attending a prestigious university included—nothing would change the fact that she belonged here.

The old man nodded in understanding and strode away. Sarah followed him and took the last available seat. Packed like sardines, they departed Fairbanks amid the threatening clouds.

With the noisy motor drowning out any possible chatter among the passengers, Sarah closed her eyes once the short trip commenced. Her mind drifted back to Greg.

As the plane taxied to a stop, she straightened her back and pushed thoughts of Greg to the back of her mind once again. She needed to focus on her homecoming and how it would affect her relationship with her father.

"Sarah, your father is home." Mr. V spoke from behind while she juggled her suitcase and backpack in her hands.

"Why isn't he in the hospital?" Sarah already knew darn well what the answer was—Ahila was stubborn as hell. His abhorrence for hospitals had to be the reason he was back at home. To make him accept confinement in a hospital, one would have to come up with an argument he couldn't win. In Sarah's absence, she imagined how difficult the situation must have been for everyone involved. Now that she was home, she'd talk him into getting the proper treatment from the hospital, while they still had time.

On many occasions in the past, he'd expressed deep animosity toward modern medicine. Despite this, he also believed his tribe deserved the best medical provisions he was able to obtain. Therefore, when Sarah showed an inclination to go into the field of medicine, he'd pushed her to follow her dream.

Mr. V rolled his eyes. "You know how he is. Besides, Dr. Ancheta believes there's nothing he can do anyway, given your father's refusal to go under the knife. All he is able to do is give him medication and hope it'll help." Mr. V seemed unsure and rolled on the balls of his feet, his hands tucked into his jeans' pockets.

Upon hearing this news, Sarah's blood turned icy in her veins, and she had to force her next words from her mouth. "What do you mean he *refused*?" Tears pooled in her eyes, threatening to spill over.

"He needs a heart bypass. He denied consent to be transported to the mainland for surgery."

The statement left Sarah sick to her stomach. Her strides faltered, but Mr. V caught her arm before she stumbled. He held her arm until she managed to stand on her own rubbery legs.

"He doesn't want it? *Why*?" Ahila's pride, or whatever the reason for his refusal, made her want to give her father an earful, but his precarious condition might not allow her to do so.

"We'll never know. Your father is a very private man. He gave no explanation, none whatsoever." Mr. V shook his head and gave her a sympathetic look. "Just hurry home. He'll be so happy to see you."

With trepidation in her heart, she walked the mile home in confusion. It was impossible to understand why her father would throw his life away in such a reckless manner. Sarah knew that refusal of treatment would lead to more complications and even death. The latter possibility shattered her already-frayed nerves, and she began crying again. Ahila would be a walking time bomb, ready to go off at any time, and there were no guarantees of a better outcome. She preferred him alive, but he sounded as if he had a death wish. The idea of losing her father made her stomach coil in fear.

When she saw their house in the distance, her footsteps quickened, and she wiped her face free of tears. The lights in the windows burned in the darkness, calling her home. *Oh, Dotson'Sa, please make him understand how much he needs the surgery. Give him a reason to live.*

Sarah broke into a run and burst through the front door like a whipping hurricane, intent letting her father know how much she loved him.

"Papa?" Sarah's hoarse voice echoed in their little house. Dropping her suitcase onto the wooden floor, she raced across the hallway. When she didn't find him in the living room, she ran for his bedroom, heart thrumming against her ribs. This was the other place he could be in their little house.

Not bothering to knock, she turned the knob and pushed the door open. The jamb rattled against the hinges, startling her father from his reverie. He sat up straighter when he saw her, and his arms opened, beckoning her to walk into his welcoming embrace.

Sarah rushed forward with a sob, and Ahila wrapped his thin arms around her. "You're home." His tender voice warmed her and broke her heart into million pieces.

"Papa, how are you?" Sarah sobbed against his chest, just like she had when she'd been a child. How long had it been since they'd held each other this way?

"I'm good, *Vichi*'." With his solemn tone and his arms giving her comfort, Sarah's tears flowed unchecked. When was the last time he'd called her his daughter in their native tongue? "Sarah, no tears, my daughter. No tears for me."

"Papa, I . . ." She hiccupped. "I . . . missed you so much. I'm glad you let me come home."

Pressed hard against his chest, Sarah heard his heartbeat skip at her statement. She looked up to see his weathered face crumple into a sad, weary expression. His eyes glistened when he met her gaze, and she could see fear, shame, and remorse in their depths. But his love and pride shone brighter.

"Can you forgive an old fool his mistakes?" A single tear trickled down his leathery skin, and Sarah's heart ached for him.

"There wasn't a day that I blamed you for what you did."

Ahila traced his fingers along her cheek and smiled. "What have I done to deserve a daughter like you?" His mouth quivered.

Sarah gave him a grateful smile. "You've got yourself to blame for who I've become. All the talks about loving all living beings, giving ourselves fully and selflessly—does that ring a bell?" She kissed his cheeks, and his lips twitched up into a smile.

"You're too smart for your own good."

Funny, she'd heard that before. Greg had said the same exact words the day before. She missed him so much already.

Shaking the melancholy threatening to cloud her homecoming, she led her father back to his bed. Now that she was home, she'd try to make each day with him count to make up for her absence. "Lie down and rest. Let's catch up tomorrow. I don't want you walking around and tiring yourself. If you need anything, call me." Sarah lifted the blanket while he climbed into bed and placed it back on top of him.

"I can do things for myself. I'm not an invalid—"

Sarah shot down his mild protest. "No buts. I'm going to be in charge from now on. Remember, you asked for me, and this is what you're going to get." She bent down and kissed his forehead, loving his scent of musk and pine.

Before she left, she turned off the little light on his nightstand and said, "I love you, Papa."

"Thanks for coming home to see me." Then, in a softer voice, he added, "I love you, too, *Vichi*'."

I'm going to make him say it louder next time. Sarah promised herself as she crossed the hallway to her room. Reality hit her as soon as she entered her room, which held so many memories. She was back home.

Sarah went through the motions of unpacking her luggage and got ready for bed. Once she was tucked underneath the covers, she stared at the ceiling for some time, unable to sleep. Greg kept popping into her mind.

Tortured by the memory of his blue eyes staring at her and the delectable taste of his lips, Sarah turned and reached over her nightstand for her cell phone to dial his number again.

"Please answer, please answer." One ring was all it took before voice mail kicked in again. Her heart sank, and she hung up, not bothering to leave a message. If cell phones weren't so expensive in Beaver, she would've hurled the stupid phone across the room. Feeling her disappointment rising to the surface, she returned the phone on her nightstand after she turned the damned thing off.

Forcing sleep proved impossible, and she lay on the bed, eyes wide open, mind reeling with negative thoughts. Minutes turned to hours, and her restlessness grew. The only sounds she heard were the crickets chirping and Ahila's steady snore from across the hallway. Sleep came at last in the wee hours of the morning when Sarah's unhappy thoughts succumbed to her exhaustion and let her rest.

Getting back into the swing of things in Beaver had come naturally to Sarah. She hadn't even skipped a beat. Although she missed the bustle of the big city, the peace and tranquility of their little town gave her the respite to lick her wounds. She had been gone for a week, and Greg hadn't even phoned her.

Sarah began to wonder if she'd imagined the last night they'd spent together. Had she made those things up? Greg had said he loved her. Had that been a figment of her imagination, too? Had her brain conjured up those words to rationalize her actions that night? She knew it wasn't true, but his failure to call her had begun to build up doubt in her head.

"What's wrong, Sarah?" Ahila's concerned tone forced her out of her mental torture.

She looked up at him while he lowered himself onto the chair next to her on the porch. "Nothing's wrong, Papa." Sarah put down her mug on the small wooden table and rose to her feet. "Let me get you some coffee."

Ahila reached out and patted her arm. "Sit. I'll get it later. Tell me what's bothering you. And don't tell me it's nothing." Though his voice retained the authoritative tone she knew so well, it had lost the firmness and edge. Their conversations were more like a father talking to his daughter, having a normal heart-to-heart talk, than a leader dictating to a tribe member.

Sarah hesitated, picking up her coffee cup. Discussing her situation with her father would be awkward, and speaking about Greg out loud would cement truths she wanted to deny and delay facing. She avoided Ahila's gaze and pretended to blow the rising steam from her cup.

"It's the man who called me, right?" By his tone, he sounded as if he already knew the answer.

Sarah closed her eyes and took a long sip of her coffee. She let the warmth trickle down her throat before she nodded. "Yes."

"Tell me what's bothering you. Why isn't he with you?"

The question startled her. Was this the same man who had forbidden her to be with someone other than Trimble?

Sarah decided to come clean. If her father wanted to hear about it, she'd tell him. Who was she fooling, anyway? Greg wasn't there because there wasn't anything for him in their tiny town. His rich blood wouldn't last a day here, away from all the comforts money could buy.

"Greg was shot by his wife's—" Sarah floundered and tried again. "He's going through a divorce. His wife's lover was the man who shot him here. This same man shot Greg again in New York, and he was in the hospital when Lily called for me to come home."

Sarah watched her father's reaction, knowing he'd have something to say about it. Ahila's face turned grim, and he stared straight ahead. Sarah held her breath.

"It sounds to me like your friend got the short end of the stick."

His reflective tone gave her the courage to bare her soul even further.

"I haven't heard from him since I left. His father is very prejudiced and was angry that I was involved with his son. I'm beginning to think his influence changed Greg's mind." She shook her head. As much as Greg had given her no reason to doubt him, the lack of recent communication began to tear apart her belief in his words.

Ahila watched her with those keen, intelligent eyes. Deep in her bones, she believed he could read her mind. "Don't let anyone lead you to believe that you're less than they are. If this Greg is worthy of you, he'd be here if he were able."

She had no reason not to trust her father's advice, but her insecurity clouded her judgment. Everything pointed to Greg having realized that he was better off without her.

When she didn't answer, her father continued. "I can't believe you left his bedside to be with me." He sounded surprised, and Sarah stared at him.

"Why wouldn't I come back for you? You needed me."

"And so does Greg. Remember, Dotson'Sa said that we leave our nest to be with our beloved. Our allegiance changes, and this applies to our priorities, too. I can't say this often enough, but I'm glad you're here, because it gave me the opportunity to fix my mistakes. I get a chance to tell you how wrong I've been about many things."

"But, Papa—"

He raised his hand to stop her from talking. "Hear me out first. I was mistaken to force you into an arranged marriage, which I now realize was doomed from the start. Trimble and I had a long talk after you left, and he told me about his feelings for Lily. At first, I refused to accept his sentiments, but after I thought about it, I saw that I haven't been fair to you and Trimble. After the heart attack, I called him and released him from the arrangement."

Ahila rested his head against the cushion of the chair and glanced upward. "I also stepped down as the tribe's chief and handed the reins to Trimble. As they say, 'out with the old and in with the new.' " He laughed and rubbed his hand across his face.

Sarah hadn't realized she had been holding her breath until she blew it out in a relieved sigh. Giving her father a wistful smile, she wondered why she still didn't feel happy. She had been accepted back into the tribe, and her marriage betrothal had been dissolved. Why did she feel no sense of victory?

"Papa, are you sure this is what's best for all of us?"

"Trimble is a good man. I'm sure he is capable of leading our tribe in a new direction. I trust him to make the best decisions for our people."

Words escaped her while she stared at her father. The realization hit her that Ahila had been giving up, giving in, and getting ready to accept his eventual fate. *Dotson'Sa, please give me more time with him. He's all I've got.* Out of nowhere, tears came in a furious rush, and before she knew it, she was crying in her father's arms again. She wept for the too-short time she had with him, as well as for the loss of the one man she'd ever loved other than her father.

"Shh . . . don't cry, my precious child. This is all for the best. I'm happy for this opportunity to hold you again. And I'm thankful for the chance to ask for forgiveness and make peace with you."

"I love you, Papa." Sarah burrowed her face in his neck.

He rubbed her back in slow, gentle strokes, and she knew that she meant more to him than anything. "I love you, Sarah. Don't ever forget that," he murmured in a soft voice.

⁂

As the weeks passed by, Sarah spent most of her time with her father, watching him with close attention that drove him up the wall. She dreaded losing him, and she often found herself checking on him every few minutes to make sure he was breathing.

Many times, Ahila forced her out of the house to check out the new hospital, which would soon be ready for its grand opening. One ordinary day, Sarah wandered around the building, waving to several people she recognized and stopping for an occasional, short conversation before resuming her survey.

She walked the corridors with their new, painted walls and tiled surfaces, and she smiled to herself. This was what their small town needed—a hospital geared to serve the increasing needs of the people.

The structure was small in comparison to the bigger cities' trauma hospitals, but it came complete with a triage desk, brand-new computers, an in-house lab, and an emergency room, as well as several in-patient rooms. It was a far cry from the little clinic it would be replacing.

When she reached the end of the long hallway, the automatic double doors opened, leading her to the trauma section. She gasped at the small but prominent sign, which read SARAH JONES—TRAUMA DEPARTMENT.

Her breath hitched, and her throat closed against her tears. Cupping her mouth to hold in her cry, she rested her head on the wall that bore her name. Greg, she thought, couldn't have given her a better gift. If she could have him, as well, her life would be complete.

But she couldn't have her cake and eat it, too.

With heavy footsteps, she continued to wander around the building. Sarah walked out of the hospital and covered the quarter mile to Lily's house. There, she not only found her best friend but Trimble, as well.

As soon as Lily spotted her at the door, she squealed so loudly that Sarah's ear drums almost shattered. They hugged and jumped up and down, to Trimble's amusement. After greetings were exchanged, Lily pulled Sarah toward the kitchen, leaving Trimble to his own devices. The scent of *Dinjik* wafted throughout the room, and Sarah closed her eyes and inhaled deeply, taking in the aroma of one of her favorite dishes. *Dinjik* was the local name for the moose, a popular fare in Gwich'in gatherings. Lily planted her on a chair and rushed to check the pot on the stove.

"Why are you visiting me just now?" Lily's tone, though accusing, made Sarah smile in understanding.

Sighing, she stood and walked over to her friend. "I'm spending as much time with my father as I can."

Lily replaced the pot cover and turned to look at Sarah with sympathetic eyes. She nodded. "I understand. I figured you needed every minute you could have with him."

"I hate it, Lily. It's like watching a ticking time bomb, waiting for the inevitable explosion. Thing is, I can force him to go for the surgery because it's what I think is best for him . . . but that just takes us back to the issue of making a decision for another person, regardless of their feelings." Ahila had expressed his wishes, and no matter how wrong she believed his choice to be, she must respect it.

Lily pulled her down onto a chair. She took Sarah's hands in hers and squeezed them. "Your father is at peace with himself now that you have returned."

Sarah nodded. He'd found his peace, but here she was, still tied in a tight knot of worry and filled with fear about his health, her future, and life in general.

⁂

The following weeks rushed by with the same crush of activities. These preoccupations gave Sarah a shallow respite from her fears. There hadn't been a call from Greg. After a month of waiting, Sarah had shut off her cell phone for good. With a terrible ache in her heart, she went through her new routine of watching and spending time with her father. She tried to forget Greg, banning all thoughts of him from her mind.

Sarah often caught her father watching her in silence or glancing in her direction with a worried expression during their short walks around the neighborhood. She'd hold his hand, and he kept her close with his arm around her shoulder. Even if her longing for Greg still filled her with emptiness, she cherished this time with her father.

Ahila hadn't brought up Greg again, and she was thankful for his sensitivity. She'd called Columbia, and they had granted her a leave of absence for two months before they would have to give her spot to another student on the waiting list. Thankful for their understanding, Sarah realized there was no way she'd ever get back to New York anyway. Aside from her duties in her father's home, funds were also a concern. The decision to ask for extra time from the university had more to do with her hope that she and Greg could be together again.

It had been a delaying tactic on her part—her way to end the beautiful and unforgettable chapter of her life on her own terms.

The more time passed without word from Greg, the more Sarah believed that everything that had happened between them had been a dream. Maybe it had been a nightmare instead, considering the pain each memory of him gave her.

Snap out of it, Sarah! her small, inner voice scolded with authority. Saying was easier than doing it, though. She knew that from experience. No matter how often she reminded herself to move on, each step forward proved difficult. Leaving behind the good memories she'd shared with Greg was just as painful as the spear of longing that had been lodged in her heart since the day she'd left him.

Chapter 24

Greg's life for the minutes, hours, days, and weeks that followed Sarah's departure from the hospital had been hell on earth. When he thought he'd hit rock bottom, more problems came his way.

When Sarah left his hospital room, his life had turned into a nightmare—except he had been awake through it all.

"I'm not putting up with your attitude anymore!" Greg Jr. shouted at the top of his lungs before he pushed Greg onto the floor, without considering his injury or that his mother was trying to support his weight. When they fell to the ground, Greg screamed one obscenity after another at the hellish pain that radiated everywhere. "You bastard." Greg lashed out, his voice dripping with hatred. "Get out of my room."

"Stop fighting!" Chelsea cried. They continued their tirade as if she didn't speak.

"You're calling *me* a bastard? Haven't you looked in the mirror and wondered why you and I bear no resemblance to each other?"

"What the hell are you talking about?" With of the little energy he had left, Greg crawled to his mother and held her in his arms.

"Your whore of a mother had an affair with a loser and came home pregnant with you. That makes you a bastard in the fullest definition of the word, don't you think?"

Greg glanced at his mother and saw the answer in her eyes. "It's true," she said in a small voice.

The shocking disclosure was like a falling domino, setting off a chain reaction that toppled the rest in succession. With startling clarity, Greg found the answers to the questions that had haunted him all his life. He wasn't his father's son. No wonder love had been hard to come by. His father couldn't find it in his heart to forgive his wife for her indiscretion, but he'd loved her enough to give her bastard son a name.

Although the truth hurt, Greg now understood his father's misgivings, realizing that, in many ways, Greg Jr. had been a slave to his love for Chelsea. It was time to free them both from the shackles of their unfortunate connection.

"Yes, I guess you're right." The admission stung, piercing through the recesses of his entire being. Everything he had known and believed in just disappeared in a cloud of smoke. "I will make it easy on you and Mom. Forget about me, and I will leave you alone. I'll resign my position in the company. You won't have to worry about me taking your money. It'll be an amicable separation. Let's relieve each other of any further emotional burdens and social ties."

As easy as that, Greg walked away from everything he'd ever known despite his mother's pleas. The freedom should've made him feel better, but the ache remained long after his parents walked out of his life. It was better this way, he tried to convince himself.

When Sarah left, Greg finally got a glimpse of his life's reality: past, present, and—if he dared hope—the future. With startling clarity, he found nothing was carved in stone, and he still held the key to his own happiness. If he tried harder, the possibility of stirring his destiny was still well within striking distance. He must figure out a way to start anew, to cut the bad memories from his past and forge ahead to replace them with new and shining experiences.

He had nothing to offer Sarah—not a name, not even the freedom to offer his hand in marriage. Even his body had rebelled against him. Bruised and battered, he'd be more of a liability than an asset for any young woman. Greg took steady breaths in order to calm himself. It was time to right all his past mistakes, and he needed to move forward with an untarnished slate. In order to move on with the future, he'd have to change.

❧

It had been six months, ten days, thirty-four minutes, and forgotten seconds since she'd last seen or spoken with Greg. Who was counting, anyway? One sniff of her runny nose gave her away, and Ahila got to his feet, disappeared down the hallway, and came back with a roll of toilet paper. Yeah, it was toilet paper for them, not the soft tissues that the well-to-do used. He handed the roll to her without a word, running his fingers through her hair and kissing her forehead before he lowered his body back into the chair.

Staying silent, Sarah watched the magnificent view of the sun setting behind the icy mountaintops from their favorite perch on the porch. Winter had made an early entrance this year, and the weather had been unpredictable. The hunting and tourism, on the other hand, was in high gear, with most visitors looking to find some brown bears.

She and her father had fallen into the habit of ending each day there. They would sit next to each other and gaze at the wondrous sight. It was the highlight of their day. Ever since Ahila had stepped down from his position as chief, he'd had more time to spend with Sarah, and they'd been inseparable since her return.

To Sarah's sorrow, Ahila's health condition continued to deteriorate, although she'd known not to expect a miracle. She had still hoped that somehow, with enough rest, the medication would improve his condition without surgery and they could delay the inevitable. The changes had been subtle at first—the loss of appetite, spending more time in bed, and the recurrent shortness of breath. However, as the days passed, his gaunt features and his thinning body told her he was losing the battle.

She agonized over his refusal to visit the hospital, even for further testing and checkups. His acceptance of his condition and his resignation to his ultimate destiny infuriated Sarah more than anything, but there was nothing she could do about it. It had been a devastating experience to watch someone waiting for death the way her father did, but it was even more terrifying when your hands were tied. Helplessness and fear went hand-in-hand, and for the most part, Sarah couldn't do more than sit, watch, and cry.

Ahila passed away in his sleep on a Friday morning, three weeks before Christmas and almost eight months since he'd welcomed Sarah back home. It was a silent, gentle death, devoid of the physical suffering associated with the disease. Despite the heartbreak that rammed into her at the discovery of her father's lifeless body, Sarah found comfort in the belief that Ahila had found peace and everlasting glory in his reunion with her mother. He was now enjoying his afterlife after a fruitful existence here on earth.

When burial arrangements were underway, Sarah wandered into her father's bedroom a day later, feeling the full brunt of his loss for the first time since his body was removed from the house. Lily's voice and continued chatter came from the kitchen, where she was busy whipping up meals for Sarah to last the next few days. Trimble and Mr. V were in the living room, discussing the services before internment.

Sarah took stock of her father's desk. A few parchments with his messy scribbles sat in a neat stack to one side. A Gwich'in book written by one of his friends lay open on the desk, its spine showing years of wear and tear. A picture of Sarah taken at her high school graduation had pride of place next to the penholder.

She sat down in his chair, catching the remnants of his scent. Sarah closed her eyes, letting the memory of his warmth caress her. Pushing past the anguish sweeping through her, she picked up the book and closed it, revealing an envelope that had lain underneath it. Her name was written on its surface in Ahila's handwriting.

With shaking hands, she lifted the envelope and held it close to her heart. Sarah stared at it for what seemed like forever. Once her tears had waned, she pried open the flap and stared at her father's handwriting. It took a monumental effort to make herself read his final words to her.

My dearest Vichi',
The days following your return have been some of the happiest moments of my life. You have returned to our native soil as a matured human being and a changed woman. I know the strength you possess will carry you through the most difficult times to come, and you will always prevail.
I say this because I have always believed in you. I am a

better man and father because of you. Your forgiveness enabled me to live the last of my days feeling like I hadn't been a total failure as a father.

It hurts me to write this letter because I know that I won't be around to hold your hand in your darkest hours. Believe me when I say that each one of these trials shall pass, and the days of smiles and happiness will soon be knocking on your door.

I love you, my dearest daughter. I love you so very much. When I meet our creator and he asks me if I have any regrets, the one thing I could say is that I wish I'd said those words more often. But know in your heart that I do love you and forever will.

Take good care of yourself. Live your life in joy, love, and tranquility. But most of all, live it as you see fit.

I shall see you in the afterlife.

Much love,

Papa

P.S. This check is my last gift to you. Excel in your chosen endeavor, and help whomever you deem worthy. Remember, we are all equal in the eyes of our maker.

Through her tears, Sarah stared at the enclosed cashier's check and the staggering amount written across it in big, bold numbers. She gasped at the enormity of the gift. Another succession of tears dripped from her eyelashes and made their way down her cheeks. She clung to the crumpled paper as she would have her father if he were still around.

"I love you, too, Papa," she whispered.

A gentle knock came at the door. Sarah stood and turned around, wiping the tears from her puffy eyes. "Come in." Her voice sounded hoarse and foreign to her ears.

The door squeaked open, and Greg stood in the doorway.

"Hello, Sarah."

Her hand shot up to stop her loud cry from escaping from her mouth. Had Ahila known this was coming? She turned the paper and read the portion again. *The days of smiles and happiness will soon be knocking at your door.*

Sarah folded the letter and stared at Greg, who remained on the threshold, watching her with sad, blue eyes. She noticed his hollow cheeks, his gaunt jaw, and the slumped shoulders underneath the blazer he wore.

"Greg, what are you doing here?" She choked back the sob in her throat.

"May I come in?" he asked, his eyes never leaving her face.

Sarah gestured for him to enter and placed the check and letter on her father's desk. From the corner of her eye, she caught the sight of Greg walking in her direction with the aid of a cane. He leaned on the device as if he would stumble without it.

He stopped a few feet away. "I'm sorry to hear about your father." Greg leaned against the wall and watched her with a somber expression.

"He led a full life." She tried to swallow the lump in her throat.

"I want to—"

"Greg, why aren't you walking better?" she interrupted. "Rehab should have done wonders for your gait by now." Sarah couldn't tear her eyes away from his leg.

He looked down at the floor. "I had better things to do."

"Better things to do?" she spat out and took a step back.

"I want to talk to you about the future, Sarah. That's why I'm here." Greg's voice was low and deep. He raised his eyes to meet her own.

"I'm still stuck in the past, and the present isn't looking great right now." Sarah picked up the letter and strode past him, her back ramrod straight. Stopping by the door she added, "I don't know what games you're playing, Greg, but I have a funeral to arrange and a new life to live here."

"No games, Sarah."

She turned, leaving him in her father's bedroom, and stomped to the living room. Her chest rose and fell while she tried to quell the rapid beating of her heart. He was here and wanted to talk about the future? How dare he think she could move on without an explanation? Who did Greg think he was?

She reached the living room, where Lily sat huddled with Trimble and Mr. V, poring over paperwork from their pastor. They all looked up at her.

Amid the specter of emotion whirling inside her, she straightened her shoulders and took a deep breath. “Mr. V, can you fly Mr. Andrews to the mainland right now?” Without waiting for the old man’s answer, she turned to Trimble. “Can you make sure he leaves town?”

Both men looked at her in bewilderment, but neither one said a word. When they both nodded, Sarah marched out of the house, intent on getting away from the presence of the man whose memory kept her up at night.

She’d gotten about half a block away when she heard footsteps behind her. Sarah quickened her steps, refusing to get sidetracked. Confusion and hurt warred inside her, but she had other things to worry about. Find Mrs. Smith so they could plan on the flower arrangements. Get the funeral schedule, and choose the coffin. Her mind whirled with the devastating details clamoring for her attention, and Greg’s arrival had just added to her inner chaos.

“Sarah, will you stop?” She heard Lily panting from behind.

She hadn’t realized she’d been running. She stopped and spun around. “What?” Sarah gritted her teeth until her jaw clenched.

“Why are you sending him away?” Lily stopped next to Sarah, hands resting on her knees while she tried to catch her breath.

Sarah didn’t need to ask who Lily was referring to. “I don’t know why he even bothered to come now, after all this time.” She shook her hand in disgust.

Lily lifted her head and tried to speak in between breaths. “I . . . am so freakin’ tired. Why don’t you let him tell you what’s on his mind? I’m sure the man has a lot to say.”

Sarah glared at her friend. “I don’t have time to talk right now. I have a funeral to arrange,” she snapped and resumed walking.

Lily groaned before she tried to catch up. “Will you stop, please?”

When Sarah stopped, she propped her hands on her hips. “What do you want from me, Lily?”

“I want you to stop running and give him a chance. You’ve been moping around for months, and now that he’s here, you won’t even give him a minute of your time. What’s going on, Sarah?”

Sarah pressed her hand over her mouth and turned away. “I’m scared,

Lily. I don't know what to do with my life now. Papa's gone, and I'm all alone." Her voice caught on a sob.

"Oh, Sarah . . . you're never alone. I'm here. Trimble's here. We're your family." Lily's hands went around Sarah's waist and pivoted her around. "We're always going to be here for you."

"You have no idea how hard it is to lose a parent, Lily. I lost Mama, and now Papa's dead. I feel lost."

Baring her soul to Lily in the middle of the deserted road, Sarah felt a little relief at having had the chance to voice some of her fears, yet the stirring of emotions brought on by Greg's sudden appearance remained. She clung to her friend for strength, and Lily began rubbing her back.

"I understand. You're going to grieve for him, but you'll be all right. We'll be with you every step of the way." Lily continued stroking her back, easing the tension in Sarah's taut muscles.

The whole afternoon flew by in a frenzied blur while Sarah finalized the necessary arrangements. The service and funeral would be held the day after tomorrow. Sarah found it pointless to prolong the process of saying goodbye. Her father had passed on with peace in his heart. Sarah had to believe that her own peace would come, too, in its own time.

While she lay in bed that night, her mind drifted off to Greg. She couldn't deny how much she still wanted him, but things were different now. This was her home—the place where she meant something, where people saw her for who she was and not for the color of her skin or the price tag on her clothes.

She turned over on the bed and pounded on the pillow. Why did these things matter anyway?

Because you want to be accepted for who you are, the tiny voice inside her said.

"It's not important. Greg and I don't have anything in common. Pretty soon, one of us would make the other miserable because of our differences."

Are you sure about that?

She was, wasn't she?

Her inner doubts continued to torment her until the morning. Sarah fell asleep just as the rest of the world was waking, her mind still reeling from her father's death and Greg's unannounced appearance. It had been too much to wrap her tired mind around, and it was stretching her emotions until she was ready to snap.

Chapter 25

The funeral service was held at the town hall, where the flag flew at half-mast as a reminder that the town was grieving the loss of a respected leader. The entire population was in attendance, so they convened in the largest room, which almost couldn't accommodate the huge turnout. With several Alaskan dignitaries in the audience, Mr. V eulogized his friend with somber and sometimes funny reflections on the years they'd known each other.

Sarah's mind wandered for most of the eulogy, thinking of the last six months of Ahila's life, sitting with him on the porch, sharing a comfortable silence, or talking about life's lessons. In her short life, that had been the best gift, the best times she'd ever had with her father. For once, they'd talked like equals, maintaining a healthy respect for each other's opinion. Oh, how she'd miss him. As much as she hated the brevity of their time together, the opportunity had given her memories to last a lifetime.

The service went as smoothly as expected. Sarah sat in the front row, flanked on either side by Trimble and Lily—her family. They held her hands while the mournful weeping of a fiddle filled the room. When the last note faded, the pastor beckoned her to say the last farewell. Sarah dabbed her eyes with a sodden tissue before she rose. She pulled at the hem of her lace dress before she strode to the podium.

When she stood in front the hundreds of people sitting and waiting for her to speak, her hands began to tremble. She stilled them by wringing her fingers together. She looked around the sea of faces and collected her thoughts. One figure caught her eye.

Greg.

He stood at the far end of the room by the door, watching her. From that point on, Sarah forgot about everyone else and delivered her speech with her gaze locked on Greg alone. She shared the quiet moments she'd had with her father, her words stumbling over tears she had no way of controlling. When she finished her grateful and love-filled farewell, it was answered with a touching silence. Stepping down from the podium, she rushed into Trimble's sympathetic embrace.

After the last rites and ritual ended, everyone began spilling out the crowded room for the short walk toward Ahila's final resting place. Sarah's eyes roamed across the room in search of Greg. Why had he stayed?

Once she stepped out of the building with Lily and Trimble, she found him standing on the steps, waiting for her. Dressed in a dark suit underneath a heavy trench coat, he seemed out of place. Sarah's heart pounded when their eyes met. He gave her a wan smile when she reached his side.

"Sarah . . ." He tilted his head and offered his hand to her.

Not trusting herself to say a word, she nodded to him and slipped her hand in his. His warm skin felt good, as it always had. They descended several steps to follow the rest of the crowd to the nearby graveyard.

The wind had picked up, and the sky showed threats of rain. The mourners walked behind the coffin, which was held by eight pallbearers consisting of Trimble, Mr. V, Mr. Compche, Mark, and other close friends of her father. Greg, despite his pronounced limp, walked the length of the road leading to the graveyard. He held her hand and lent her the strength she needed now that her own had dissipated into thin air.

Strings of mournful melodies played while they walked to Ahila's place of rest. Sarah remained standing when the final blessing was bestowed on him and the process of returning him to earth commenced. Her cries rose then, but Greg wrapped his arms around her, offering her comfort and his solid chest to cry on. He rocked her to the cadence of the woeful music, while her despondent cries intensified.

After each one of the mourners had paid their last respects, Sarah sat down in one of the white plastic chairs and watched while several men packed the earth on top of Ahila's coffin.

"Goodbye, Papa," she murmured, pain ripping through her heart.

Greg stayed close to her until the last of the mourners left. Sarah stared at the new grave, still grappling with the inconceivable fact that her father was gone. Her mind was numb and her body was tired, but she couldn't leave. Not yet. Even when raindrops started falling, she remained seated.

"Sarah, do you want me to get an umbrella for you?" Greg leaned his cane on the chair and sat on his haunches next to her, resting a hand on her knee.

"No . . . why don't you go ahead?" She glanced at him and saw the hard lines around his mouth.

"I want to stay here with you," he said in a gruff voice.

Sarah swallowed hard, trying to clear the arid taste from her mouth. "I don't know why you stayed. There's nothing for you here."

Greg flinched at her statement. He studied her face, lifting a finger to trace the contour of her cheek. "Everything I love and want is here."

She closed her eyes at his revelation. "You didn't call me back. I waited for your call, Greg." Her accusation was laced with an all-too-familiar sadness.

The rain continued its steady downpour, but neither one of them paid attention to their drenched clothes or the chill in the air.

"Sarah, so much has happened since you left. I made a life-altering decision." Pain crossed Greg's features, and he cupped her face in his hands. "All I know is I love you so much."

"Love, Greg? How can you say the words as if you're free to give me what I want?" She turned away, not wanting him to see the hurt and longing in her eyes.

"I am free now, Sarah. I'm free to give you myself." He shifted on his haunches, but his healing leg buckled underneath him. He levered his body up and sat on the chair next to her, reaching for her shoulders and turning her to face him.

"After you left, all hell broke loose. I got a clearer picture of why my father hated me so much. I knew I needed to remove all the negativity in my life, so I finalized the divorce with Cassandra and settled the lawsuit with the cab driver and the lawsuit against Cade's estate. I was a total mess, and I thought it was best for you not to have to cope with that."

Sarah stared at him in surprise, and her breath hitched in her throat. "Your di—vorce?" Her question came out in a stutter.

"Yes, just three days ago. That is why I didn't call . . . I wanted to surprise you. I know it might sound like a lame reason, but it's what I've got. I have nothing to offer you. After I straightened out everything, my first instinct was to come here and offer to share my life with you, whatever is left of it." He threw a disgusted look at his leg. "Would you accept damaged goods?"

She swatted him on the arm. "Stop it. You've always been perfect in my eyes."

"Is that a yes?" Greg bit his lip, but the corner of his mouth twitched into a grin.

Sarah hesitated. Despite the good news, she still had doubts. She shook her head. No matter how much she wanted to revel in the possibilities, the glaring differences between them would be a tough hurdle to crack. Impossible. She wouldn't dare agree to another arrangement. "No . . . we can't make this work," she replied, her voice hoarse.

Anguish tore at his expression, and his face dropped. "Why not?"

Sarah needed to talk fast before she lost her resolve. As much as she wanted to be with him, a long-distance relationship wasn't possible, and it wasn't enough for her.

She jabbed a finger into his chest. "You and I are so different, Greg. I realized that when I was living under your roof. You're rich, and I don't have a penny to my name . . ."

Her words came to an abrupt stop when she thought of the check from her father. She might not be a millionaire, but she wasn't a pauper anymore. That would take some getting used to.

"We are from two different worlds. You live in a city, which can offer you the best of everything. You're filthy rich and successful. I live in this town no one has even heard of. I have nothing, and I haven't made a name for myself. I'm nobody. How can you not see how this wouldn't work?" She shook her head in disbelief.

"If it makes you feel any better, I'm not as rich as I used to be. I don't care where I live—I just want you. We'll make it work, Sarah. I'm not asking you to give up your life here."

Sarah looked up at the sky, wishing answers would pour down on her. Rain and tears mingled on her face. She wiped them dry before returning her eyes to Greg. His forehead was wrinkled in confusion.

"I don't like long-distance relationships." Her head continued shaking, and her lips jutted out in a stubborn pout.

"It doesn't have to be a long-distance relationship. I intend to be wherever you are."

Denial congealed into disbelief. She blinked. And then blinked again.

"Don't tease me with false promises. I'm not built for a roller-coaster relationship. I want forever." Moisture filled her eyes once more.

"Baby, I never tease about love." He gathered her face in his hands once more and brushed his lips against hers in a tender motion. "I can't live without you, either. If you stay here, I'm going to be here with you. When you go back to school, I'll be wherever you need me to be."

Sarah clasped her hands around his neck. She was about to kiss him when an important detail popped in her head. Greg stiffened when she hesitated. "What about work? Your parents?"

"I don't work for my father anymore." He smiled at her shocked reaction. "Don't worry. I have enough for us to keep living comfortably until I set up my own business. And as far as my parents are concerned, we've parted ways."

She brought her hands down and cupped his face. "I don't want to be the reason for the falling out between you and your parents." She scowled at the thought of Greg severing his relationship with his parents for her sake.

He took her hands and kissed them, one after the other. Then, he pulled her back until her body was crushed against his. "They managed to break everything apart years ago. It's all right, Sarah. In time, we'll see if we can work it out. For now, my parents and I need a break from each other."

Sarah smiled up at him, dragging her fingers through his hair. "I love you, Greg. And yes . . . I want you to be with me, wherever I go."

The kiss that followed was hungry. Filled with tenderness and love, he explored what she had to offer with sweet, lingering strokes. Greg groaned against her mouth before he tore himself away. Sarah's skin burned, despite the chilly wetness from the rain. She was helpless to do more than cling, but he inched away from her. Greg struggled to get down on his one good knee.

"What are you doing?" Alarmed, she tried to brace his arm on her thigh.

"I want to do this right." Greg's expression turned solemn, and he slid a hand into his pocket.

Sarah watched him with nervous anticipation, not daring to hope. *Oh could it be?* Greg straightened his body and produced a solitaire ring, and her eyes widened even further.

"I have no idea when the perfect time would be . . . but I think this is good as any. Your father is here, and he can hear me when I say I want to marry you, Sarah Jones." Greg glanced at Ahila's grave as if seeking permission before returning to her face. "Please, be my wife."

Greg's piercing gaze followed her every movement despite the trickles of water cascading down his face. Sarah's mind spun, but her mouth refused to form an answer. Happiness filled her heart, and she managed at last to bob her head up and down.

"I'm down on bended knee, and you have nothing to say?" His mouth curled up in a smile.

"Yes." Sarah's response came out in a rush. Her mind tried to grasp the unfathomable joy Greg had given her. "Yes . . . I want to be your wife."

When Greg slipped the ring on her finger, her heart thrummed against her chest at the thrill of having this man with her for the rest of her life. She glanced at her father's grave and laughed with pure delight. "Papa, you said happiness would come knocking soon . . . and it did."

How could the saddest day in her life turn out to be the happiest one, too? It was amazing how life's intricacies had thrown one curve ball after another at them. In the end, the karmic balance played a huge part in how the grand scheme had worked out.

Sarah breathed an ecstatic sigh before offering him another sweet kiss. Her blood heated and her body awoke when Greg kissed her back with unbridled passion. This time, forever poured out of him, infusing her with the promise of a happy tomorrow.

Epilogue

Three years, ten months, and four days after the day they'd first met in Beaver, Sarah stood in front of their floor-to-ceiling window, rubbing her belly with pride. The window had been one of her concessions to Greg's idea of comfort and aesthetics for their home. Her sole concern was their safety. In reality, her needless anxiety was quite laughable. For crying out loud, they were in the middle of nowhere. Unless she was worried about Peeping Toms, which in their case would be of the four-legged and wild variety, they couldn't be safer from potential harm.

"How can you refuse a big window when you have the mountains as your backdrop?" he'd argued, while the New York architect he contracted for the job had scratched his head in disbelief. "No one can see us anyway—we're so close to the wilderness, and our nearest neighbor is a quarter mile away."

She remembered huffing in agreement. "Fine . . . but I want deadbolts, locks, you name it." Her fear for their safety—to be more precise, Greg's safety—hadn't ebbed even with the passage of time. Nightmares of losing him still haunted her from time to time, and as much as she knew that the past was a distant memory, she couldn't shake the fear altogether.

Between Greg's proposal and her return to Columbia to finish med school, the time following her father's demise had been a whirlwind. Not long after, they'd moved back to New York so she could finish her final year before beginning her residency, and Greg had plunged into a flurry of activity in building his own business. Although Sarah regretted the outcome of his relationship with his parents, she continued to hold out hope that, someday, they'd find common ground on which they could build a decent relationship. They were going be grandparents very soon, after all.

Med school took precedence over other concerns, and her residency even more so. They were lucky to have Matilda and Simon staying with them while they juggled their lives together through school and business meetings and the other hosts of activities that sprouted left and right. Their friends' help made the adjustment period bearable.

It had been a year since they'd return to Beaver to stay. Greg had left Simon in position as his right-hand man in his business dealings in New York, and he maintained an office in town in an effort to boost the tribe's flagging economy. Greg's successful endeavor had brought many new businesses to the town, and to Trimble's delight, their once-unknown home rose to prominence as an alternative shipping port in the state.

"Hey." Greg walked into the room, supported by a cane, an aid he still needed to help him get around. Physical therapy had helped some, but the bullet had done irreparable damage to his thighbone, making it impossible to maintain a secure gait without pain. At least, that was Greg's excuse. Sarah suspected that Greg had just chosen to accept his limitations and his injury.

"Hi." Sarah glanced over her shoulder and grinned. "They work fast, don't they?

Greg stopped behind her and propped his cane on the sofa before wrapping his arms around her rather round belly. "I told you not to worry about anything. I've got everything all taken care of. So all I want my almost-wife to do is rest and be pretty tomorrow." He skimmed his mouth along the back of her neck, and a shudder rose from her tailbone up her spine.

"You expect me not to worry. I've waited for this day for over three years." Sarah sounded breathless to her own ears. Damn him for creating havoc in her mind. Her body vibrated with every movement of his lips when they grazed her skin.

A rustle of footsteps sounded behind them, and Matilda cleared her throat. "I'm going to the grocery store. Is there anything you need before I go?" Her usual smock had been replaced by a flowered blouse and jeans, but her fussing and mothering remained the same. If anything, she'd become more fierce with Sarah's pregnancy.

Sarah glanced up at Greg and smiled. "Matilda, you can give me the grocery list, and I'll take care of it for you." She knew the older woman would refuse. There was no stopping her from doing chores, even if they only intended her to be the baby's nanny.

Matilda snorted. "I'll see you lovebirds in a few." She turned on her heel and exited through the front door.

"How are you and the baby?" Greg rested his chin on Sarah's shoulder, and they both gazed outside. Beaver weather promised glorious days ahead, and they couldn't be happier. They watched the efficient movement of the workers while they brought chairs and tables inside the big, white tent.

"We're fine. If she doesn't stop kicking, I'm afraid I'll be going for restroom breaks every hour tomorrow." Sarah smiled at the thought of their daughter somersaulting non-stop inside her.

"She's an active baby, isn't she?" Pride and happiness radiated in his tone, as well as the smile she detected on his face. "I wonder who she'll look like."

"I'm hoping she'll take after you, blue eyes and all." Sarah turned around to face him. "Let's not talk about Senaya yet. You know she gets all wired up from the attention. We have to get through the wedding first."

Greg beamed and planted a kiss on her lips. "Yeah, I'm dying for you to hyphenate your name, Sarah Jones-Andrews. I love the sound of it."

It had been a mutual decision to postpone their wedding until Sarah finished her residency, and also in deference to her father's death. Getting married right after the funeral hadn't sat well with them. Having it close to Ahila's death anniversary hadn't seemed right, either, so they'd waited. The news of Sarah's pregnancy had jumpstarted the whole process and sent them scrambling to make arrangements for a rushed wedding, just in time for the baby's arrival.

Well, *rushed* wasn't the word Sarah would use. Greg wanted a wedding big enough to accommodate their neighbors, which in Gwich'in terms meant inviting the whole tribe. Planning the wedding itself was Greg's task —he only came to her for specific choices like linen color, flower arrangements, and music.

Everything else, Greg relegated to his new assistants, who were all eager to help out. The caterers, wedding coordinator, and even the DJ were all coming from the Big Apple. Greg wanted the best for his bride, or so he said.

Sarah chuckled and pinched his nose playfully. "I think we may have to change the sign on the trauma section soon."

"I got that all taken care of. As soon as you sign on the dotted line, someone is going to put up the new sign right away." Greg's hands loosened on her waist and moved up to her face. "I'm going to love every minute of being married to you."

"Me, too." Sarah stood on her tiptoes and pressed her body against his muscular one, being careful to avoid crushing her belly in the process. "But first, I want to show you what I'm going to wear tomorrow."

Greg's brow furrowed. "Isn't it bad luck to see the bride's dress before the wedding?" His concern palpable, and Sarah couldn't help from laughing out loud.

"For someone who had such a modern upbringing, you sound like an old-fashioned guy. Sorry, but I don't believe in old wives' tales." She smothered Greg with little kisses until he relented.

"Fine . . . fine . . . I'm an old-fashioned guy. But taking me to the bedroom is a bad idea, because I have something else in mind." He waggled his eyebrows and kissed the tip of her nose. "Let's go so I can take a good look at you."

In response to his teasing, Sarah clapped him on the back before they walked hand-in-hand toward their bedroom. "We're just looking at the dress, Greg. Will you get your head out of your pants for a change?"

"You must never ask for the impossible." Greg licked his lips in the playful manner Sarah had grown to love over the years. Without a word, he swept her off her feet as if she weighed nothing.

"Your legs, Greg!" Sarah tried to wiggle free, but his steely arms were protectively wrapped around her. Greg shook his head.

“My legs are fine. I’m getting some help from a third one.” He barked out an honest-to-goodness laugh when Sarah turned beet red. His mouth descended on hers as he kicked the door to their bedroom open.

The moment they reached their bedroom and the door was shut, the dress was the last thing on their minds. Even Sarah couldn’t remember the reason why they had gone in there in the first place. She responded to Greg with heated passion.

He laid her on the bed and hovered above her, his eyes glinting with amorous desire. Greg removed her sundress with one quick sweep of his hand, and it landed together with his shirt and shorts on the wood floor with a soft thud.

“Sarah, I don’t know what I have done in this life to deserve you, but I’m glad we found each other.” His voice was hoarse, and he settled on top of her. His legs braced his weight, and he was careful not to put too much pressure on her stomach.

Sarah focused on the gratification of skin-to-skin contact, loving the sensation of Greg’s body on top of hers. “You know I feel the same way. I’ve been thanking Dotson’Sa every day for the letting me meet the man of my dreams.”

Smiling, Greg lowered his mouth and brushed his lips against hers. The indivisible line between them was now a mere imaginary divide they’d already conquered.

Minutes later, her body still reeling from the intense workout, Sarah’s hospital ringtone went off. Rolling his eyes, Greg scooted over to grab the device from the nightstand.

He handed her the beeper, and she read the text from the answering service.

Emergency surgery—ruptured appendix. Patient is in severe pain.

Sarah groaned, cursing the timing. “I’ll have to run to the hospital.”

Greg gave a deep sigh, which was his way of dealing with the constant demands for Sarah’s time. He eyed her with the thirst of a dying man, and Sarah kissed his pouting lips. “I love you. I’ll be back as soon as I can, but for now, I've got to run."

Restraining her arms before she got up, Greg pulled her palm to his face and kissed it. "I love you more. No wife of mine is running. I'll drive you to the hospital, darling." He grinned, and his eyes sparkled.

True to form, Greg had been what she'd hoped for and more. Her father's wish for her had come true, and her life had changed just the way he'd said it would. Ahila had told her to live life in joy, peace, and tranquility, and she'd been doing just that.

Acknowledgments

Thank you so much, Wendy Depperschmidt, Lucia Morales, Kristen Giles, Trenda Lundin and Judith Somera. You gals have come through for me once again. Luck smiled on me when it surrounded me with such a supportive bunch of ladies. You've stayed up with me while I wrote, listened patiently when I went off on one of my tangents, and kept me sane.

To Claudia Trapp — you astound me with your talent. Thanks for bringing the picture in my head to life.

To my Sensei, Mavvy Vasquez — can I keep you?

About the Author

A professional daydreamer, Lorenz Font discovered her love of writing after reading a celebrated novel that inspired one idea after another. Since being published in 2013, she has been conspiring, butting heads, and enjoying her spare time with vampires, angels, samurais, and other creatures she has created in her head.

Her perfect day consists of writing and lounging on her garage couch (a.k.a. the office) with a glass of her favorite cabernet while listening to her ever-growing music collection. She finds writing urban fantasy exhilarating and places an intense focus on angst and the redemption of flawed characters. Her fascination with romantic twists is a mainstay in all her stories.

Lorenz lives in Southern California with her supportive family and three demanding dogs. divides her time between a full-time job and her busy writing schedule.

www.ingramcontent.com/pod-product-compliance
Lightning Source LLC
Chambersburg PA
CBHW070915180626
46817CB00003B/1067

9780997782301